Under Your Skin

My True Blood

Neelia Jacobi has a problem: She can't remember two years of her life since a car accident. Instead, a huge tattoo adorns her entire back, and she suffers from mysterious bouts of weakness.

Then she meets Rob and falls in love with him, but at the same time dark dreams about life and death appear in which she doesn't seem to be herself.

The solution to this mystery is unbelievable and changes Neelia's whole life. But Rob has a dark secret that could take everything away from her ...

Kristin Wöllmer-Bergmann

UNDER
YOUR
SKIN

My True Blood

Bibliografische Information der Deutschen Nationalbibliothek: Die Deutsche Nationalbibliothek verzeichnet diese Publikation in der Deutschen National-bibliografie; detaillierte bibliografische Daten sind im Internet über dnb.dnb.de abrufbar.

Verlag: BoD · Books on Demand GmbH, In de Tarpen 42, 22848 Norderstedt
Druck: Libri Plureos GmbH, Friedensallee 273, 22763 Hamburg

ISBN: 978-3-7693-1173-0

Part 1

Dark Promises

Chapter 1

I'm just heading to the bank, Neelia. Can you hold the fort?" Helmut asked from the door.

I peeked past the shelves and waved. "Of course. You know I will. See you soon!"

My boss left the antiquarian bookstore, and the old-fashioned doorbell chimed. I loved that sound; it was like something out of an old film. When I closed my eyes and breathed in the scent of paper and old leather bindings, I felt transported to another time. I half-expected the next customer to walk in wearing a top hat or for a lady in a lace dress to enter.

That was what I loved about my job. I could have worked in a modern bookstore or any other shop. Finding a better-paying job wouldn't have been a problem for me. But I didn't want that.

I wanted to be right here, at *Helmut Hilmers' antiquarian bookstore* in Hamburg. My heart would lift whenever I looked into the boxes of "new" books Helmut had brought back from his latest buying trip. I lovingly stroked the leather spines.

It wasn't an easy business in the era of online sales and second-hand books, but we had adapted. That's why the antiquarian bookstore also offered other items that brought in money: handmade bags from a local fashion designer, special teas and coffees, unique bookmarks, and smaller accessories - anything that made a book lover's heart beat faster.

In addition, we hosted themed evenings, readings, and tried a few other activities, which we were increasing. Helmut was approaching sixty; convincing him hadn't been easy, but now he was passionate about it. And grateful for any idea that ensured the shop's survival.

We needed every cent, that much was clear, but the core business remained the books, which I now carefully lifted out of the first box. I pulled the laptop closer to catalog them into our digital inventory. I introduced that system. Helmut preferred index cards.

"How much longer do you need?" Klara asked. She was a literature student and helped once or twice a week. I liked her a lot and pleased she seemed happier again. Two months ago, she had gone through a tough time, and, for a while, it seemed like she might quit.

I knew tough times, unfortunately. All the better that things had straightened out for her.

"I'm just getting started," I said mysteriously and waved the first edition in my hand. Klara smiled and went to the counter, so she'd be seen when someone entered the shop. Another book lover. I liked to surround myself with such people.

Smiling, I looked at the book in my hand and caressed the cover.

Whenever I held a book, I had to restrain myself from curling up in one of the comfy armchairs and getting lost in it. That would take me at least several hours.

I had driven my parents to despair with this habit as a child, but by now, I knew my weakness. I knew when I could allow myself to get involved with a story from Emily Bronte or Charles Dickens.

My smile faded as another familiar and very unwelcome feeling surfaced. I quickly put the book aside and clung to the antique writing desk where the laptop sat. My head throbbed, and I felt nauseous. Then my legs started shaking. *Damn, why now?*

Black spots danced before my eyes, and I had trouble breathing. My throat tightened, and the feeling left my hands, which began to tingle terribly.

"Klara!" I called out, but I wasn't sure if I only had thought it or really did it.

Carefully and as slowly as I could, I went to my knees, trying to avoid a fall. If I could sit down and rest my head on my knees, I'd almost have made it. Just a little more. Just a few more inches.

My fingers slipped off the desk, and I landed on my tailbone. The pain took my breath away, and I couldn't even scream.

"Neelia?" Finally, I heard footsteps. Klara came around the shelf and knelt in front of me. "Oh crap, is it happening again?" She took my hand and stroked my back.

It was good to have someone with me, even if it wasn't something anyone could fix. No one understood these attacks. For the pounding head and numb limbs. For the flashes dancing before my eyes and the weak knees. I could only hope that someone was nearby to make sure I didn't hurt myself. And if I was alone, that nothing happened when I fell.

Klara wrapped her arms around me and held me tight. I gasped for air and breathed through the pain. The fall had been rough despite the short distance.

The doorbell rang as someone entered.

A customer. Of all times.

"I'll be right there!" Klara called; her voice choked.

A man peeked around the shelf and saw us on the floor. "Is everything okay?"

"My colleague isn't feeling well. I'll be with you shortly," Klara said. He came over and helped her lift me into an armchair. I couldn't even protest, I was so weak.

"You should see a doctor about this," he said, concerned.

I smiled weakly. As if I hadn't already thought of that!

Klara guided the customer away from me and assisted him while I closed my eyes and leaned heavily against the cushion. It always took a while for the attacks to pass. They came quickly and suddenly, but they left slowly.

The tingling in my hands subsided, and I took a deep breath. I've been dealing with this for eleven years now. They appear suddenly - usually once a month, sometimes more often. Eleven damn years, and the doctors couldn't find anything.

"Post-traumatic stress disorder," was the diagnosis that came from their helplessness.

To some extent, it made sense, as the dizziness first occurred after the accident. The accident that had cost my mother her life. Since then, my father had been in a wheelchair. Since then, two years of my life have been missing from my memory.

I woke up in the hospital, thinking I was fifteen, but I was already seventeen and had to learn that my mother was dead, and my father paralyzed from the waist down.

And then there was the tattoo that had adorned my back since then. It stretched from my shoulder blade to my hip. It was beautiful, consisting of Sanskrit characters, flowers, and lines that were clearly of Indian style (my mother was from

India), but it was huge. Who would tattoo something like that on a seventeen-year-old?

I pushed those thoughts away, straightened my spine, and rounded it again to relax my muscles. Slowly, it got better. I regained feeling in my hands, and my legs no longer felt like jelly.

Klara handed me a glass of water as she passed, which I gratefully drank. It helped with the pounding in my head, and I felt better. Finally.

"Neelia, are you okay?" Helmut was back. He pulled up a chair and sat beside me.

"It's better now," I said. "Just the usual, unfortunately."

He patted my hand. "I'm sorry. Do you need anything? Tea?"

"Tea would be great. I can get back to work soon," I said, closing my eyes again because I felt dizzy once more.

"We'll see about that. First, tea," Helmut said and looked around. Klara was just saying goodbye to the customer who helped me. He had a bag, so she had made a sale. Luckily, my bad conscience would have been even greater if not.

Helmut made tea, called Klara over, and added some cookies. "We'll continue in ten minutes," he said, but I noticed he kept an eye on the door. He didn't want to miss any customers either.

"I know how terrible it is to feel so exhausted," Klara said, blowing into her cup. "That's how I felt all the time in November. When I think about you dealing with this for ten years…"

"It's usually not that bad," I waved it off because I didn't want the conversation to revolve around that. "I only get it once or twice a month. You see how quickly it passes. I can live with it." Better than with the flickering, fragmented memories of the accident and the thoughts of everything I had lost.

I pulled the sleeve of my tunic over my right arm. There was a scar, almost as long as my hand. The one on my hip was twice as long. I didn't want to think about those either, so I drank my tea and got back to work. Although I was feeling better, I was glad when the end of work came, and I could go home.

I spent the evening alone on the couch.

Sometimes, being single annoyed me. Especially on days when the attacks happened. It would be nice to have someone with me then, someone to hold me and give me a sense of security.

I had been single for three years now. Occasionally, I had dates, but lately, even those had become rarer. A few bad experiences had made me wiser.

Tomorrow evening, I was invited to my friend Skadi's place. She and her boyfriend Emil had gotten engaged last year and now wanted to finally connect their friend groups before the wedding.

"Besides," Skadi had said when she invited Mira and me, "Emil has a few friends who are quite cute. Maybe one of them will click with one of you."

The problem was that Mira wouldn't be there with me tomorrow, and I didn't know anyone except Skadi and Emil. I always found small talk difficult. It just wasn't my thing, and sometimes I said incredibly stupid things because talking to strangers stressed me out.

Having Mira by my side would have been comforting because she could talk non-stop and was even funny. However, she was busy tomorrow and couldn't reschedule. I had to manage Emil's "cute" friends alone.

Grumbling, I nestled into my sofa cushions and pulled my wool blanket up to my chin. It would be fine; Skadi wouldn't let me down.

I got through Friday at work without any issues. That was another phenomenon with my attacks: they disappeared without a trace, as if they had never happened. I usually didn't even have muscle soreness, just the occasional bruise from falling. Unfortunately, that didn't apply to the memories and the fear of new attacks.

I finished work at six on the dot and went home. "Just one more chapter," I told myself and retreated to the sofa with my book. Before that, I set an alarm so I wouldn't lose track of time.

As always, it took only seconds for me to get lost in the story.

I startled when the alarm rang. I had forgotten everything around me.

"Just one more page," I thought and read on quickly. Then it rang a second time. Now it was time. I set the book aside with a sigh.

"Alright, here we go."

I should approach this differently, looking forward to a nice evening and being open-minded.

That brought me to the next problem: my wardrobe. When it came to clothing, I was practical: jeans, T-shirts, tunics, or sweaters filled my closet, but party outfits? Skirts, dresses, glitter tops? None.

I rolled my eyes. As if there were no alternatives! I just had to find and combine them sensibly. I could manage that. Hopefully.

I finally chose black jeans and a black tank top, with a red leather jacket over it. I brushed my long black hair and applied mascara. After a moment's hesitation, I also put on some tinted lipstick. Not bad.

I put on my black leather boots and threw on my coat, then set off.

Emil and Skadi only lived about twenty minutes away from me on foot. Of course it was cold today, because it was the middle of January. I shivered despite my warm coat and wished I had brought a hat. Naturally, I had also forgotten my scarf.

That was typical for me. My head was in books, often leaving little room for reality. Sometimes I could barely distinguish between what I had read and what I had experienced.

My father and friends always smiled indulgently. They knew the routine.

I hurried, breaking into a sweat despite the cold, and got annoyed with myself. I should have left earlier! I should have laid out my things beforehand!

Now it was too late.

I finally reached Skadi's building and rang the doorbell. In the hallway, I had to open my jacket and cool down a bit.

"Neelia!" Skadi stood in the doorway as I panted up the stairs. My friend raised her blonde eyebrows. Naturally, she looked impeccable, that was Skadi's special talent. Her blonde hair was perfect, and her blouse wasn't the least bit wrinkled.

"Bathroom, it's an emergency," she said, dragging me through the appropriate door. In the mirror, I saw the problem: sweating had smeared my makeup across my face. I almost looked like the Joker from Batman.

Skadi handed me a makeup wipe and then the necessary items: blush, eyeshadow, eyeliner, mascara, lipstick. "May I?" she asked and did the finishing touches with a small brush.

"Thanks, but was that necessary?" I asked.

"Sweetie, you should always look as good as possible, you deserve it. You're so beautiful that anything less is a waste, and I'm not letting you face people all sweaty." She nodded contentedly. "Those eyes... your skin... you don't even know how pretty you are." She smiled and tossed the makeup into her bag. I thought she was exaggerating, though it flattered me. Compliments always felt good.

"It's a shame Mira can't make it today," I said.

She smiled even wider. "You'll manage on your own, don't worry. Emil's friends are very nice. It's a shame you haven't met them in all these years."

"It's not my fault," I said with a shrug, as Emil's friends often couldn't make it to parties. Travel, family matters... Mira and I had joked about it, saying Emil didn't have any friends.

Skadi knew that. She had joined in.

"So, they're really here?" I asked, just in case.

Skadi nodded and examined her manicured nails. "Yep. They exist. Promise."

"What are you up to?" I asked suspiciously. I knew her too well for her to fool me.

"Nothing much. Just come along and behave, okay?" She pushed the door open, and I followed her into the living room. Four men and two women were already there. I greeted Emil and the other guests, but I was never good at remembering names.

Only my neighbor's name stuck: Rob. It was short enough for me to remember.

"How do you know Skadi?" he asked.

"From school. We graduated together," I replied. Skadi smiled, handing me a drink. "And how do you know Emil?"

"Our families are friends, we basically grew up together," he said. "And we even work together."

"In the furniture business," I boasted. It had taken a while for me to understand what Emil did: he traveled the world in search of unique pieces to supply the company he worked for, either on speculation or by customer order.

I had been to the store once when I was out with Skadi. The furniture was beautiful. Antique or handcrafted. Almost all one-of-a-kind. There were no assembly instructions or cardboard boxes. I had fallen in love with a dresser until I saw the price. Two months' salary. Gross. I couldn't afford that.

Since then, my enthusiasm had cooled a bit, but in principle, it was like the books in the antiquarian bookstore: the rarer and older, the better.

"Exactly," Rob nodded. "I compete with him to find the crown jewels for every client."

I had to smile at the wording. "You definitely need a trained eye for that, or you might miss the crown jewels."

He paused for two seconds, then laughed. "True. That would be a real shame." When he laughed, a scar on his chin became visible. I hadn't noticed it in the dim light before.

I liked him. He was nice and funny. And his humor seemed similar to mine.

At his request, I told him about my job. Most people found it boring. I was used to that, but his eyes lit up.

"An antiquarian bookstore? Which one?" he wanted to know.

"Hilmers' Antiquarian Bookstore," I said. "We're in between the hairdresser and the little café with the nice cupcakes."

"I've been there a few times," he paused. "Do you hide when customers come in?"

"No, but I'm not there all the time," I said. "Otherwise, you should call ahead."

"I will," he promised, grinning and pulling out his smartphone. "Number, please."

I stared at him. "That was a good one."

"Setup, and scored, I'd say," he said, looking at me attentively. "So? Can I visit you at work, Neelia?"

I hesitated but entered my number into his phone. There was nothing wrong with that. He was nice. I liked him. And seeing Skadi's triumphant look, I suspected I was being set up.

That was typical of her. She had been waiting for this forever.

Rob told me his family owned a furniture antiquarian store.

"Why don't you work there?" I asked, puzzled. "That would make sense, right?"

"Some distance does my father and me good," he said lightly. "My sister works there; that's enough. I can always join later if I want to."

I understood that. I had a great relationship with my father, but I wasn't sure it would be the same if we worked together. It was best when everyone had their own space.

"Aren't you usually a trio?" Rob asked.

"Yes. Mira couldn't make it today. She's at an event," I said. Skadi, sitting across from me, rolled her eyes.

"Not your band?" Rob guessed.

"Not my taste," she replied. "It's not a concert. Mira is into esotericism and the occult. It's her hobby. If she were here, she would have read your palm by now."

I knew Skadi was annoyed that Mira couldn't make it today. Skadi was so pragmatic that she couldn't understand Mira's passion, as she called it.

I sometimes lost interest at a certain point, but until then, it was often fascinating what she told us.

"She's at a Wicca convention," I explained to Rob.

He raised his eyebrows in surprise, then shrugged. "Everyone as they please."

There's nothing more to add, I thought, and enjoyed the rest of the evening. Later, as I lay in bed, I was happy that I had met Rob. I hoped that we would see each other again soon.

Then I closed my eyes and sank into a deep dream.

Blue lights shimmered through my closed eyelids.

I heard sirens. Voices. Shouts.

The screeching of a saw biting through metal.

I felt the vibration in my entire body. It even cut through the pain.

Pain. It was everywhere. It flooded me, washing everything else away. Except the vibration. It stayed.

It was a swirl. An endless swirl of darkness, pain, and vibration.

I opened my eyes. I closed them again immediately.

The blue light hurt my retinas.

And I had seen the blood. The blood dripping from my mother's black hair.

The pain intensified.

So much that the darkness swallowed me.

I woke up with a headache. They always accompanied the memories of the car accident and lasted all day.

Slowly, I sat up and rolled my head from side to side. Sometimes that helped. Not today.

I dragged myself out of bed and went to shower. As is so often the case, my gaze lingered on my reflection in the mirror as I undressed. On my back. On the scar and the tattoo. My eyes clung to the lines, the shades. To the symbols and the flowers that looked so real I could pick them. Then the human eyes that reminded me of my mother. And the animal eyes that watched me like a predator from the mirror.

I even had the Sanskrit characters translated. I knew they were blessings and something that read like a prayer for protection. To this day, I didn't know why I had chosen those motifs. And when.

My father said I had started when I turned seventeen, and the tattoo was finished shortly before the accident. But that couldn't be true because it was positioned as if to embrace the scar I had had since the accident. How could that be?

I feared that only my mother could have answered that question. I didn't even know where I had the tattoo done.

My mother had tattoos herself that resembled mine. The knowledge had died with her. Now my back was one big mystery. It intertwined with the gaps in my memory, forming a web that made me sad and puzzled.

Quickly, I got into the shower, turned my back to the mirror, and defiantly closed my eyes. I had mulled over these thoughts in my head so many times. They had never gotten me any further.

Today would be no different.

When I returned to the bedroom, a message blinked on my smartphone. It was from Skadi in our group chat with Mira: *"Neelia, did you exchange numbers? Are you meeting up?"* she wrote. Skadi never used emojis; she hated them.

Unlike Mira, who had already added a bunch of confused, excited faces, hearts, and question marks.

"With whom?" was her clear message.

"You'd know if you hadn't been growing crystals," was Skadi's snarky reply.

"Very funny. Who did Neelia exchange numbers with? A friend of email?" wrote Mira. *"Sorry, damn autocorrect."* I had to grin. This mistake happened to her so often that it almost seemed intentional.

"Yes, his name is Rob," I wrote before they could argue. I didn't know any friends who were as often at odds as Skadi and Mira.

Luckily, they made up just as quickly.

"Are you meeting up? When and where?" Skadi asked.

"We didn't set anything up," I replied.

"Text him!" Mira wrote with hearts and muscle arms.

"No! How would that look?" Skadi said.

"Hey guys, we just had a nice chat. There was no talk of a date," I quickly typed.

"As if. You two were so engrossed in conversation that no one could get between you. I had to ask you three times if you wanted another drink." Skadi exaggerated, I thought.

She had only asked twice.

"Are we meeting this afternoon?" Mira wrote.

"Yes," I replied. I had no plans and was curious to hear about Mira's Wicca gathering. Those events always made for a good story.

"I can't, we have to go to the location for the wedding," Skadi wrote.

"Then I'll save you the secret witch's brew. Maybe you can join later," Mira responded, adding some hearts and cocktail glasses.

"I'll try," Skadi replied.

I promised Mira I'd be at her place at five and then got ready.

On my free Saturdays, I always visit my father for breakfast. That was the plan for today as well.

Dad lived near the antiquarian bookstore; I knew the way by heart. I rang the bell and let myself in.

He was waiting for me in the kitchen, where he was frying scrambled eggs. "Good morning, sweetheart!"

I bent down and kissed his stubbly cheek. "Good morning, how are you today?"

"Good as always." He swung the pan. The barrier-free kitchen was an expensive but absolutely good investment. I admired my father for his zest for life. It had taken a while, but now he had come to terms with his fate. He no longer struggled with his paralysis but accepted it and spent his time figuring out what was still possible. Basketball was his passion.

In the living room was a framed picture of him, my mother, and me. Though I don't recall the day it was taken, the three of us look happy. He calls it his 'anchor', because it reminded him of his previous life. He had let go of everything else. For the past three years, he had been in a new relationship. I was happy about that too. I liked Annaya; she was good for him. I couldn't wish for more for him.

We had breakfast and talked about the past few days, during which my headache subsided. Scrambled eggs and coffee usually helped.

My father worked as a sworn auditor, examining company balance sheets. What sounded boring was sometimes a real detective job, which he entertained me wonderfully with. He was just telling me about a particularly hairy case in a dog salon (he had made the joke himself) when I received a call.

"Hello Helmut," I greeted my boss and already knew what it was about. It was Saturday at half past eleven. That could only mean that Amira, the part-time employee who worked on Saturdays, was unavailable.

"Hello Neelia. Sorry for the disturbance. Amira's daughter is sick, and she can't come in. Could you come over to cover three or four hours? It's very busy today; I don't know why."

"It's because of the neighborhood festival," I said. The Quartier 21, as the trendy redevelopment of the former hospital grounds was called, was a few hundred meters from the antiquarian bookstore, but if the festival brought customers, we welcomed it. I looked at my watch.

"I can be there in half an hour." I gave my father an apologetic look, but he nodded understandingly. He knew Helmut only called when it was serious.

I finished my coffee and headed to the antiquarian bookstore. I arrived just before twelve and helped Helmut until four when it got quieter.

"Thank you," he said, wiping sweat from his forehead. The last customer had been demanding, but he had made a sale. That was what I admired about him: he usually came up with a brilliant idea at the last minute to make people happy. In this case, it was a colored edition of Goethe's love poems.

"You know it's a given for me," I said. "I love this shop too."

"That's why I want you to take it over when I'm too old for it," he said. My heart leaped whenever he said that. I really wanted that, but I hoped there would be a few more years to learn from him.

"Take your time getting old," I said. "Things are going well." And besides that, I prefer stability as a nice counterpart to my complicated past. Helmut in the antiquarian bookstore was a big part of that.

"We'll see. But have a nice afternoon. I'll treat you to cake on Monday."

"But the good one from the bakery," I said.

He promised, and I headed to Mira's place. She also lived nearby, right between Skadi and me, but I took my time and bought some snacks for the evening on the way.

I arrived at a quarter to five and grinned when Mira greeted me with a long drink.

"It's Saturday, after all," she said with a shrug.

"Is this the witch's brew you promised?" I asked, slipping off my boots.

"No, I'm saving that for Skadi," she waved it off. "She'll need it. It's half absinthe."

"Oh God, that can only end badly. I just got rid of my headache. Oh well." I hung up my coat and took the crystal glass with the deep blue content. "Blue Curaçao?"

"Too simple, right? It's called *Oriental Night.* Can you smell the cloves and cinnamon?" she asked enthusiastically.

I could, and it tasted good. We went to the living room, which, as always, smelled strongly of incense. I adjusted a crystal coaster and snuggled into her handmade cushions. The scent of cinnamon and cloves reminded me of my mother. She often used those spices when cooking. They evoked bittersweet memories of my childhood that I had to breathe away.

"How was work?" Mira asked. I had texted her in the afternoon, so she'd know if I'd be late.

"Good. Busy today. And your convention?"

"Oh, you know, I really enjoy going there because most people are really cool," she said, playing with her silver rings.

She wore at least one on each finger. I noticed a new small tattoo on her left wrist. A rune, probably a souvenir from yesterday. She had several of those.

"But some overdo it a bit," she continued. "I like to immerse myself in this mystical world, but you have to find your way back." She pushed back her red-dyed hair and looked thoughtful. Then she grinned. "But the wizard who showed me his potion brewing was still cute."

"Is 'brewing' a Wicca code for sex?" I asked.

"Yep. It was needed and appropriate." Mira sipped her drink. "He got my cattle boiling."

"Oh boy, what a metaphor. Thank you for that. Are you meeting him again?" I wanted to know.

"No, he's one of those withdrawn types, but that's okay. He put in an effort." She shrugged. "I also think I shouldn't look for a partner in the scene. That would probably be the final proof for Skadi to have me committed."

"Possibly. If you were that detached from the earthly world," I said with a smile.

"Exactly. That's why I don't do it. And what about the mysterious Rob? Tell me more." She leaned forward, holding her drink like a holy grail.

"He's not detached," I reported with a grin. "He works at the same company as Emil. His family owns a furniture antiquarian store. And he loves books, just like me. We had a long conversation about Fontane." I felt my cheeks redden under her gaze. "I know, you find that odd."

"Me? Odd? Not at all," she waved it off. "I had a serious conversation with the wizard about potions. Though we probably talked about different things. I was more about effective herbs and plants rather than love spells from virgin hair. Whatever. If the way to your heart is through Fontane, so be it."

My phone vibrated. "Probably Skadi," I said. It would be nice if she could come. Our girls' nights were rare these days due to her wedding preparations.

The message was from Rob, as I realized with a pounding heart: "*I just stopped by the bookstore, but your boss said you already left. Annoying, I wanted to surprise you. So then as a message: Dinner next week?*"

"Rob?" Mira asked. I nodded and waved her over. She scooted next to me and read the message with me. Her eyes lit up. "Ooh, I like that. He's got humor and style. Do you want to meet him?"

"Yes." I smiled. "I can invest the time, don't you think?"

"He probably doesn't have a potion brewing, so go for it. I'll mix the next drinks. I hope you don't have any plans for tonight."

"No, the next twelve hours are reserved for you," I said and replied to Rob that I was free on Wednesday. I could hardly wait for our date. What a lovely end to the day. I was more than ready for good times without fainting spells and dark dreams.

Mira laughed loudly in the kitchen. "A whole twelve hours of Wicca drinks? Challenge accepted!"

Chapter 2

*I*t's night, and I'm walking through empty streets.

It's quiet. I am alone.

The movement feels good. While running, I stretch. My spine aligns like pearls on a necklace. I sway my head and stretch my sides.

A pleasant shiver runs down my back, like a warm trickle through my entire body.

The asphalt under my feet is cold. Damp. The air is crystal clear and fills my lungs with refreshing coolness.

In the distance, I hear a sound. I tilt my head slightly in its direction but lose interest. It's far away. It doesn't threaten me.

Above me, the full moon hangs in the sky.

My gaze lingers on it. It's magical. It's been a long time since the moon and I met. It's like a secret rendezvous. I flirt a bit, turn my gaze away, and pretend not to notice it. Meanwhile, I listen to the promises it makes to me.

"We haven't seen each other for too long. Come to me. You know what I can give you. You know what I can show you. You know what I can make you become."

Yes, I know. Deep inside, I understand exactly what it's saying.

My mind doesn't know what to make of its words, but who needs a mind when they can feel? And I feel good in its presence. Too good to question this feeling it fills me with.

A breeze picks up, and I close my eyes for a moment to enjoy it.

"You and I, Neelia, we have a date. For the hunt." *I smile inwardly. That sounds good. Intimate. More like what I want. What I deeply need.*

Another sound.

I pause mid-step and listen. I turn to find where it came from. What it is.

The hair on the back of my neck stands up.

Danger.

Danger!

And it is close.

My instinct tells me that I have already been spotted.

That I have been targeted.

I look up at the moon.

"We have a date. For the hunt."

I look forward to finding out if I am the hunter or the hunted.

I woke up with a terrible hangover.

Mira was serious and mercilessly filled both Skadi, who arrived around eight, and me with her witch cocktails. We sat together until three in the morning, drinking concoctions with melodious names like "*Walpurgis Night*," "*Poisoned Apple*," "*Love Spell*," and "*May Moon*," catching up on all the gatherings we'd missed in the past few weeks.

"Admit it, you went to a cocktail seminar for Harry Potter fans," groaned Skadi around one in the morning. She was already squinting slightly. It must have been the absinthe.

"Then they'd be called '*Troll Snot*' instead of '*Love Spell*'," Mira cheerfully dismissed and mixed the next one. And then the next after that.

Accordingly, I spent Sunday recovering from my hangover - and Monday, too. Luckily, my date with Rob was on

Wednesday. By then, I should be able to drink a glass of wine with dinner without groaning from a headache.

Because of the headache, I forgot about my dream, even though it had felt so real. It wasn't until Tuesday night in bed, when I looked out the window and saw the waxing moon, that I remembered it.

I rarely had such extraordinary dreams, and I liked it. It was exciting. I had felt so good. So balanced and expectant.

Maybe I should look for a book on dream interpretation at the antiquarian bookstore. Helmut sometimes accidentally bought such books. They ended up in our so-called esoteric corner, where Mira was a regular customer.

Maybe the moon was a metaphor for Rob, and the hunt referred to our date. My subconscious was likely telling me I was ready for something new and should dare to embrace it—to be brave and comfortable in my own skin.

I snuggled into my blanket and smiled. That sounded like a good plan.

The next day, I was surprised at how excited I was about the date.

Rob and I exchanged a few more messages since Saturday. I liked his style; even in the chat, his humor came through. And I was glad he communicated with words—not emojis. His choice of words told me much more about him than comic faces.

We were meeting at a tapas bar he had suggested. I was immediately thrilled. I loved tapas, and I had heard of this bar but never made it there. Now that my hangover had subsided, I was looking forward to Spanish wine and good food.

Still, I had another problem that called Skadi to action, half an hour before I had to leave.

"Why didn't you say anything on Saturday?" she asked as she stood at the door. "We could have taken care of this long ago. Now we're pressed for time."

"The 'Poisoned Apple' is to blame," I said, moving to my wardrobe.

"Yes, that could be," she murmured. "I didn't get out of bed on Sunday. Emil had to go to the pharmacy for me." She opened the sliding doors and cracked her shoulders. "Let's get started then."

I arrived at the restaurant on time, smoothing my hair back as I walked through the door. Skadi had done a great job. In my outfit of black jeans and a purple blouse (which I'd completely forgotten I owned), I felt comfortable. Skadi had helped with my makeup, so I felt pretty but not overdone. If she ever gave up her job at the bank, she could become a stylist. She had talent.

Rob was already waiting for me. He saw me come in and stood up from the table. I liked that, as if he were a gentleman. I clearly read too many old books.

He kissed me on the cheek to greet me. I felt warm, and my face tingled. I was really looking forward to the date, the pleasant evening we'd hopefully have together. And maybe what could come from it.

After three years as a single, I longed for a new relationship, the excitement of good dates and the chance to get to know someone intensely.

"Nice to see you," Rob said casually and led me to the table.

Maybe he was the right one for that.

"I'm glad to be here too." We sat across from each other at the table, and I studied his face. It was narrow, with a pronounced jaw and high cheekbones. His dark hair fell over his forehead in a way that seemed undoubtedly intentional. His brown eyes sparkled mischievously as he opened the wine list with a grand gesture.

"Is it okay if I choose the wine, or do you have a preference?" he asked.

"I usually stick with Tempranillo, but if you have another recommendation, go ahead," I said.

He studied the list with feigned seriousness. "The lady knows her wine."

"The lady just likes drinking wine," I corrected him.

"The man likes that." He laughed. "And now let's stop sounding like a TV show from the eighties, okay? Or do you value that?"

"Not at all. Eighties dialogue isn't exactly top-notch," I replied.

"Exactly. And before you stop taking me seriously, I need to change course." The waiter arrived, and Rob ordered a Primitivo and a mixed plate of tapas. I watched him as he did. He was friendly and exuded a confidence I liked. He seemed unflappable. I liked that because hyper people (except Mira) quickly got on my nerves.

In my mind's eye, I saw us in other restaurants. In beach bars on vacation together. Sitting together at our dining table in our apartment.

"Everything okay?" he asked, and I realized I had been staring at him.

"Yes, sure." I smiled, embarrassed.

"And here I thought I had missed a spot while shaving or something."

"You did. There." I pointed to a small patch of stubble on his left cheek. The touch electrified me, and I found myself keeping my finger on his skin longer than necessary.

He took my wrist and held it. His eyes locked onto mine. "Good catch. Thanks." He leaned in a bit, a silent invitation I could accept if I wanted.

I wanted to. I placed my other hand on his cheek and kissed him.

As our lips met, heat surged through me like a wave. We didn't kiss on Friday. I regretted it afterward. Now it didn't matter.

His lips were soft, but the forgotten stubble on his cheeks scratched my skin. They tingled at my fingertips. He still held my wrist. I closed my eyes and inhaled his scent. Fresh yet earthy. Like a promise that there was more to him than met the eye.

I wanted to find out. I felt good with him.

He touched a part of me that had been neglected for a long time. I wanted to know more about him and see where this would take us. If he was someone who fit me.

I felt like he was.

Warmth filled my chest and mingled with the heat in the rest of my body. I moved even closer to him, wanting to feel more of him. I forgot where I was. I forgot that the drinks hadn't even arrived yet.

Someone cleared their throat.

Startled, I pulled back and saw the waiter standing by our table, holding the wine bottle and barely suppressing a grin.

"That could have taken another three minutes," Rob said calmly, while my cheeks burned.

"I see, but I have to keep going," the waiter said and poured the wine. It was nice that the two of them took it so lightly. I breathed out and smiled as well, especially when Rob turned to me and solemnly raised his glass.

I raised my glass to my lips and tasted the wine. It was heavy and velvety, just as I liked it. The flavors tickled my palate and spread through my nose.

"It's good," I praised.

"Thank you. Only the best for a wonderful woman," he said with a mock-serious air, though he grinned.

"Don't make fun of me."

"I'm not. I've been kicking myself since Friday for not kissing you and have been looking forward to tonight. We've been here for fifteen minutes, made up for it, and I couldn't feel better."

My cheeks warmed again. "Thanks, that's really..."

"If you say 'nice,' I'll drink the wine alone and run away to hide," he informed me.

I raised my hand as if swearing. "I wasn't going to, I promise."

He caught my fingers with his and smiled. "Lucky for you. How was your day?"

It was so easy to talk to him. We jumped from topic to topic effortlessly. My heart fluttered when he asked if we could see each other again after dinner.

"Of course."

He pulled me close and kissed me again. I felt the kiss down to my toes and wrapped my arms around his neck.

"When?" I asked. I didn't want to let him go.

"Next Saturday? I'd like to see you sooner, but I have to go to the airport early tomorrow. My next client assignment takes me to Colombia."

"Colombia?" I widened my eyes.

"Yes, a special order – just a cabinet." He shrugged. "That's one of the reasons I love my job. It takes me to the most exotic places to pick up furniture pieces custom-made for our clients. I'd be happy to show you pictures next time. They're incredibly beautiful."

"They must be if you're flying halfway around the world for them," I said.

"As I said, that's why I like my job. Except today. I would have liked to see you sooner. Actually, I don't want to let you go at all."

Heat flooded my body and set me on fire. New images appeared in my mind's eye. Another dining table, but this time we were lying entwined on it. Naked and sweaty.

I never had sex on the first date, but with Rob… maybe I'd make an exception. Though that question wouldn't arise until next Saturday at the earliest.

"Then Saturday, the fourth of February," I confirmed. "I'll pick a restaurant. Be excited."

He kissed me again, and it was hard to pull away. "I can't wait."

Waiting for our second date was tough.

Rob and I stayed in touch via messenger, but it wasn't easy due to the time difference. He entertained me with photos from Colombia, and I felt I wanted to visit that country someday.

Some photos reminded me of the pictures from my mother's childhood. She had grown up in Madras, and the vibrant colors in Colombia reminded me a bit of India.

I had only been there once. Unfortunately. But hopefully, I could repeat it someday and visit my relatives. My grandmother and my aunts with their families. Maybe it would help heal the wounds from my mom's death if I were there.

With Rob?

I had to smile at myself when that thought crossed my mind. I should wait for the second date before planning trips to the other side of the world. The crazy thing was how natural it felt to think about a trip together.

"That's how it is when you're in love," Mira said wisely when the three of us met at Skadi's on Friday. Skadi was thrilled about our date.

"I knew it!" she said triumphantly.

"Then why did you keep him from me for so long?" I asked.

She shrugged. "Because one of you was always unavailable. Emil and I have been together for ten years, and you never met him. I only realized it could work a few weeks ago when we planned the party. And what can I say? My gut feeling was right." She looked at Mira. "Your turn."

"Never mind," she waved it off. "I'm working my way through all the crazies out there. Or do you have another Rob you can pull out of your hat?"

"No, not another Rob." Skadi looked at Mira thoughtfully until she laughed.

"See? I'll find someone myself."

"A wizard?" I teased.

"Who knows? Or a werewolf?" Mira said with a grin.

Skadi choked on her drink. "Are there people in the community who think they're werewolves?"

"Wouldn't surprise me, honestly," Mira said casually, stirring her glass. "But no one has offered to show me their fur yet."

"That sounds mega creepy when you say it like that," I said, laughing.

"And after you've finished being creeped out, you wonder how hairy the guy must be," Skadi shook her head.

"But you'd never be cold at night if your wolfie was lying next to you." Mira laughed so hard that tears streamed down her cheeks and smudged her green eyeliner. I laughed with her; it was just too contagious. My brain conjured up the corresponding images, and it took a while for us to recover from this fit.

On Saturday, I worked, and on Sunday, I visited my father. We spent a relaxed day together, and I told him about Rob.

"I'm curious," he said. "If he's a friend of Emil's, I don't have to worry about you."

"No, you can keep your imaginary shotgun in the closet," I smiled and kissed his cheek. "Besides, I can take care of myself."

A shadow passed over his face. I knew he still tortured himself about the accident, even though he had been proven not at fault. It must still be terrible to live with that feeling.

My impairment was so much smaller than his, and I was so proud of him for being so full of life.

"Dad, really. As long as I have you, nothing can happen to me." I hugged him, hoping it would help. I was so glad he was with me, and I couldn't bear it when he felt bad. Dad hugged me and smiled. "I feel the same way, sweetheart. I'm here for you. And if I ever need a shotgun... I think I have a good chance in court."

"Oh, Dad, you're silly," I said lovingly and kissed his cheek.

There was a lot to do at the antiquarian bookstore. On Monday, we received a huge delivery. Amira and I stood silently before the ten boxes of Helmut's purchases.

"What was he thinking?" she finally muttered. Her gaze slid over the shelves, some of which were already sagging under the weight of the books.

"I don't know," I sighed. "And he's out on another buying trip today."

"I sense something terrible," she said with a deep sigh. "What do we do now?"

"Sort and catalog," I replied resignedly. "Maybe we'll come up with a way to store them while we work."

So we got to work and didn't finish on Monday, Tuesday, or Wednesday. On Thursday, I opened the last box with Klara. Helmut stood by, scratching his head sheepishly.

"Do I want to know how much you bought in the last few days?" I asked. His eyes grew even bigger, and his smile more apologetic.

"I got a good discount," he said. "The estate sale was huge, and the sellers just wanted to get rid of the books. I almost felt guilty for paying so little. And then there were the other things..."

I sensed trouble. "What other things?" I asked cautiously. Klara held her breath next to me.

Helmut grinned sheepishly. "Well, a few items for the esoteric corner. And some jars. And..."

"Helmut!" I wrung my hands in despair. "Did you secretly rent more store space? Because I don't know where to put the books and other items!"

"You'll think of something," he said and took a few steps back. The bell rang at the door. "I'll go take care of that." He ran off.

Klara exhaled deeply. "My God," she muttered, rubbing her forearm. She had been doing that constantly lately, as if there was something under her skin that didn't belong. I understood that feeling all too well.

Disheartened, I turned to the last box. "Let's keep going. Maybe I'll come up with a saving idea."

"If necessary, we can have a sidewalk sale," Klara suggested. "A sale for antiques and curiosities."

"That's a great idea," I replied and picked up the next thick tome. "Do you think we could combine it with mulled wine or pastries? Then we could ask the bakery next door."

"Why not? Mulled wine has never hurt shopping," she said.

I smiled and stepped to the laptop to enter the book into the inventory. Suddenly, everything went black before my eyes, and my hands went numb. The book slipped from my fingers and fell to the floor with a thud.

I gasped for air and tried to hold onto the table but missed the edge. My knees buckled, and the table corner rushed toward me.

"Neelia!" Klara grabbed my arm and broke my fall. Nevertheless, we both crashed to the floor. I hit my knees and left elbow with a groan. Pain shot through my body, and everything spun before my eyes. My head felt like it was about to explode.

Klara lifted me into a sitting position. I tried to look at her, but the black spots blocked my view. I leaned heavily against a sales table and closed my eyes.

Just a moment more, then the dizziness would hopefully pass. Breathe calmly. In. Out. In. Out.

"Neelia? Are you okay? Should I call a doctor?" Klara asked tentatively.

"Give me two minutes," I groaned, holding my aching arm. "Then I'll be fine."

"Are you sure? You're pale as a ghost, and sweat is pouring down your face."

"I've definitely looked better." I felt nauseous but didn't want to admit it. I didn't want to be taken away by an ambulance. I hated hospitals. And I hated feeling like this right now.

'It will be over soon. For sure.'

I clenched my fists and stretched my fingers to get rid of the numbness. I rotated my ankles and moved my spine. Somewhere inside me was a blockage I had to release to feel better. At home, I had an acupressure mat that helped in such cases. It was miles away.

"What happened?" I heard Helmut ask. Then warm hands wrapped around mine. "Can you get up?"

"Two minutes," I repeated.

"We should call an ambulance," said Klara.

"Please don't. It will be over soon." I opened my eyes and focused on the worried faces in front of me. "Really. I'm all right. You know that happens sometimes."

"But that doesn't mean we worry any less," Klara said, rubbing her forearm. "You scare me every time." She was pale. I knew that her boyfriend had almost died of an allergic shock in the winter. The fear was still in her limbs.

"I'm sorry about that. I hope it stops one day." I struggled to my feet and closed my eyes again as the room spun frantically.

"Can you go to the doctor again about this?" asked Helmut. "Maybe they can find something if you don't wait too long."

It didn't make a difference; I had already seen all the specialists. I just wanted them to stop worrying, so I promised to call my doctor. Then Helmut sent me home.

For once, I accepted the offer.

I went home and immediately lay down. By Friday, I felt better and finished the remaining work at the antiquarian bookstore. In the evening, I had plans with Mira and Skadi. It was about time.

Mira had been at a floristry fair all week, Skadi and Emil had taken a short trip to Oslo. So, we hadn't yet caught up on my first date with Rob.

Mira snuggled tiredly on my sofa. She had come straight from the fair to my place. She had to go back tomorrow.

"I thought I had a stress-free job where I could unleash my creativity," she groaned. "Instead, strict guidelines and deadlines."

"You signed up for the contest yourself," Skadi said with a shrug. "Your bosses didn't force you."

"They would never do that," Mira said. "And yes, I chose it myself. For good reason, the first prize is a trip to Madeira."

"And?" I asked.

Mira shrugged. "Only fourth place, but that doesn't mean I'm giving up. The winners were really good. I'm proud of the fourth place. It was my first contest, and somehow I'll make it to the flower festival in Madeira."

I smiled at her. Mira was talented in her job, and her bouquets and arrangements were popular gifts. I knew she could go far if she dared to enter more competitions. This was a good start.

"And choosing it myself doesn't mean I can't complain about the stress. At least the guy from the electrical team was really cute," she concluded with a grin.

"I can imagine and hope you stayed away from the control panel," Skadi said dryly.

Mira laughed. "That would be a thrilling adventure. What do you think of me. I only flirted with him. No sex in the control room."

"Because you didn't have time," Skadi guessed. Mira laughed even louder. Bullseye.

Her laughter was infectious. I admired how confidently she did everything she wanted. Mira disliked constraints and imposed none on herself. She trusted that she would always find a solution and dared much more than Skadi and I did. If she wanted a tattoo or piercing, she got it. If she was at the train station and suddenly wanted to go to Berlin, she bought a ticket and went. And in all the years I knew her, she had never regretted anything, even though not everything always went smoothly.

I didn't always understand her, but I accepted that Mira was just like that. Skadi, who was way more structured and safety-conscious, had bigger problems with it. The two sometimes argued, but I knew they were safety nets for each other.

Skadi ensured Mira didn't do anything completely crazy. Mira, in turn, prevented Skadi from acting like an old lady already. And I enjoyed knowing two such great, different women. I was the calming influence in our trio. The reliable one who was always there but ensured we got home safely.

Occasionally, I wished I could push my limits. Then often came the fear. The memory of the accident and the certainty that sometimes you couldn't control your fate. That second could destroy everything and take away people you thought would always be there.

Unfortunately, this fear paralyzed me. I couldn't laugh in its face like Mira. And I couldn't stoically control it like Skadi. I quickly sipped my drink and shook off the thoughts.

Skadi shook her head at Mira and turned to me.

"I want to hear about Rob."

I felt my mouth stretch into a broad grin. They hung on my every word. "It was a lovely evening."

"Did you have sex?" Mira asked breathlessly. Skadi snorted. "What? That makes every evening even better!"

"No, we didn't. He had to go on a business trip the next day," I said. "We have our second date tomorrow, and you need to be able to top things. I don't think we'll run out of conversation topics, but I can keep this ace up my sleeve."

"But you did kiss, didn't you?" Mira asked.

I felt my grin widen. "Yes, right at the beginning. The waiter interrupted us."

Mira laughed. "That's the way I like it."

Skadi looked at me searchingly. "You're in love with him!"

My cheeks warmed, and I lost control of my mouth corners. It felt like they were reaching my earlobes. "Yes, maybe."

"Definitely," she countered.

"Yes, definitely," I admitted.

Mira smiled. "How lovely, sweetie. Skadi picked the right man for you. I feel good vibes with you two. Maybe matchmaking is your calling, Ska."

Skadi snorted. "You and I could rule the world. You're the pendulum, and I'm the matchmaker."

We had to laugh.

"I'm glad you like him so much," Skadi said. "I thought you'd like each other. That it's going so well is great."

"We'll see, we've only met twice," I waved it off, even though I wanted to admit how hopeful I was.

"You must call us on Sunday and tell us how it was. In detail," Mira demanded.

"I will," I promised and could hardly wait to see Rob again.

Chapter 3

I stand in the street. It is night again.

The asphalt glistens wet beneath my feet.

I shiver as I sense the invisible danger. A chill clings to my skin, but I sense something warmer - a presence, lingering and waiting for me to slip. A scent both familiar and unsettling fills the air. My pulse quickens, caught between recognition and dread.

My pursuer. I know he is there. He has me in his sight.

I listen to pinpoint his location.

I am strong and fast.

No matter what he tries, I will outwit him.

He can try to sneak up, aim his weapon at me. I will be faster than him.

A sound reveals his location.

A hasty breath shows his nervousness.

A breeze carries his scent to me.

I twist my mouth, then my eyes widen. I know this scent. But from where?

Who is my pursuer?

Why is he here now?

After all these years, now, of all times, he wants to finish what he failed to do back then.

Well, let him try.

My muscles are tense, ready to spring.

This time, he will fail again.

I jerked awake. The dream hung heavily in my head. I placed my hands on my temples and tried to clear my thoughts.

What the hell was that? I felt like I'd been pulled back to those years after the accident when strange dreams and dark thoughts followed me all the time.

The dream rattled me—a complete understatement.

It scared me. On many levels. The feeling of being pursued frightened me. Standing alone on the street and not knowing what was happening stressed me out. Waiting for someone to attack and try to kill me (for that's what my instinct told me) caused a deep-seated panic that made it hard to breathe.

I hadn't had such dreams in years.

I remembered having nightmares after the accident. The psychologists who treated me said it was related to post-traumatic stress disorder. The shock of my mother's death.

They were confusing and frightened me. I repeatedly had the feeling of being pursued. A latent fear that accompanied me even when I was awake. It was hard to bear, especially with all the grief, pain, and amnesia.

I was in therapy for two years until I felt somewhat better and had adjusted to the new life that confined my father to a wheelchair.

Eventually, the dreams disappeared on their own, and I stopped thinking about them. I simply forgot them or pushed them into the depths of my mind. Along with everything else that hurt.

Now, I dragged myself to the bathroom and looked in the mirror. I was pale, with dark shadows under my eyes. Not a good start for my date tonight. I wanted to look forward to it. Strange dreams didn't fit into that.

I showered and stretched my tired limbs. Then I did yoga exercises to stretch my muscles. Afterward, I lay on my acupressure mat. The pain quickly faded, and a pleasant warmth spread as my circulation got going.

After half an hour, I got up feeling better. I made tea and had a quiet breakfast. A message came in on my phone. It was from Rob.

Hopefully, he wasn't canceling!

"I'm looking forward to tonight. I can make it a bit earlier if that's okay with you."

My heart made a little jump. *"Sounds good. The table is reserved, but we can meet before then."*

"Perfect, that's what I hoped. I'll pick you up at four at your place. See you later."

That gave me enough time to tidy up. I had taken some of Helmut's purchases home to look at and read. It helped me get to know new books and better advise customers. However, it also meant I constantly had to climb over stacks of books. Helmut always said my apartment was his external warehouse. Sometimes, I believed it too.

Rob was punctual. Too punctual, as my hair was uncombed, and I had grabbed some random sweaters from the closet. I had made the mistake of sitting down with one of the books "briefly." The story captivated me so much that I lost track of time and jumped up at a quarter to four.

"Damn," I muttered as I stumbled over my shoes. "Always the same." I opened the door and saw Rob's surprised face. "Hey."

"Hey. Everything okay?" he asked.

"Yes, why?"

"You, um... have two different shoes on."

I looked down at my boots. One brown, one black—definitely a new trend in clueless fashion.

"If I'd known, I'd have matched you with a flip-flop," he joked, shaking his head, instantly disarming my embarrassment.

"Sorry. Next time." I kicked off the leather boot and pulled on the second winter boot, then grabbed my coat from the wardrobe and slipped it on. At the last moment, I grabbed a scarf and hat. Rob waited at the door, grinning as I finally finished getting ready.

"Very nice. One more thing before we go."

I stopped and looked at him. He put his arm around me and pulled me close. I stood on my tiptoe to kiss him. Again, our kiss electrified me. Warmth shot through my body, making my hands and feet tingle. I snuggled against him, imagining all the annoying clothes out of the way.

I could just unlock the apartment door, drag him inside, tear the clothes from his body, and kiss him more when I felt his skin against mine.

His fingers ran through my hair, brushing it back, then he moved to my neck to pull me even closer. I sighed and leaned against the hallway wall. My hand groped for my apartment keys. Mira was right: I should take some risks. Why not now?

I wanted it. And judging by how his hands glided over my hips, he wanted it too.

I reached for my keys and groped for the front door. "Do you want to...," I began and sighed as he pulled me even tighter.

Then I heard footsteps. I immediately knew who they belonged to. Oh no. I broke the kiss and gave Rob an apologetic look. He heard it too and slowly pulled away from me, his eyes gleaming.

"This is how I envisioned it. A great start to the evening," he whispered.

My upstairs neighbor walked past us with her heavy step, giving us a curious look. I couldn't stand her. She was terribly finicky and posted snide notes next to the front door for every little thing. She was also a terrible gossip. Seeing Rob had given her enough ammunition for the next three weeks. Now she would stop me every time she saw me and bombard me with questions.

I greeted her and pulled Rob by the hand down the stairs. Just get away from here because she had already taken a breath to start talking. "No need," I thought and slipped out the front door.

Rob looked at me with raised eyebrows. "Neighbors like that are in every building, aren't they?"

"Do you also have someone who knows the house rules by heart and annoys everyone with them?" I asked.

He nodded. "Not anymore since I have a condo, but before, there was a prime example living below me. She banged on the ceiling with a broom at every step. Didn't understand that you always hear something with parquet flooring."

"That sounds exactly like my neighbor." I paused as he took my hand. Warmth spread through me, and I remembered what she had interrupted.

I was so close to taking him back upstairs.

Maybe later, after dinner. I wasn't sure what I craved more at that moment, honestly.

Take it easy. Waiting a bit longer never hurt anyone," I told myself. His hand in mine felt good. Like we were a couple. The thought was beautiful. It sparked my imagination and showed me pictures of us together again. Lazy weekend breakfasts, shared glances on a crowded street. Ordinary days that feel special now. Because of him.

I hadn't felt this way in ages when meeting a man. Normally, I was cautious and waited. But with Rob, it was like loose pieces coming together into a picture.

I shouldn't read too much into it. This was only our second date. It could still turn out that we weren't a match. Even though I didn't believe that.

"Do you want to get a coffee and walk around a bit? Or is it too cold for you?" he asked.

Too cold! I was still so hot from the kiss that I almost wanted to take off my coat!

"Coffee sounds good," I said.

We got a coffee to go and strolled through the neighborhood. Rob lived in Eilbek. That was too far to walk, so he came by car.

"Luckily, my apartment has a garage," he said. "Finding a parking space otherwise is unbearable."

"That's one reason I don't have a car," I said. I preferred to walk. I also had a bike, but I was usually too lazy to get it out of the basement.

"What are the other reasons?" Rob asked.

"The environment, the money, and my accident," I rattled off. He stopped and looked at me, startled.

"Your accident?"

"Oh, crap, that's not a good topic for a date. Just forget it," I said.

"Do you want to talk about it?"

"Yes, but only briefly. It ruins every mood: Shortly before my eighteenth birthday, I had a car accident with my parents. My mother died, and my father has been in a wheelchair since then. I can barely remember the two years before the accident." I shrugged. "That's it. I'd already spent too many days letting the accident define me."

'That part of me is buried—just what I should do with those dreams', I thought.

"So next topic, please."

Rob looked at me, speechless. I could see the thoughts running through his mind. "I'm really sorry," he finally said.

"Thanks, that's kind. But it can't be changed."

"That must be awful."

"Yes, sometimes. Mostly I've gotten used to it." I avoided his gaze and feverishly searched for a way to change the topic. I didn't want to talk about it. I wanted to enjoy the evening and see where it took us.

The accident was part of my story, but by no means the only thing he should know about me. And I didn't want Rob to pity me. I couldn't handle that. It gave me a sense of helplessness. That I was a victim of circumstances. I didn't want that. Breaking free from that had cost me a lot of time and effort in therapy.

"What does your family do?" I asked.

Rob blinked, but he understood. "I already told you about my parents' antique shop," he said. "And about Cecilia."

"Your sister," I nodded.

"Yes. We get along well. So well that she's currently living with me because her landlord evicted her."

I raised my eyebrows. "You must really get along."

"Yes, but we're a better match than her and my parents. When kids move back home..."

"They revert to being kids," I nodded. "I can imagine."

Although my father and I had a great relationship, it was good that we each had our own lives. Living together would only be a last resort.

Rob and I finished our walk and went to the restaurant. Again, time flew by. We talked as if we had known each other forever. I felt incredibly comfortable around him.

We were just putting on our coats, and I was already gathering the courage to invite him back to my place when his phone rang.

"Sorry, it's Cecilia." He took the call. The female voice on the other end sounded excited, even though I couldn't make out what she was saying. "Hey, calm down. What's going on?" He listened and sighed. "Yeah, okay, I'm coming. I'll tell her." He hung up and rolled his eyes. "I must go. Cecilia urgently needs my help. It can't wait."

"Sounds dramatic for a Saturday night at half-past nine," I teased, swallowing my disappointment.

"Yeah, she apologizes profusely." His expression softened, and he pulled me close. "I'd love to continue what we started in your stairwell."

"It's much nicer in my apartment," I whispered.

He grinned and kissed me. "Next time?"

"Definitely. Say hi to your sister for me. She owes us one."

"I'll remind her," he promised, kissing me with a grin before leaving.

Mira and Skadi looked disappointed when I video-called them the next day.

"That's never happened to me," Mira said, stunned. "A lot has gotten in the way, but never a little sister."

"You'll manage that too," Skadi said sharply. Mira just laughed. "I'm really sorry, Neelia," Skadi continued. "That's really frustrating."

"Oh, it's not that bad, really. We'll meet again soon," I waved it off.

"And when?" Mira asked curiously.

"Unfortunately, not until next week. He must go on another business trip tomorrow and is too busy today."

"Get used to it," Skadi said, looking at her hair tips. "Emil also left for Norway this morning. Sometimes his job is really annoying. We were supposed to choose the wedding invitations."

"Do you need help?" I asked.

"I could bring champagne," Mira immediately offered.

Skadi hesitated only for a second before agreeing. Day saved.

The week dragged on. I had a lot to do at the antiquarian bookstore, finding space for Helmut's purchases. He had gone overboard on his last two trips. Some of the books had to be stored at his house because I couldn't fit them in. That was typical of him, and I worried about the expenses.

"We'll recoup it all," he promised.

I was skeptical. Helmut was a gifted bookseller, and yes, he always found the right book for anyone who walked through the door. Rarely did anyone leave empty-handed. But as a businessman, my boss had his weaknesses. Finances were never my strength, but I had made them so because of him. I handled the accounts and inventories sometimes so much that I barely had time for the books.

It had to be done. And that was why Helmut wanted me to take over the bookstore when he retired. One distant day, when I had hopefully learned everything important. For all I cared, he could take fifteen more years.

On Friday, I met with my friends. I looked forward to a relaxed evening, but the mood was tense when I entered Mira's door. I was the last to arrive; it had taken longer at the bookstore.

"Hey, what's wrong?" I asked. Skadi grimaced, and Mira shrugged. "If you don't talk to me, we can't solve it," I said.

"There's nothing to solve," Skadi said tightly.

"I think we can discuss how pointless and stupid you find my job and calling," Mira said snippily. I sensed trouble.

Skadi shot up. "I have nothing against your job," she said, emphasizing the word 'job.' "But you have to let me honestly say what I think about your esoteric hobby: It's a hobby, nothing more. I don't understand most of what you're into. But okay, you like it and are passionate about it, so that's fine by me. But if you tell me you're taking a course in rune reading, I'm allowed to say I think a seminar in business management or floristry would be more useful."

"It's a course in dream interpretation," Mira retorted, agitated. "And I find your macramé deadly boring."

"My hobby doesn't cost hundreds of euros for some nonsense. Everything I make, I have in hand afterward. But fine, you'll never see those things again if you find them so annoying." Skadi's cheeks were red with anger, and her voice was getting louder.

Speechlessly, I looked from one to the other. "You're fighting about this?" I asked, bewildered. "Because Mira wants to take a dream interpretation course? Are you serious? Don't you have any other problems?"

The two looked at me angrily, then I saw the anger dissipate from Mira's face. Skadi took a few seconds longer, then she hung her head.

"I...," she began, looking at Mira. "I don't think you're stupid."

"That would be something," Mira said.

"I just don't understand your enthusiasm for these topics. But that's no reason to attack you. I'm sorry." Skadi twirled a blonde strand of hair.

Mira took a deep breath and then flipped her red hair over her shoulder. "Thanks. Forgotten already. I know you're too pragmatic to get into it." She rolled her eyes. "So what do I do now? I wanted to read palms and lay tarot cards at your wedding. Now my gift idea is ruined."

Skadi looked horrified. It took her a few seconds to realize Mira was joking. I saw her genuine relief. Now I sat down with them, glad they had made up.

The rest of the evening was relaxed. We worked on preparations for Skadi's wedding, choosing colors and flowers for the table decorations, and coming up with a few more details for the decor. There was plenty of wine, and the mood was good again.

Luckily, because I couldn't stand it when they fought.

On Monday, Rob contacted me. "I'm coming back tomorrow night," he said crackling. The connection was terrible. "Unfortunately, it'll be so late that we can't celebrate Valentine's Day. Are you free on Wednesday? We can make it up then."

"Wednesday works," I replied. "And I never cared about Valentine's Day. I buy flowers all year round."

He laughed. "Maybe we can think of something better than flowers and chocolates."

My insides vibrated at his words. "Definitely," I breathed. My brain conjured up the appropriate images, and I got hot. I could hardly wait and had to restrain myself.

I couldn't set my expectations too high, or it would only lead to disappointment. But the way he kissed promised a lot. If he was the same in bed... Again, my brain supplied the corresponding storyline. I already felt his hands on my skin, his lips wandering over my neck. His breath gave me goosebumps. His gaze as our bodies came together...

"Neelia?" His voice brought me back.

"Yes?" I asked, distracted.

"Is everything okay?"

"Yes, why?"

"You made a weird noise just now. Or do you have a cat?" Rob asked.

Oh God, what had I done? My cheeks burned. The line between sexy and crazy was sometimes thin. I feared I was balancing on it.

"Are you coming to my place?" I quickly changed the subject before it got more embarrassing. My inner movie should take a break; my life wasn't a romance novel. Even though I was ready for it.

"Sure. Do you want to order food?" he suggested.

"Maybe I'll cook," I said.

Maybe that would help me stay cool. Besides, I liked cooking. Did Rob like Indian food? I had a collection of recipes from my mother that deserved more attention.

"I'm looking forward to it. A lot." His voice got deeper. Maybe it was the terrible connection.

"Me too," I said, feeling hot again.

We hung up, and I snuggled contentedly on my sofa. I closed my eyes and tried to keep my inner movie in check. It didn't work; I got lost in it. It was nice too.

On Wednesday, I left work early and forced myself to cook for Rob and me. I even tidied up a bit. Just a bit, then I found a book and lost track of time. Fortunately, the lentil dal on the stove was patient.

He arrived at seven o'clock, just as I was desperately looking for a top. Time had caught up with me once again. I quickly put on a cardigan and opened the door.

He came in smiling, then his eyes widened, and his smile grew broader. "Hey."

I looked down at myself. The cardigan had no buttons, and the neckline of the spaghetti top I wore underneath sat dangerously low because I had pulled at the hem. My breasts were clearly demanding his attention. And Rob found it hard to tear his eyes away from them. Honestly, I felt the same way about his butt.

I kissed him to diffuse the situation and subtly pulled up my top. I didn't get far because he wrapped his arms around me and pressed me to him.

"There's that sound again," he whispered against my lips. I hadn't even noticed I had made a noise. "So that's what it means."

I leaned against my hallway wall and sighed as he slipped the cardigan from my shoulders.

"Why don't you take a moment to get settled," I said, dazed.

He let go of me, grinning, and took off his coat and boots. "You're right. This okay, or more?"

He wore black jeans and a gray long-sleeved shirt with a button placket.

My lips parted, and my cheeks warmed. He looked me straight in the eye and waited for my answer. He wasn't joking. If I wanted, one word, and we could go straight to the bedroom.

I still had the dal on the stove. "More."

Did I just say that?

Holding my breath, I watched him pull his shirt over his head. My heart pounded, and I took a close look at him. Rob was slim, his body defined as a lightweight athlete's: firm muscles clung to him, flexible and sleek. His stomach was flat. I paused when I saw the long scar on his side. As I traced it with my thumb, he pulled me closer.

I inhaled his scent, feeling the warmth of his skin under my hands. "I've been through some stuff too. Want to see more?"

"Absolutely." My brain had no control over my mouth. I wanted to approach it differently, but I said the opposite of what my mind advised. Instead, I did what I really wanted to do. I felt bold and daring, simply telling him what I wanted.

I dared. Rob made it easy.

I led him into my bedroom and kissed him again. His hands slid to the hem of my shirt and pulled it over my head. I looked into his face and stroked his cheek. Today he was clean-shaven. I liked that too, though I found the stubble even hotter on him.

I ran my hands over his chest, his ribs, the scar, and his flat stomach to his hip bones. His skin stretched softly over firm muscles. The scar was a notch as if he had escaped an attack. I imagined the exciting story behind it.

He slipped the straps of my bra from my shoulders and kissed my collarbone. Then my neck.

He turned me around and wrapped his arms around me. Then he paused and straightened up. "Oh."

I looked over my shoulder at his surprised face. He had discovered the tattoo. "Everything okay?" I asked.

"Yes. I just didn't expect you to..."

"Have such a huge tattoo?" I offered. Most people didn't expect that from me.

"Yes." His fingers traced the lines slowly, as if piecing together the layers of my story. "But it's beautiful. It suits you," he said, with a sincerity that softened his gaze. Then he discovered the scar on the other side. "Is that from your accident?"

"Yes." I turned around and wrapped my arms around his neck. I definitely didn't want to talk about the accident now. Not when we were half-naked in front of my bed. I stood on tiptoe and kissed him, while I fumbled with his belt buckle.

He wasted no time and unbuttoned my jeans. I sighed as we fell onto my bed, and I felt his naked skin against mine. I explored his body with my hands and eyes, pressing myself to him, enjoying his touches.

I found more scars on his arms, back, and even his left thigh. I also discovered that Rob had a tattoo too: an intricate symbol on his right shoulder blade.

Before I could ask about it, he rose and lowered his lips to my breasts. We would have plenty of time to talk later. Now I focused on what I wanted to do.

Something stirred in me, pushing to the surface. It made me climb onto his lap. I wrapped my legs around his waist and looked deep into his eyes. "More."

Rob's brown eyes darkened. He reached behind him and pulled a package from his pocket.

"So you planned this?" I asked.

"I hoped I'd need it," he replied, tearing it open. Then he gripped me tighter and positioned me. I let out a loud moan as I sank onto him.

Again, I felt that urge to take control. I wanted to show him how to proceed. How to touch me and which movements I liked best. My brain was screaming 'slow down,' but my heart said otherwise. I gave in, letting instinct guide me, and found myself daringly asking for more.

That surprised me because usually, it was hard for me to say what I wanted in bed. I often let my partner take the lead. Not tonight. Tonight, I was fully engaged and wanted to decide what happened to me. I wanted to show him how to treat me so this night would be unforgettable for both of us.

The first of many,' I reminded myself, guiding his hands to my hips, claiming the moment as my own. He liked it; I could see that immediately.

Our bodies merged perfectly, and I no longer knew where he ended, and I began. Heat filled me, and I kissed him passionately on the mouth. He held me tight, and we found our rhythm. My breath was shaky and ragged. Sweat ran down my body, and all my muscles tensed.

I felt his every movement, lost myself in his kisses, and our union. My moans excited him, and I savored every sound he made, showing how much he enjoyed it.

It felt like I had waited forever for him. For this first night we spent together.

I clung to his shoulders as the heat inside me coiled and then exploded. I let out a loud scream and had to be held by him. My head throbbed, and I had no control over my body.

Rob gripped me tighter and increased the pace. I could barely keep up. Stars danced before my eyes, and my arms and legs felt numb.

He held on for a moment longer, then his grip became almost painfully tight, and he let out a suppressed cry. I held him close, closed my eyes, and lost myself in this moment that should last forever.

"Neelia," he whispered. I snuggled against him, feeling his heartbeat against my chest. Or was it my own? I couldn't say for sure.

"I wasn't planning to ask this now, but whatever." His voice was lazy, but his gaze was alert as he looked into my face. "I know it's early, maybe a bit impulsive, but I just can't shake it—I want to be with you, constantly. If you're ready for that."

"You mean, you want us to be a couple? Officially?" I asked for clarification. He nodded, and I saw a hint of uncertainty in his face.

Yes, it happened quickly, and no, this was not the best time to ask this question. But practical wasn't what I wanted—he felt like the missing piece I didn't know I needed. It just felt right.

"I want that too," I said, kissing him as I fell back onto the mattress. Rob leaned over me and placed my leg back around his waist.

"Then let's make this official—properly."

Chapter 4

*M*y breath rises in clouds.
*Each sense, painfully sharp. My breath, cold clouds against the night.
My muscles tense, coiled. Ready. My heart beats heavily. My gaze
catches every corner.*

*Where are you, my invisible observer? How close have you already
come to me? How heavy is the weapon in your hand? Do you like what
you see? Are you sure you can do it? And do you really think you are
faster and more dangerous than I am?'*

*I feel his eyes on me. He is waiting for the right moment. A shiver
runs through my body and my heart pounds even more. I can hardly
stand it. Waiting and patience have never been my strengths.*

I am ready. Ready for him. Ready for the fight for life and death.

I want to find out who is stronger. More cunning.

Who will survive? And how?

This time, the hunter and I are close. Close enough to smell his nerves.

*I hear footsteps. My blood rushes through my veins. Finally, he reveals
himself to me. Finally, he steps out of his hiding place.*

The corners of my mouth curl into a smile.

*I know that I will be the one who triumphs. Surely, he thinks the
same of himself.*

He is wrong.

I am not.

The steps come closer.

I draw up the corners of my mouth and growl.

Finally.

Finally, we bring it to an end.
The moonlight reflects on the blade of his knife.
He will regret choosing this weapon.
He has no chance.
I growl even deeper, and anticipation fills me.
It is time. The revenge is mine.

I blinked into pale light and flinched when I noticed the arm over my naked waist. Then I felt the breath on my neck.

'Oh God, where am I? And who's that?"

Frightened, I disentangled myself and turned around.

My heart skipped a beat when I recognized Rob. Of course, it was him. Of course, he was lying here in my bed.

My boyfriend.

It has been official since last night. I wanted to be happy about it, but the dream still held me captive.

Waking felt like surfacing from a heavy fog, every shadow from my dream clinging as I slipped off the mattress.

A deep breath. It was just a dream, just old memories stirring. On the way, I grabbed my bathrobe from the hook by the door. The cold kitchen tiles jolted me fully awake. Normal. This was normal.

It was cold in the apartment, and a glance at the clock told me it was five in the morning. Outside, it was still deep at night, the light came from the streetlamp in front of the house.

Shivering, I got something to drink from the fridge and sat down at my table. My body felt like it did after an intense workout. Normally, I would assume it was from the sex, but after this dream, I was unsure.

I felt strained, as if the tension I felt in the dream was still in every muscle. Taking deep breaths helped release some of the inner restlessness.

I noticed that I was listening to every little noise.

As if the hunter were somewhere around here.

The hunter. I didn't even know if he was really a man. I just assumed so.

These dreams were a mystery to me. I had no clue what they meant. They scared me. Because of their content, but also because of the intensity with which I experienced them.

Tonight, I would meet Mira and Skadi. Although Mira hadn't had her dream interpretation workshop yet, maybe she still had some advice for me.

I rolled my eyes. This was going to be fun if Skadi found out.

Next door, I heard a noise and stood up. That was Rob. I pushed the thoughts of my dream to the back of my mind and went back into the bedroom.

What lay ahead of us was much more important than fantasies. I opened the bedroom door. In front of me lay my new boyfriend, stretching his arms out to me.

I let my bathrobe fall to the floor and walked to him with a smile.

By evening, I had forced the morning's weight back into the shadows. The lighthearted chatter with Skadi and Mira felt like a welcome escape from whatever haunted my nights. Skadi beamed at me as I told her about last night.

"Oh my God, I'm so happy for you!" she cheered. "This is even better than I thought."

"The guy must be a beast in bed. And... does he bite? Did you do it here too? Are there any virgin places left? Or do you want to keep that to yourself?" Mira teased, dancing around my sofa. I laughed and threw a sofa cushion at her. "We'll save that for next time, once you've told me your favorite spot," I replied.

Mira burst into laughter and clinked her glass with mine. "I'm glad it's going so well. You deserve the best man."

"We'll see," I said, taking a sip of wine. "But the start was pretty good."

'*More than that*,' I corrected myself. There was something in the way he looked at me - a kind of acceptance I hadn't felt in a long time.

He didn't know about my past, my shadows. What would he think if he knew about my dreams, my inner scars? I wanted to keep them at bay, keep him from seeing this part of me. But some shadows don't stay hidden. Could I really let him in, even with the parts of myself that frightened me?

I pushed those feelings aside. This wasn't the time to deal with dark thoughts. This was the time to be happy.

Skadi sipped her glass contentedly. She deserved it. Her intuition was spot on, and I was grateful for the push she had given me.

"There is one more thing I wanted to ask you, Mira," I started on the second topic.

"Please, always," said Mira, relaxed.

"I've been having strange dreams lately that I don't understand," I continued.

Out of the corner of my eye, I saw Skadi raise her eyebrows. "I'll get some wine from the kitchen," she mumbled and stood up.

Mira watched her go and then turned back to me. "I'm listening."

I quickly described the dreams to her. About the hunter, about my desire to duel with him. About my certainty that I was more dangerous than him. Mira's eyes grew wider.

"Well, I didn't expect that," she admitted.

"At first, I thought the dreams were about Rob," I said. "That they were subconsciously telling me to embrace the relationship and be brave. But now I don't think that anymore."

Mira slowly shook her head. "No, I wouldn't interpret it that way either," she said. "I think the whole thing sounds like a danger you're not yet aware of."

"Danger?" I asked. Skadi returned and sat down with a tense expression. "Sorry, I know this isn't your favorite topic," I said to her.

Skadi shrugged. "It's up to you. I always think that the subconscious can only process what the conscious has perceived – whether it left an impression or not. I don't believe in omens or anything like that."

"Neither do I," Mira said dismissively. "But it's not always easy to figure out what's behind it. That's why I took the course. Dream interpretation has a lot to do with psychology."

"And what comes next? Hypnosis?" Skadi asked dryly. Another thing she didn't believe in.

"Yes, that would be the next step, you're right." Mira turned back to me. "Is there anything that scares you?"

"Nothing new," I said. "I also dreamed about the accident recently, but that can't be it. I've worked through that well."

"That doesn't mean it can't still play a role subconsciously," Mira said, and for once, Skadi nodded. How nice that they agreed.

Mira sighed. "Maybe it helps to keep a diary. If you sit down in the evening before bed and reflect on the day, it might help you find the cause. But I do think it could be related to Rob. I can see how much in love you are with him. Maybe that scares you a little. It will surely subside in the next few days and weeks."

Again, Skadi nodded in agreement. "That sounds plausible."

"Then I'll try the diary," I said. "And just wait and see what happens. They're just dreams. They have no influence on my actual life."

"Good idea. And speaking of influence: I'm going to Madeira!" Mira announced so loudly that I jumped.

"Congratulations," Skadi said, hugging her. "How did that come about so suddenly?"

"Dumb luck," Mira said and let me hug her too. "The winner of the competition at the fair was disqualified. He cheated, who knows. They couldn't reach second place, and the third declined the prize because she couldn't take the trip. So I'm the lucky one to go to the Flower Festival in Madeira. A dream comes true!"

Skadi poured more wine, and we toasted each other.

"I'm so happy for you," I said. "I know how long you've wanted to go there."

"'Long' is an understatement," Mira replied cheerfully. "Thanks, girls. I knew we could celebrate this properly. I brought a bottle of 'Moonlight Love'. You're going to love the shot; I can feel it."

I knew we couldn't resist and got the shot glasses. At the same time, I had a feeling we would regret it.

The next morning, I woke up with a terrible hangover.

My hunch was right: 'Moonlight Love' knocked us all out. And mischievously, this stuff was so delicious that you couldn't stop. Mira just kept pouring. When the first bottle was empty, she 'accidentally' found a second in her bag. Skadi and I loudly celebrated and drank with her.

I remembered being dizzy and Mira's idea of doing a moonlight session naked on my balcony only failing to materialize thanks to Skadi's remaining sanity. Otherwise, we would all have pneumonia now. It was the eighteenth of February, that would have been madness.

So we continued drinking with our clothes on and laughed so much that I got even dizzier. We sang songs we used to party to as teenagers and danced to them. It reminded us of the time when we still thought we could achieve anything. For me, that was the time when I neither knew who I was nor what I wanted. My whole life was a mess I had to deal with. Dad and I went to Berlin for a while, but I always kept in touch with Skadi and Mira. Thanks to my two friends, I managed to get out of that phase. They visited me as often as they could. And then we really let loose. They were my anchors.

When I told them that again with a heavy tongue, we cried and hugged. Then Mira poured more. What happened after that, I didn't remember exactly. Maybe that was for the best.

I sat up and rubbed my sore head. Apparently, I would never learn when it came to my girls. We almost always escalated. And those were always the best evenings and nights.

I wouldn't know what to do without the two of them.

Skadi lay next to me in bed, Mira had fallen asleep on the couch. I could hear her through the open bedroom door. Mira didn't snore, but she always made funny noises that I had never heard from anyone else. You might think a little cat was next door.

Skadi lay there like a statue as always.

"Oh God," I murmured, rubbing my eyes. Every beam of light hurt like a stab.

Skadi twitched and woke up. The remnants of her makeup were smeared across her face. Her eyes were bloodshot as she blinked now. "I'm going to kill Mira," she whispered, pressing her hands to her eyelids. "If she brings that stuff again, I'm pouring it down the toilet."

"It did taste good, though," I pointed out.

Skadi shuddered. "Just the thought makes me sick." Yeah, I felt the same way.

"The aspirin is in the kitchen. I'll bring a round," I said and groaned as I sat up.

Skadi crawled out of bed and smoothed her tousled hair. "Never again," she muttered.

When I walked into the hallway, I stopped short. The smell of coffee greeted us, and the kitchen exhaust fan was on. Cautiously, I peeked around the corner and widened my eyes: Mira stood at the stove, making scrambled eggs. She saw me and waved cheerfully. Had I just imagined hearing her in the living room?

"Wasn't she just in bed?" Skadi whispered. She was still squinting slightly. "What the hell," she growled, stomping into the kitchen. "How are you so chipper?"

"Because I drank the elixir of cheerful health, which you both foolishly declined," Mira said casually, pouring coffee into three mugs. "I told you it prevents a hangover."

Skadi snorted and went to the bathroom, closing the door firmly behind her. Shortly after, I heard the shower running.

"I thought you were joking," I said tiredly, accepting my coffee mug gratefully.

"Oh, sweetie, you should know me better. When it comes to hangovers, I never joke." Mira sipped her mug and stirred the pan.

"I'll remember that," I promised and took an aspirin. "Despite everything, it was a great evening."

"Absolutely. I've been thinking about your dreams," Mira said over her shoulder. "If something is bothering you, please talk to us about it. There's something strange about your dream, I just don't know what. It's driving me crazy. This whole fight thing. A duel to the death. If you had only dreamed it once, it wouldn't worry me, but they're basically episodes. A serial story."

"I've noticed that too. Some things repeat, but it always leads to this duel. I wonder what happens when I meet my pursuer," I said, staring at my coffee.

"Yes, me too," Mira replied. She looked at me seriously. "Neelia, please be careful. I don't believe in omens either, but it's never wrong to be careful."

"Promise." My phone rang. Rob was calling. We had a date tonight. I looked forward to it and hoped I would be fit by then. I wanted to enjoy every moment with him.

"Hey, Neelia." Wherever he was, it was loud. Still, I could tell he was stressed. Hopefully, nothing bad happened.

"Hey. Where are you? Is everything okay?"

"Yes, I'm fine. I'm at the airport because I must go to Casablanca short notice. An important assignment came up that I couldn't refuse. I'm sorry, I can't make it tonight." Rob sounded terribly frustrated.

Disappointment spread through me. Was this going to be a regular thing? Would I always have to expect to be stood up?

"I'm really sorry," Rob said, and I believed him. "I know you were looking forward to tonight. So was I. I'll make it up to you. I'll be back on Tuesday if everything goes smoothly. Reserve the rest of the week for me. I will make up for it thoroughly."

Now I laughed. "Well, since you admit your mistake, I won't be too hard on you. And aside from Friday, you can have every evening."

"Then I'll arrange a table for Tuesday. And I have an idea for Thursday."

"What about Wednesday?" I wanted to know.

"Wednesday, you won't be able to leave the house."

A pleasant little shiver ran down my spine. He couldn't say things like that when I wouldn't see him until Tuesday. That was three evenings and three nights alone, waiting for this 'penance.'

"Don't promise too much," I warned him.

"Never. I must go; my boarding is starting. I'll call you when I'm in the hotel. Maybe we'll have time for a hot phone call."

"We'll see. Bring me something from Casablanca."

"As long as it's not Humphrey Bogart…." Rob said good-bye and hung up. I stared at my phone and tried not to take it too hard. Mira patted my hand and took a breath to say something.

"Get used to it," I heard Skadi say before Mira could. She stood in the doorway with wet hair, just unpacking an aspirin. "That's the price you pay for choosing a guy with a job like that. I know it all too well."

"I know." I shook off the rest of my disappointment. It made no sense, and I had to accept it. "There are worse things than a boyfriend who travels a lot for work. I can handle it."

"Absolutely!" Mira said cheerfully, piling mountains of scrambled eggs onto plates. "So, enjoy your hangover cure!"

Mira and Skadi had no plans on Saturday, so I told my dad I would visit him on Sunday. The three of us spent a relaxing day together, and I recharged with strength and peace. We had a long breakfast, went shopping, and spontaneously decided on half a wellness day. Afterward, I felt better than I had in a long time. I treated myself to a massage, which, along with a sauna session, melted all the tension out of my body.

"We should do this more often," Mira sighed, floating on her back in the pool. She was absolutely right. We rarely treated ourselves to such breaks.

Later, we ordered food and spent the evening on Skadi's couch watching a movie, most of which we missed because we couldn't stop talking.

Without alcohol, even though Mira asked multiple times.

"Boring!" she said.

"Sensible," Skadi countered.

"Sensible *is* boring," Mira retorted.

"Maybe, but this way we'll still have a Sunday," I said.

"Fine, without it then," Mira conceded.

"I hope you're not always so easy to convince," Skadi teased. Mira stuck out her tongue.

"If someone convincingly tells me that a contraceptive spell also prevents gonorrhea, I usually give in."

"You're impossible," Skadi said.

"You started it."

"Enough, or I'll need wine after all," I said. They both laughed, and we managed to focus on the film for another five minutes.

On Sunday, I walked to my dad's and cooked with him and Annaya. I liked my dad's girlfriend; she was just right for him: balanced and full of life. They were both delighted when I told them the news about Rob and me.

"When do we get to meet him?" Dad wanted to know.

Annaya laughed. "And you always claim to be such a relaxed father, Abel. You've just shattered that illusion for us."

My father smiled ruefully and rubbed his neck. "You're right. Take your time, Neelia, there's no rush. I know you've chosen him carefully."

Now Annaya laughed even louder. "You're not making it any better, my dear." She looked at me with twinkling eyes. "Your father is more nervous than you."

"I can see that," I said calmly and patted his hand. "Don't worry about me."

"Easier said than done," he grumbled. "I'm your father; that's my job."

"You're right, but you can relax about Rob. He's absolutely harmless. And if nothing else, Skadi can assure you he's not crazy."

"I'll think about it," he said, smiling.

"Is he away a lot for work?" Annaya asked, setting the plates out.

"Yes, that's the only downside. But I get cool photos from him." I took out my smartphone and showed them the latest picture he had sent. "He's in Casablanca right now."

I kept the other photos to myself. Along with the chat history. Neither was for fathers.

"A job like that does have its perks," Annaya laughed, as Dad gave her a reproachful look. "Don't worry; I'm not leaving you. I know you need me."

"Alright," he grumbled. "I know I can count on you."

I served the food on the plates and was happy for the two of them. That was the kind of relationship I wanted too. And I was sure it was possible with Rob.

In the evening, I fell into bed, exhausted. Rob texted me and sent a few more pictures from Morocco. *It's beautiful here; you absolutely have to see it someday.*

'Someday, definitely,' I replied, wondering if it would be over the top to ask him if he would travel there again with me.

'I'll be your tour guide,' he wrote.

I snuggled into my pillow with a smile. *'That would be great. Do you know when you'll be back?'*

'Tomorrow evening. Is Tuesday still on?' he asked.

'Definitely. You still have a few promises to keep,' I texted and sent a little devil emoji.

I will, so get ready for something. Come over to my place? I miss you.

My cheeks warmed with joy as I read that.

'I will. I can't wait for you to be back.' I thought for a moment, then added: *'You said I should get ready. For what?'*

I can't write that; I'll be arrested immediately. In some countries, what I plan to do with you is forbidden.

Sounds dangerous. Do I need a safe word?

He sent a grinning devil emoji. *'Let yourself be surprised, chérie.'*

We exchanged a few more messages, his words promising, filling me with warmth.

Yet in a quiet part of my mind, a question lingered... Could I truly let him in, knowing what might come out? And if I did, would I risk losing him?

'*Yes*', I realized. *Because I want this, and I will do everything to make it work. I deserve it. And I will cherish every moment we have.*'

Both of us had to get up early the next day. Reluctantly, we wished each other goodnight. I put the phone away and closed my eyes. I fell asleep with a smile on my face.

It's that dream again.

I recognize the scene immediately. The place where I am. But above all, how my body feels: supple, strong. As if nothing could defeat me.

No one, except one. I have an equal opponent.

He's out there. Watching, closing in. I feel it - his need to strike, his patience thin. My muscles twitch, a beast coiled, waiting.

This time, the hunter and I are close.

Steam rises from the asphalt. My neck tingles with anticipation. I take a few steps and check the surroundings one more time.

I know where he is lurking. I sense how he will attack me. I smell his excitement.

It mingles with mine. My heart beats loudly.

He takes another step.

I hear him draw breath.

'I know what you're planning. I will beat you to it.'

My heart pounds, yet despite the danger, I feel no fear. This must happen between us. We must finish it.

Another step. Now he comes out of the shadow.

My sharp eyes recognize his outline. He is wearing a long coat. His face is in half-shadow, but I can see the glint in his eyes.

His face doesn't matter to me. Neither does his name or his origin. The same was true of him. We were anonymous mortal enemies.

We know why we are here. At the end of our encounter, only his story will remain. I don't grant him a future, just as he doesn't for me. The most important thing is the knife in his hand. That's why he must come to me. I expected a gun. How foolish of him. In close combat, he has no chance against me.

"There you are," he says. His voice doesn't match him. Its melody doesn't fit an ice-cold killer.

He and I, we both deceive our opponents.

We are too clever to fall for that.

It will happen. Now.

We both know it.

I crouch slightly, ready to jump. My eyes keep the blade in view.

The corners of my mouth curl. But tonight, uncertainty flickers - a warning in the shadows. I must be sharper, faster.

Surely, he thinks the same of himself.

He is wrong. I hope I am not.

I mustn't make a mistake.

I won't make a mistake.

I push off from the ground and leap at him.

I surfaced, gasping, as if clawing out of the dark. The dream's grip still clenched around me, shadows stalking the edges of my vision. Cold sweat clung to my skin, and every creak in the quiet room felt like a whisper from the other side.

'*Just a dream,*' I told myself. A part of me didn't believe it.

The dream was so real that all the impressions were still present. The fight to the death had begun. I dreaded dreaming it further.

I didn't want to see how it ended. I was afraid of the bloodbath this encounter would end in.

Him or me. There was no alternative.

Breathing heavily, I looked at the ceiling. I didn't understand these dreams. What did they mean? Why did they keep playing out in my head?

If this continued and I couldn't handle it alone, I would have to go to Dr. Singh. She had helped me after the accident. Maybe she would show me a way out of helplessness this time too.

It felt good to have an option. Slowly, my heartbeat calmed down. I looked at my clock. It was almost time to get up; staying in bed made no sense.

Besides, I wanted to shake off the dream.

I swung my legs over the edge of the bed and stood up. I noticed the numb feeling too late. The tightness slammed into my chest, a wave crushing my lungs. Air… where was it? My body tingled. Numb. Everything slipped and left me gasping.

My legs gave way, and I lost control of my body. With a dull thud, I hit the floor, barely cushioning my fall with my back against the bed. Then I lay on the floor, choking. I felt nauseous, and my whole body tingled. My head felt like I wasn't getting enough air.

Panic rose within me. I was alone. No one could help me. I didn't know how long the attack would last. My breathing was labored and wheezing, I made a terrible noise. I had to cough, but it didn't make things better. Panic overwhelmed me again.

Breathe!

I coughed again, then took a deep breath. It took all my strength to maintain control.

Then, finally, it got a little easier. The pressure on my chest lessened. The throbbing in my head subsided.

The numbness was still there, but the panic was fading. I had to hold on and wait until I regained control of my body. That would happen. The calmer I was, the sooner. At least, I hoped so.

My eyelids grew heavy with exhaustion, but I had to prevent myself from dozing off. Another dream would only make things worse, and I sensed it lurking in my subconscious.

The floor of my bedroom was cold. I lay only with my hip and left leg on the carpet in front of the bed; the rest was on the parquet. *'I should carpet the whole room,'* I thought dully. I felt sick again and breathed against the nausea.

Time passed, and finally, I felt the numbness leaving my limbs. I waited until I could move my hands and feet, then cautiously tried my arms and legs.

Groaning, I pushed myself into a sitting position and leaned against my bed. My legs wouldn't hold me yet, but I somehow pulled myself onto the mattress.

My teeth chattered with exhaustion and cold. I couldn't stand up. The attack had drained all my strength; I felt like an empty shell. With the last bit of energy, I grabbed my phone and called Helmut. Only the voicemail answered. "I can't make it today," I whispered. "I'm sorry." Then the phone slipped from my hand.

My eyes grew heavy, exhaustion pulled me under, but I forced my mind to steady.

I sensed it - a darkness pacing, watching, waiting.

Just like in my dream.

But this time, I wouldn't face it unprepared.

Chapter 5

Iwoke up feeling better, though every movement pulled at sore muscles. As I placed my feet on the floor, a dull ache ran down my side where I'd hit the floor - probably a bruise forming.

Tired, I pulled myself up and cautiously placed my feet on the floor. There was no way I wanted to risk another fall. This time, my legs held me, but I still sat on the edge of the bed and took a deep breath. My smartphone lay on my nightstand. With heavy limbs, I picked it up and saw that I had received twenty messages. Helmut had called too. I called him back and explained what had happened.

"I'm worried about you," he said. "That it hit you so hard and you're home alone, it can't be good."

"That's kind, but nothing happened," I said. "And who should take care of me? I'm hopefully far from needing a nursing service. I can manage on my own. I'll be back at work tomorrow. Promise."

"Only if you're feeling well. Otherwise, go to the doctor."

I promised to think about it, but I was determined to go back to the bookshop the next day. A doctor couldn't help me anyway.

After the call, I made myself something to eat; my stomach was loudly demanding attention. With pasta and pesto, I sat on the couch and tried to stay awake at least a bit.

After that, I dragged myself back to bed.

The next morning, I felt better and arrived at work on time. I took it easy, and everything was fine. Helmut agreed, though he nervously hovered around me the entire time, constantly asking how I was. I assured him and Klara, who came in the afternoon, that I was fine.

In the evening, I finished work on time and took the bus to Rob's place. He was my ray of light; I had been looking forward to seeing him all day. I eagerly anticipated our touches, his kisses. I had brought my toothbrush and fresh clothes for the next day.

It felt wonderful to go to my boyfriend's place.

Using my navigation app, I found his apartment building and rang the bell for "R. von Lindenstein." What a cool last name. Definitely cooler than mine, Jacobi.

It was far too early to think about such things.

The buzzer went off, and I climbed the stairs to the third floor, wanting to prove to myself that I was fit enough for the elevator. When I reached the top, I was drenched in sweat and had to admit I had overestimated myself.

Rob stood surprised at his apartment door. "Are you okay? Why didn't you take the elevator?"

"Because I look best when I'm drenched in sweat," I panted. He hugged me and kissed me. Now I could hardly breathe, but it felt good.

He took me inside and handed me a glass of water. I leaned against his kitchen counter and looked around. The room was beautiful. Modern and tastefully furnished. I remembered that Rob owned his apartment.

Of course, it was nicer than my rental.

My kitchen had seen better days.

"Do you like my kitchen?" Rob asked as I tested the pressure mechanism on the cabinet doors.

I stifled a grin. "Is that a macho comment? Are you about to say I fit perfectly here?"

"Never. I just took forever to decide on this kitchen and I'm proud of it. So I hope for a compliment on my good taste."

"Well then: I like your kitchen, Rob. You have excellent kitchen taste. Almost as if you work with furniture for a living," I praised him effusively.

He nudged me lovingly. "I'm to blame for fishing for compliments."

"Yep, you are. Will you show me the rest so I can properly admire it and continue to praise your excellent taste?" I asked cheerfully.

He hugged me and kissed me again. "Gladly. I'll open a bottle of wine, so it feels like a soirée in an artist's studio."

"Good idea." I took the glass he offered, and Rob showed me his four-room apartment.

I was deeply impressed. Just the fact that he owned the apartment was amazing. I had lived in rentals all my life and couldn't imagine owning something so valuable.

Rob led me to the living room, and I noticed he steered me past the bedroom.

"I'll show you that later."

I felt a flush as I imagined how he planned to show me.

We stood in front of his large couch, and he pulled me down with him. "I've ordered food for eight. We have a bit of time until then." He wrapped his arms around me, and I kissed him.

"I really like your apartment. It must be great to own something all by yourself," I said.

"Well, not quite as alone as I'm usually used to," he began, just as the apartment door opened and someone walked in.

"Rob? Are you here? How was Morocco? Did you get the thing? Was it difficult? Are you…?" The voice floated down the hall, light and curious, until she entered the room and froze, her eyes widening as she took us in, a curious smirk tugging at her mouth. "Oh, fuck, sorry."

For a moment, I was at a loss as to what to make of her appearance. The situation overwhelmed me.

"Cilly, I thought you were out today," Rob said with a strange undertone. "Neelia, this is my sister, Cecilia."

"Hi!" Cecilia waved at me. I remembered then: Rob had mentioned that she was staying with him because she had been evicted from her own apartment. I waved back and now noticed the resemblance between them: the eye area and chin were similar, and as she grinned at him, the impression was reinforced.

"You could have told me your girlfriend was here."

"Then you'd be here even more," he retorted.

She laughed. "True. Nice to meet you, Neelia. So we're meeting earlier than planned. Rob always makes a big secret out of it when he meets someone."

"Always?" I asked, raising an eyebrow. Rob rubbed the back of his neck uneasily. Was his sister about to tell me he was a womanizer?

"Sounds like more than it is. But my brother is quite the secretive type," she said matter-of-factly.

"Thanks for making every effort to make her think poorly of me, Cilly." Rob grimaced.

Cecilia shrugged. "Sorry, that wasn't my intention. Maybe Neelia is the woman you want to confide in. Okay," she stretched. "I don't want to intrude. I'll just grab a few things and leave you two alone. Forget I was here."

"Well, from my side…," I began. I didn't want her to feel offended.

"Are you staying out overnight?" Rob asked.

Her eyes sparkled. "Since you ask, yes. And no, it's none of your business where I'm staying, dear brother."

Rob watched her with narrow eyes as she went into his study. It was so meticulously tidy that I hadn't noticed anyone lived there during the tour.

"I don't want her to feel unwelcome," I said to Rob.

"Hey, don't worry about it. She was supposed to be out today," he shrugged.

"Does she have a boyfriend?" I wanted to know.

"Not that I know of, but she'll be sleeping somewhere," he growled.

"Well, it's not just you who has secrets, dear brother," Cecilia came back and blew us a kiss. "Have fun, you two. Don't let me bother you." She laughed and closed the door behind her. I watched her leave with a guilty conscience. I had always wished for siblings. In my imagination, it was great to have a brother or sister. If I caused a rift between Rob and Cecilia, it would weigh heavily on me.

But Rob looked relaxed and pulled me back to him. "I didn't plan on letting us be disturbed."

"Is it really okay with her?" I asked.

"Yes, don't worry. I didn't want you to meet so quickly like this, but we'll make up for it. Planned. Then it won't be so awkward."

"I found her nice," I said weakly. I still felt uncomfortable with the situation. As if I had driven Cecilia out of her home.

Rob smiled. "She is. You'll like each other. And now, don't worry, everything's okay."

He handed me my glass, and I took a sip. Slowly, I calmed down. He was probably right and knew his sister best. I smiled at him and decided to enjoy the evening. Rob kissed me, and I wrapped my arms around his neck. "How long until the food is delivered?"

He grinned. "About an hour."

"Then we can already celebrate our reunion, right?" I asked.

"Definitely." He walked backward to the couch, pulling me with him until I found myself on his lap. His hands roamed over my body. I snuggled against him and enjoyed it. My lips found his, and I let my fingers glide through his thick hair. I loved how his skin felt against mine. How he smelled. I had missed his scent. Today, his stubble scratched my cheek. I loved that feeling too.

His warm hands slid under my shirt and caressed my sides, my ribs, my back. With Rob, I didn't mind when he touched my scar. And the tattoo. I wanted to open up to him completely. I moved closer to him, and he held me tighter.

A smile crossed my face. I liked it when he touched me like that; it made me feel even more desired. As if he could barely hold back.

Fine with me.

"An hour isn't much time for everything I have planned for you," he whispered in my ear. I got goosebumps.

"We have the whole night for that," I sighed. It was as if something from my dangerous dream-self stirred within me. I felt a bold ambition to ensure he never forgot this night. The dream-self seemed somewhat delusional.

Nevertheless, it spurred me on.

I quickly pulled his shirt over his head and then started on myself. I wriggled out of my jeans and unbuttoned his. Rob's eyes widened, but he let me continue. I could see that he liked it.

"You're full of surprises. I love that," he said, stroking my shoulder. Then his fingers slipped into my bra. I sighed and ran my hands through his hair again, but then continued with his pants. Today, I wanted to take the lead.

Rob watched me, his eyes gleaming. I wrapped my legs around his waist and pressed myself against him. Then I brushed against something soft on his back. I paused and looked at it.

"What happened?" I asked, feeling the edges of the bandage on his lower back.

"Morocco is a dangerous country," he joked.

My eyes widened. "Were you attacked? What happened?"

"Nothing," he dismissed, taking my hands. "I was clumsy and slipped. Unfortunately, I was holding a teacup at the time. Don't ask how I managed it, but I fell right onto a shard. Bad luck, but nothing a tetanus shot couldn't fix. And the devoted hands of my girlfriend, of course." He pulled me back to him and kissed me until I felt dizzy.

I snuggled up to him and told myself that sometimes stories, especially when they sound completely strange, could simply be true. There was no reason not to believe them.

Rob took off my bra and continued kissing me. I dismissed my worries about his injury and focused on him. Especially now, as he removed our last pieces of clothing.

As I sank deeper onto his lap and felt him completely, everything else didn't matter and I had to hold onto his gaze. It felt so good to be with him.

I was infinitely glad that we had met.

The next morning, I opened my eyes and noticed the arm around my waist. Smiling, I turned to Rob. It was lovely waking up next to him.

With my fingertips, I stroked his arm, smoothing the hair that had gotten messy during sleep. The evening was wonderful. The food, the sex... and the long time we spent wrapped up on the sofa, talking.

I wanted nothing else.

Rob woke up and smiled. "Hey, did you sleep well?"

"Yes. You?" I whispered.

"How could I not, with you next to me?"

"Sweet talker," I said lovingly and kissed him. "Can I use the bathroom first?"

"I can come with you," he offered, his eyes sparkling. I glanced at the clock. We still had enough time. "Okay."

He jumped up and pulled me into the shower. Another point on the list of things I didn't want to miss anymore.

"I'm meeting Skadi and Mira tonight," I said later over coffee. "Do you have time tomorrow?"

"I had reserved the whole week for you. But a bit of waiting increases anticipation, of course," he said. "I'll find a restaurant, okay? How about Moroccan?"

"I can't make it too easy for you. A bit of flirtation is necessary. Moroccan sounds good. Are you into it now?" I said with a smile.

"Of course, my lady. I will admire any flirtation with awe," he said. I laughed. I liked that he joined in the joke. He grabbed my hand and kissed the back of it like a gentleman. "And as for the restaurant: Wait until you've had authentic Moroccan food. Then you won't laugh at me anymore."

"I'm open to anything," I replied and drank my coffee. I had to leave; our shower adventure had taken longer. I would never complain, but it left us less time for breakfast.

I didn't want to go, but I didn't want to be late either. Helmut was out and I had to open the shop. Besides, there were boxes of purchases in the back room that I had to figure out what to do with.

I had threatened Helmut not to buy so impulsively anymore. "Only books we can sell," I reminded him. "Remember that we can't get rid of the others, and they clog our shelves."

Helmut promised and I hoped he would stick to it this time.

I made up some time because Rob drove me to work. The bookshop was on his way.

Once there, I started with all the books in the boxes that waited for me to be brought into our system. To be safe, I texted Helmut again to remind him of his promise.

The day passed, and I had a lovely evening with Skadi and Mira. Today, they got along, and over a glass of wine (or two, or three), we caught up on the latest news in our lives.

Skadi was still stressed about the wedding. We did our best to support her. In the end, we couldn't finalize the menu without giving Emil a heart attack, but we had a lot of fun mixing up the courses. I enjoyed the evening, although I would have loved to see Rob too.

On Thursday, Helmut was back. "I bought almost nothing," he said, almost reproachfully. "Only the real treasures. But there was so much more."

"I believe you, but you know...," I began.

"I know, and you're right. It's just hard for me to say no to people." He shrugged, then pulled a book from his bag. "For you."

Touched, I looked at the first edition of *Wuthering Heights*, he handed me. "Oh my god..."

Helmut grinned. "You're welcome. I know you're a real Brontë sisters fangirl."

That was true. As a teenager, I was obsessed with Emily and Charlotte, later adding Branwell and Anne. I even went to England and visited the house where the siblings grew up, which is now a museum. An entire display case in my living room was dedicated solely to Brontë works and everything else I had collected about the four.

"Everyone needs heroes," I thought and looked at the old booklet in my hand. It was a precious gift. Not only because of its material value but because Helmut thought of me. That meant a lot to me.

Today, the bookshop was not very busy, and when Helmut noticed I had a date with Rob, he sent me home early.

This time, I had prepared for our date and already laid out what I wanted to wear for dinner, so I wouldn't run out of time again. Skadi had given me tips, but it worked on my own too. This would probably last a few more weeks, then Rob would have to get used to my normal clothing style. I assumed that wouldn't be a problem.

We met at the restaurant, and though I set off on time, a cold wind cut through the evening air, making me shiver. Something about the heavy shadows around me felt odd, like we weren't alone. I shook off the feeling, focusing on Rob waiting for me just inside the restaurant.

He was already waiting for me.

"I'm very curious about the food," I said. "Have you been here before?"

"Yes, but it's been a while. And I admit I didn't appreciate the food as much as I do now. Traveling broadens your horizons, as they say." He kissed me and pulled me close. "Are you coming back to my place tonight?"

"Sure. Maybe I should leave some things at your place, so I don't have to bring everything every time, right?" I smiled and spoke quickly, unsure if it was okay. Maybe it was too early for him.

But Rob nodded. "Of course. I'll label them with your name, so Cecilia won't touch them."

"She doesn't seem like the type to use someone else's toothbrush," I said, stepping through the door he held open.

Rob laughed. "No, but I sometimes wonder what of my stuff she uses when she's distracted. The other day, she used my aftershave as lotion and wondered about the smell. It takes her forever to wake up in the morning. You have to consider that."

"Okay, I'll keep that in mind when I leave spare clothes at your place," I said, smiling. The waiter showed us to a table, and we sat on the floor cushions. I looked around. I liked the decor. Everything was golden and colorful. It smelled of spices and coziness, reminding me of Indian cuisine.

Again, there was that small sting in my chest, a loving pain that reminded me of my mother. In such moments, I missed her the most.

Rob placed his hand on mine. "Are you okay?"

"Yes. I just thought of my mother." I explained briefly, and his eyes widened.

"I'm sorry. I didn't mean to make you sad."

"That's all right. Then I wouldn't be able to get out of bed because everything and every place would remind me of her. You know, sometimes it's even nice. It proves to me that I haven't forgotten her."

"I don't think anyone can forget their mother," he said. The waiter brought an aperitif and Rob raised his glass. "To your mother. I wish I could have met her."

I smiled and clinked glasses with him. "She would have liked to have met you too. You can look forward to meeting my father. He's very keen to find out who his daughter is hanging out with."

"The pressure's on," Rob said half-jokingly. I felt the same way about his family. I wanted to get to know Cecilia better; our first meeting had been suboptimal. And parents are a completely different matter.

I asked Rob to tell me a little about them. He did, and I learned more about his childhood and the family business. The von Lindensteins were a traditional family. They even had their own family crest, which Rob showed me on his cell phone: an oak wreath and two crossed swords, with the heads of a stag and a bear above it.

"Hunting has a long tradition in my family, hence the animal heads," Rob explained. "My father is incredibly proud of the coat of arms. It's almost embarrassing, but he places it all over my parents' house for everyone to see. I think he thinks we're an old noble family."

"That's a nice motif for a tattoo," I said. "You've got a second arm. I'm sure he'd like that."

"No way. He thinks tattoos are awful," Rob said. "Mine upset him, and he still doesn't know that Cecilia has several."

"Then I should probably avoid backless dresses when your parents are around," I said nervously.

Rob pulled me close and kissed me. "Don't worry. There are more important things in life than my father's opinion on tattoos." I could live with that, and we focused on the delicious food that was served. I immersed myself in the flavors of North Africa and enjoyed every bite. Rob was right: it was fantastic, and I got the travel bug. My last trip was a while ago. Now, a thousand ideas for the next one came to mind. I hoped I could make them happen with Rob.

After dinner, I stretched and sighed. "I'm so full. Can we walk a bit? I'm afraid I won't sleep otherwise."

"Of course," Rob said. "The way is long enough. We can always grab a taxi."

So we set off, and I enjoyed the walk despite the cold. Rob wrapped his arm around me, and I relished the evening.

I glanced at his face. I was happy. It had been a while since I felt this good.

"We can warm up at my place," Rob promised. "Best naked in my bed. Or would you like to shower again first?"

"I'll think about it," I said, smiling. "Do we have time for a glass of wine?"

"I think there's always time for that." Rob was about to say something when a man came up from the front and shoved him.

A blur of movement. Rob was thrown against the wall, his body slamming into brick. A flash—no, a knife in the guy's hand. Cold metal glinting in the streetlight.

"Hand over your phones and money," he growled, holding the knife to my face. I was frozen with fear. Beside me, Rob picked himself up and grabbed my wrist.

"Get lost, you idiot."

I was terrified. The guy was big, and his face was pure aggression. He was deadly serious.

"We should just give him our stuff," I whispered.

It was pointless to play the hero. But my boyfriend shook his head grimly. "No way."

"Last chance," the attacker snarled. The knife glinted in the streetlight. Panic gripped me, and I clung to Rob. Yet he was strangely calm. He clenched his fists and crouched slightly. Was he planning to take on the guy?

"Please don't," I whispered, terrified, and dug my fingers into the sleeve of his coat.

Everything happened too fast. I barely registered Rob's shove before I was thrown off balance, stumbling as I tried to grip onto something. A cry tore from my throat as I fell.

Rob whirled around and tried to catch me, but I lost control of my fall. With a groan, we both went down.

The man towered over us, the knife in his hand.

He growled an insult and kicked Rob in the ribs. He groaned but got back on his feet. I took longer; pain shot from my hip through my body, and my head throbbed.

Through the haze, I saw Rob lunge at the man, his fist swinging. The knife's blade flashed again, catching the streetlight, and my heart seized.

A primal instinct snapped inside me, raw and wild. My vision blurred to red, blood pounding louder in my ears. I crouched, poised, before I surged forward, hands clawed and ready. The cold night air bit my skin as I launched myself at him.

My fingernails dug into his cheeks, leaving long scratches. He howled and threw me off.

I fell, but this time I landed on my feet. I didn't take my eyes off him for a second.

"Neelia!" Rob's voice broke my concentration.

He reached for me, wanting to protect me. Instead, I missed the man's attack as he swung his knife at me again. I barely dodged in time. I turned away, then came the pain. He had hit me squarely.

Rob screamed, and I heard something clatter to the ground. I dropped to my knees, clutching my torso, but the pain radiated elsewhere, deep and searing. A wave of heat and cold washed over me, the world spinning and shrinking to the sound of my own pulse.

Next to me, Rob tackled the man, but the sounds barely reached me. I collapsed and propped myself up on my hands. Footsteps.

I looked over my shoulder. The man was running away.

Rob rushed to my side, his voice sounding distant as if through fog. Warm wetness soaked my back - blood, I realized, hot against the cold air. Black spots danced before my eyes; I felt sick. I smelled iron, sharp and metallic. Rob reached for my hand. "The EMTs are on their way!" he said. "Stay with me!"

I did, but I couldn't form a clear thought.

The pain prevented it. And at the same time, I couldn't believe what I had done.

Part 2

The eye of the beast

Chapter 6

The ambulance arrived quickly and took us to the hospital. Rob stayed with me the whole time, holding my hand. He was pale as a ghost and didn't say a word until the emergency doctor spoke to him. I lay on my stomach on the stretcher, feeling them press a bandage on the stab wound on my back.

"What happened?" the doctor asked.

"We were attacked. Mugging. The guy had a knife. My girlfriend tried to protect me, and he got her," Rob said tightly.

The doctor squeezed my hand. "Very brave of you." Her gaze flickered over to Rob, as if he had utterly failed. I gave a weak smile and said nothing. I didn't need to discuss my boyfriend's bravery with a stranger. I knew how brave (and reckless) Rob had been. The doctor had to change the bandage because my back was bleeding heavily.

Rob sat before me like a pile of misery. I squeezed his hand and felt the urge to say something. "It's not your fault. You tried to chase the guy away. You couldn't have been any faster," I said.

The doctor silently raised an eyebrow.

Rob shook his head. "Feels different right now. I should have made sure nothing happened to you."

I squeezed his hand again. It was crazy that he needed comfort now, but I saw how guilty he felt. "Are you in a lot of pain?" he asked.

"No." They had given me painkillers that were already working. "How about you?" Rob also needed to be checked because of the kick to his ribs. He had been holding himself gingerly but refused to be transported on a stretcher.

"I'm fine," he said shortly. I suspected he was lying. I had seen the kick; it was brutal.

I lowered my eyes and looked at our hands. "This is a date we won't forget anytime soon."

"You were lucky," said the paramedic next to the doctor. "The knife hit your shoulder blade and didn't go in deep." I felt him adjusting the compress. "We can fix this. Even your tattoo." I didn't want to think about what that might mean.

I found out later when I was examined. Rob took a photo of the wound at my request when we were briefly alone, waiting for the doctor. The cut ran across my left shoulder blade and through my tattoo. It needed stitches. The doctor had promised to do his best so it wouldn't look terrible, but he couldn't guarantee anything. I didn't expect it to be salvageable. They were just giving me a local anesthetic and about to start.

They had already taken blood from me, and I had received a tetanus shot. Rob looked so stricken that I almost sent him away. It moved me that he wanted to protect me, but it couldn't be changed now.

Beating himself up wouldn't help anyone.

The doctor came and stitched me up, repeatedly assuring me he was doing his utmost. I found out he was a plastic surgeon and had been called in specifically to save my tattoo.

"I had some time and thought it was the least I could do after what happened to you," he said as he made the next stitch. "You must have been terrified when the guy attacked you with a knife."

"Both of us," I corrected. Rob was in another room getting his ribs X-rayed. I hoped he was using the time to calm down. "My boyfriend took quite a hit too."

"It's never smart to play the hero in such moments," said the doctor, and I guessed he meant Rob. I found that unfair because he hadn't been there, and it was quite old-fashioned to assume I couldn't defend myself. Well, looking at my back, one might think so.

"That's unlikely to happen to us again," I said, relieved when he finished shortly after.

"It looks good," he said. "You'll see the scar, but the design isn't destroyed."

I thanked him, and Rob came back in. His ribs weren't broken, luckily. Now we just had to wait for our discharge papers.

"Neelia, I'm so sorry," Rob repeated, avoiding my gaze. His voice was quiet, and he bit his lip.

"It's okay. Really. I don't know what happened either. And you got quite a hit too," I said.

"The bruised ribs will heal in a few days. Unfortunately, the same can't be said for your wound. The scar will always remind you. And the tattoo…"

"We'll see. The doctor said it looks good. Otherwise, I'll find someone to fix the design. A cover-up isn't a problem," I said bravely. I was afraid of needles. Terrified. To this day, I didn't know how I had survived getting the tattoo. Back then. Whenever that was.

The doctor came back and brought our papers. I was glad we were going to Rob's now. By taxi, as soon as one would arrive. I'd think twice about walking late at night in the future.

I got goosebumps at the thought. What a terrible experience. That had never happened to me before. I was familiar with nighttime anxiety, but earlier, I had been terrified for Rob and myself. For a moment, I didn't expect us to get out alive.

"We were very lucky that nothing worse happened," I said. Rob flinched, his mouth tightening grimly. I didn't like seeing him look like that.

"I wish it hadn't happened at all," he said.

"There's no point in feeling bad about it," I said. "It doesn't change anything and just ruins our mood." I kissed his lips. "Okay?"

He took a deep breath and returned the kiss. "Okay. But with a heavy heart."

"The only one to blame is the guy with the knife." His grip on my waist tightened. I kissed him quickly again. "But hey, if this doesn't bring us closer, I don't know what will."

Rob hugged me carefully. "I was so scared for you. When he swung the knife…"

"Me too. Let's not go for walks for a while, okay? At least not in the dark," I asked.

"Absolutely not," said Rob. We both knew how slim the chances were of catching the guy. We had filed a report, but the officers gave us little hope.

Finally, the taxi came and took us to Rob's place. I could only fall asleep when he held me tightly. I suspected it would take a long time to process this experience.

I stare at the knife blade in his hand. It glints in the streetlight.

I have no fear of this man with the knife. I will defeat him. He can hurt me, nothing more.

He won't achieve his goal. I will achieve mine.

I relish how I feel. Confident, self-assured.

A growl gathers in my throat.

He will regret meeting me. He will regret seeking me out. Unfortunately, he won't be able to tell anyone how stupid the idea was.

"Got you," he says quietly. He misjudges the situation. He doesn't know he's as good as dead.

I have no weapon. I don't need one. My body is weapon enough. He'll feel it soon.

He spreads his legs wider, holding the knife up.

I tense every muscle. I jump.

The next morning, Rob insisted on taking me to work. Like a bodyguard, he escorted me to the door and waited until I had unlocked the bookshop. I waved to him as he left. He shouldn't make this a habit. I liked that he was attentive, but I didn't want him guarding me like a dog its bone.

I hoped this would pass quickly.

Helmut came later, so I had time to inform my dad, Skadi, and Mira about what happened.

"I'm fine," I added in the chat with Mira and Skadi. *"It was blessing in disguise."*

"That doesn't comfort me at all," Skadi wrote. *"We're coming over tonight. You shouldn't be alone."*

"What a fucking mess," was Mira's comment. *"I'll pick you up from work."*

I agreed and then called my dad. He was at a training session, but I reached him before it started. As expected, he was beside himself.

"Dad, I'm fine," I said for the third time. "It was a huge scare, but apart from a flesh wound, I'm okay."

"I'm coming to see you tomorrow. I'm so sorry I wasn't there," he said for the third time.

I knew everyone meant well, but it was starting to annoy me how they hovered around me. I wasn't fragile. I could handle this.

I didn't tell Helmut and Amira when they came. Thanks to the painkillers, I hardly felt the wound. If I took it slow, no one would notice anything. Still, I realized I wasn't on top of things. I had to take several breaks because I kept dropping things or getting upset over small mistakes. I retreated to the little kitchen in the back of the shop to catch my breath.

Obviously, the stress got to me. This would be a challenge. Helmut and Amira weren't to blame, so I didn't want to snap at them when something went wrong during the accounting.

Everything was too much for me. I wanted to leave early, but there was too much to do, and Mira couldn't leave until six. Finally, it was time, and she picked me up. Outside, she hugged me tightly. "How are you?"

I shrugged. "I think I'm okay."

"It must have been a huge shock," she said calmly. I was grateful for that. "If you want to talk, I'm here for you. Always."

"I know, thanks."

Then she let it go. Unlike Skadi, whose issue was different. She couldn't believe Rob hadn't protected me.

"But he did," I said. "He was just a second too late, and I wanted to protect him too."

Skadi pressed her lips together. "It's just awful how much security an incident like this takes away. I'm scared too, and it didn't even happen to me. You're incredibly brave, you know that? I'd be in bed crying now."

"I feel like that too, but it doesn't change anything," I said.

I told my dad the same thing the next day. He blamed himself for not being there.

"No one is to blame," I repeated. "Only the guy who attacked us. It's not your fault, not mine, and not Rob's. It was just bad luck, and I hope they catch the bastard."

Dad nodded sadly. "Can I see the wound? So I can convince myself it's not that bad?"

"If it makes you feel better, sure." I sat next to him and pulled up my sweater. He carefully peeled back the bandage. His hands froze.

"Dad? Everything okay?" I asked when he said nothing.

"It's worse than I thought," he muttered, reapplying the bandage.

"What does that mean? I think it looks okay. The plastic surgeon did his best," I said, frowning, but Dad looked even more stressed than before.

Now he gave me a forced smile. "Of course. It will look better once it heals. How are you feeling?"

"I've already told you," I replied impatiently.

"I know. But how do you feel?" Dad asked. I had no idea what he was getting at. How was I supposed to feel?

I listed: "Unbalanced, jumpy, and scared. I called Dr. Singh and made an appointment. Together we'll get me back on track." I kissed him on the cheek. "Don't worry, okay? I can handle this."

"I know," he said, but his eyes said something else. His hand gently brushed my back. "I hope so."

Dad insisted I stay over from Saturday to Sunday. I gave in because I saw how upset he was. If it made him feel better,

I'd do it. I had to postpone seeing Rob. He wasn't happy about it, but I promised we'd see each other on Sunday.

I was glad to be on my way home after breakfast on Sunday. Dad made me uneasy. It felt like he didn't take his eyes off me for a second, expecting me to have a nervous breakdown or something. It made me anxious and irritable. Again.

I didn't want that. I wanted to forget about the incident and walk around outside without getting anxious. That wouldn't happen if everyone made such a fuss. I wanted to get back to normal. And believe that such a thing wouldn't happen again.

The walk was okay in daylight, and the fresh air did me good. I got home and settled into my reading chair with a book to calm down and escape into another world. The wound on my back stung while sitting, but the painkillers made it bearable.

I didn't want to think about the attack anymore. It was pointless. The past was the past. No matter how much I dwelled on it, it couldn't be undone.

I learned that in therapy after the accident. I had to accept and let go. I was ready for that. Now everyone else just had to let me.

But there was something else I wanted to banish from my mind: The dream from the night before last deeply unsettled me. I felt good. Invincible. Like I could easily fend off a man with a knife with my bare hands. Just hours after the mugging, that was crazy.

Kill. I closed my eyes and took a deep breath.

In my dream, it was about life and death. In my dream, I was determined to kill my pursuer. I recoiled from that thought.

The mugging could have ended fatally. For both me and Rob. That thought was the worst. I couldn't focus on my book and set it aside in frustration.

"I'll get through this," I murmured, placing my hands flat on my legs. "I won't let this ruin my life. I'm happy. This is just a setback that won't derail me." I stood up and walked briskly through my apartment, wanting to feel my body. To feel my muscles as supple as in my dream.

I stopped in front of my hallway mirror and looked at my reflection. This was silly, right? *Right?*

I took another deep breath.

Today wasn't my day. I was out of balance. Unfortunately. Understandably, but I didn't want that. I wanted to focus on feeling good. That I had finally found someone I could be happy with.

I hoped Rob would make it easier for me later. We needed to cheer each other up and help each other get over this. We could only do it together. I hoped he understood that we depended on each other. If we supported each other and didn't hinder each other with negative feelings, we could get through this.

I hoped he already trusted me enough to listen to me and follow this path to make us both feel better. I rubbed my face and tried to muster optimism. "I can do this."

I passed the time with a shower and took much longer and more carefully getting ready than usual. I controlled every movement and focused on what I wanted to do. I didn't let other thoughts intrude.

"I have everything under control. I can handle this."

Uncharacteristically, I was ready an hour before our date and even had time to prepare dinner.

"Not bad. You can do it after all," I thought, pouring myself some wine while stirring the curry.

Rob was punctual. I opened the door with a smile, confident we'd have a lovely evening. But when I saw his tense face, the warm feeling disappeared. "Everything okay?" I asked.

"Not really." He wrapped me in his arms. I snuggled against him, trying to regain my cheerfulness. He needed my support. "How are you?" he asked into my hair, taking a deep breath.

I leaned against him to give him strength. "Good."

"How's your injury?" His hand gently brushed my back.

"It's okay, thanks to the painkillers." I pressed myself against him. "I'm glad you're here." He took a deep breath. I started to worry. "What's wrong?" I asked.

"I went to the police today to try to push the investigation forward. I know someone at the precinct. Things don't look good for our case." Rob was so downcast that my stomach felt like a cold lump.

"I figured as much. Without knowing the guy's name, it's difficult," I nodded.

"It's driving me crazy. I slept badly last night. It's gnawing at me." He began pacing restlessly in my hallway.

I stopped him. "Rob," I said softly, placing my hand on his chest. Finally, he looked into my eyes. "I'm so glad you're here. I've been looking forward to this all day. The mugging was awful, yes, and I'm just as shocked and angry as you. But we shouldn't let it ruin how wonderful it is to be together. Please." I took his hand. "I've had a traumatic experience before. Will you help me get through this crap?"

He hesitated. I knew he felt ashamed on top of being angry because he thought he hadn't protected me. How could I explain that I wasn't angry at him for that? I believed he had done everything possible.

"Can I see the injury?" he asked.

"I don't want you to see it and feel worse," I countered.

"I already feel bad. But I promise you, Neelia: this won't happen again. I'll protect you from now on, you can count on that."

I looked at his face. He meant every word. His expression was serious, and there was a stubborn set to his mouth that I didn't like. Maybe I would have found this promise sweet and romantic not long ago, but now I felt a resistance. It felt like condescension. Like control.

I didn't want that, and he needed to understand. The sooner, the better. "You don't have to." I searched for the right words to avoid offending him. I definitely didn't want a fight.

"First, you can't always be with me; second, it's too much to ask; and third, and this is the most important point: I'm an adult and can take care of myself. I want you as a partner, not a watchdog. And I don't like being protected like a helpless child. My dad tried that after the accident. I don't handle it well. Just be there for me, okay? I'll do the same for you. That's all I want."

Rob raised his eyebrows. I let him sort his thoughts and feelings and took care of the curry. He could take all the time he needed. Sometimes that was better than saying the first thing that came to mind.

"It's not easy," he finally said. "It goes against my manly instincts."

My mouth twitched. At least he hadn't lost his sense of humor. "I'm sure there will be other opportunities for you to prove your manliness. My feminine instincts rebel against being protected. But maybe I'll rescue you sometime."

"I'll gladly look for opportunities for your femininity." He pulled me close and smiled. "I'm not a macho, but sometimes there's this urge, you know? I want to go out with my spear and bring you back a saber-toothed tiger."

"That's charming, but I'd prefer if we hunt together. I'm a big girl."

He kissed me. "More like an amazing woman. And I have big plans for us tonight." I wrapped my arms around his neck, relieved we had resolved this conflict.

Hopefully for good.

I fly. My muscles are taut. My pursuer is getting closer.
Now he opens his mouth in surprise. He didn't expect a direct attack. How foolish of him.
I keep the knife in view. I won't meet it.
I hit the hunter with full force and throw him to the ground. He lands under me, groaning, and I push him to the ground with my weight. I bare my teeth, ready to finish him off. I seek eye contact, relishing his realization when he realizes he's lost. But he squirms, tossing his head back and forth, trying to shake me off.
I smell his fear. It intoxicates me, making it hard to focus. His face is a blurry spot. It doesn't matter.
A surge of heat fills me. Victory is mine, and he knows it.
He's helpless under me, his hand with the knife lies motionless on the ground. Is it my weight or did I break his arm? Either is fine with me.
A metallic smell fills my nose. Blood.
I close my eyes briefly and breathe it in deeply.
His blood.
I want it spilled across the asphalt, every last drop blending with dust. He gasps with effort as he struggles again. He has no chance.

Suddenly, pain explodes in my body. I howl and let him go.

Out of the corner of my eye, I see him swing the knife. Not broken after all.

I get to my feet and stomp on that damn knife arm with full force. Now it's broken.

My adversary howls in pain, and I step back to see what he used to hurt me. Warm blood trickles down my side.

Now I see the smaller knife in his other hand. My blood clings to the short blade.

This cowardly bastard! That was his last dirty trick!

He gets to his feet, bent over and clutching his arm. His breath is labored. "Bitch," he whimpers. "Then I'll just make a hole."

He pulls something from his belt.

Mesmerized, I stare into the barrel of the gun.

With a jerk, I woke up. My heart was pounding, and I was drenched in sweat. My hands trembled as I pushed my hair back.

Rob lay beside me in bed, sleeping peacefully. Carefully, I pulled the blanket back and crept out of the bedroom. Again. What was wrong with me?

I touched my right side where the attacker had stabbed me in the dream. The pain had felt so real that I would have sworn the wound was genuine. My body was full of adrenaline, my muscles warm as if I had already run three kilometers. I felt like a predator on the hunt, just missing its prey.

If the guy from Friday attacked me at that moment... The jump from the dream was in my muscle memory; I was sure I could repeat it immediately. I would take him down like the hunter in the dream. I would hurt him. His screams of pain were already in my head, and I could smell his blood.

Horrified, I clamped a hand over my mouth.

What were these thoughts?

Anger and vengeance didn't help anyone; I knew that from therapy. You could only be happy if you let go of what held you back.

Violent fantasies certainly weren't part of that.

"Damn, what's wrong with me?" I whispered. My thoughts scared me; I didn't recognize myself.

I looked at the framed Om symbol on my wall, a sign of peace and balance. I didn't feel that. Something was wrong with me, but I had no idea what it was. That scared me too.

It took a while to calm down enough to return to bed.

Rob woke up and asked what was wrong. I didn't know what to say and swung my leg over him. Sex was a good way to get rid of the dream. I was still hot, so I might as well use that energy.

Rob's eyes widened but he quickly caught on. His hands moved over my hips. "In the middle of the night? I like it!"

I turned off my mind and surrendered to his touch. My nails glided over his skin, eliciting a moan from him. It sounded like music to my ears. I didn't want to think about why.

I took the opportunity and gave him everything I had. My shirt and panties disappeared as quickly as Rob's clothes, and I started to really enjoy myself. I could forget the dream and turn it into something good.

Rob was more than willing to help me with this plan, doing his utmost. When I threw my head back and screamed, I didn't think about it. At least not for a while.

On Monday, I met with Skadi and Mira. They looked at me thoughtfully and a bit scared.

"Please stop," I said impatiently. "You don't need to treat me like I'm fragile. I'm fine."

"Are you sure?" Skadi asked. "I don't think I could handle it so easily."

"Me neither," Mira agreed. "And I've been through a lot of shit."

"Oh, girls..." I shrugged because I didn't know what else to say.

"You seem different," Mira continued. "So restless. Like something's driving you."

"It's nothing," I insisted. "I'll process the mugging, and the dreams will stop soon."

"You still have them?" Mira asked. "How unusual. Your subconscious is trying to tell you something. Are you keeping the dream journal?"

"No, I didn't have the nerve for it. And if the dreams are trying to tell me something, what is it?" I asked.

"Can someone fill me in?" Skadi asked impatiently. "And do I even want to know?"

"We talked about this the other day," I reminded her. "I've been having weird dreams for a while. I'm standing in a street, and someone is chasing me. He wants to kill me, and I'm looking forward to the duel."

"That's a bit twisted," Skadi said, surprised. "I remember the conversation, but I didn't catch that detail."

"Sorry, yes, that's possible. I didn't think it would bother me for so long," I replied.

"And you think her subconscious is trying to tell her something?" Skadi asked Mira. "Like 'stop watching horror movies'?"

"Of course, you make fun of it," Mira said, annoyed.

"Hey, no fighting, okay? Let's not talk about it anymore," I said. "It's pointless."

"Our dreams are a mirror to our soul," Mira insisted. Skadi snorted. "Do you even dream?" Mira asked irritably.

Skadi smirked. "Yes, but more normal stuff like my wedding cake being ugly. Wanting to kill someone is rare. Maybe that's the next step if the cake is actually ugly."

Now Mira made a face. Such jabs hit her where it hurt the most.

I had to intervene. "Okay, come on, this isn't helping," I said before they could argue. "I'm fine. And maybe Skadi is right that my imagination is playing tricks on me. I'll stop watching mystery series. It will be fine." The problem was that none of us looked convinced. And neither was I.

Chapter 7

After a few quiet evenings at home, I managed to settle down a bit. Good books and tea (or wine) could fix just about anything. I had an appointment with my therapist, Dr. Singh, and started working through the attack with her to put it behind me.

I felt better and less driven by my fear. The dream didn't return, and I knew I was getting better. I just needed some time. Dr. Singh confirmed this, and we developed strategies to help me cope. I planned to explain to my loved ones how they could help me at the next opportunity.

Rob was in Latvia for work all week. There was a cabinet that his client absolutely wanted, so Rob went to examine it and negotiate a fair price. Some people's eccentricity knew no bounds; I supposed I just didn't have the money to understand them. Besides, the client covered Rob's commission and expenses. Still, it financed Rob's lifestyle.

I missed him, but the break helped me focus on myself. I looked forward to Saturday, when he'd finally return, and we'd meet at his place.

I worked at the bookstore on Saturday. With the weather improving and days getting longer, I started a collaboration with the café next door. We called the combination of cakes and books *'Appetizers'*.

The smell of cake filled the air, making my mouth water all day; I had to shoo Helmut away from the sample bites a few times.

It worked; by evening, almost all the books Layla had set out for us were sold. Our concept was that customers could browse the books while having coffee and buy the book if they liked it. I didn't give valuable first editions and rare pieces over there, but books that appealed to the café's clientele and made a nice gift for a maximum of ten euros. Layla earned twenty percent commission, and we received the samples for free.

Layla was already at my counter for the second time wanting to pick up the next box of books. She had to wait briefly because the store was full. Soon, our stock of Jane Austen books and similar works would be sold out.

"This is perfect timing," I said, taking the tray with the sample bites from Layla. The mini cakes, muffins, and cupcakes looked delectable and tasted divine.

"I don't know how many more I can make," she said, wiping flour from her cheek. "It's rare that I have to bake during the day. We're busy too. Many single people today, who love to browse books. One woman took four books and three pieces of cake earlier."

We shared a quick high five. Helmut wasn't convinced the idea would work at first. Now, he eagerly put together more boxes for Layla and even approached the hairdresser next door about a collaboration. That was also a good idea.

"For customers with perms," he said wisely, stacking dime novels for which I had scolded him.

"If you can still find anyone for that," I said amusedly. "The eighties are over, Helmut."

"It all comes back," he called out. "Mark my words."

I stifled a grin and continued working.

Rob picked me up in the evening. I had just come from the stockroom and saw him and Helmut standing together, chatting animatedly.

"There she is!" Rob kissed me. "Can I take her right away, Helmut?"

"She's yours, Rob," said Helmut cheerfully.

"Oh, you're already on a first-name basis? I've been waiting for that for two years," I said half-jokingly. Helmut called me Ms. Jacobi for what felt like forever, making it hard for me to switch to informal when Helmut finally offered it.

My boss laughed. No wonder, the day had gone incredibly well. We hadn't counted the takings yet, but they were high. We could celebrate on Monday.

I grabbed my bag and said goodbye.

"Busy day?" Rob asked, holding the door open.

"Yes, but in a good way. We made excellent sales today. The last week was a bit difficult, but we made up for it. Thankfully." I waved to Layla through the café window. "That's also thanks to Layla. We're connecting in the neighborhood. It's working well."

"I'm happy for you." Rob pulled me close and kissed me again.

"How was Latvia?" I asked.

"Surprisingly nice," he replied. "Another country I definitely want to visit again. I'll show you some photos later. And everything went wonderfully. I even completed a second assignment because it went so quickly. The sushi I ordered tonight is well deserved."

"I'm looking forward to it," I said, taking his warm hand in mine. Maybe we'd visit Latvia together someday. One thing at a time.

Rob was there by car. I preferred that, even though it wasn't dark yet and the street was full of people.

We parked in the garage under his place and took the elevator up to Rob's apartment. In the living room, Cecilia was sitting on the couch with a laptop. She waved when she saw us come in. "Hello!"

"Hey, you're still here," Rob said slowly.

She rolled her eyes. "Yes, but I'm leaving in half an hour. Can you tolerate my presence for that long?"

"If you behave," he said.

"Keep it up, and you'll be sorry." She stood up and held out her hand to me. "Now I can say hello properly. Nice to officially meet you, Neelia."

I smiled and took her hand.

A chill shot through me as my insides twisted with fear and aggression. The feelings rushed through me so quickly I couldn't grasp them. I widened my eyes and flinched.

Adrenaline shot through my legs, but at the same time, everything in me resisted running away. My instincts went crazy, and cold sweat broke out.

"Danger!" screamed all my senses, but I was paralyzed.

Cecilia let go of my hand and said something to Rob. I saw her lips moving, but I couldn't hear a thing. My hands tingled, but life slowly returned to my body.

I fought against the urge to run, which grew stronger, stronger than the urge to defend myself to the death.

"Panic," I thought dully. "I'm panicking, it's the adrenaline. But why?"

"Neelia, are you okay?" Rob asked, snapping me out of my spiral of thoughts. I jerked violently and looked into his eyes. His face calmed me. My racing pulse slowed down.

"Yes, sure. I'm just tired. It was a long day," I lied, brushing a strand of hair from my face with a trembling hand. My thoughts whirled wildly because I didn't understand what was happening.

Cecilia didn't notice anything. She left the room to get something, talking non-stop. It couldn't be because of her, but where did the panic come from?

What had just happened?

It was almost as bad as during the mugging.

I looked at the door through which Rob's sister had disappeared. Was it her? How could that be? She had done nothing to me, I barely knew her. It was crazy and couldn't be the reason.

"You look like you've seen a ghost," Rob said cautiously. "Are you really okay?"

"Yes, I think so." I steadied myself. "Sometimes I don't understand what's happening. These fainting spells I've had since my accident are getting more frequent and worse." I shrugged. "You've got a damaged girlfriend, unfortunately."

He took my hand. "It's things like these that make a person interesting. Of course, I wish you hadn't had to go through such a terrible experience, but it doesn't scare me off. It's clear it still affects you. I'd be more concerned if you had forgotten it."

"You're sweet, thank you." I kissed him and felt better. Cecilia returned, and nothing happened. I remained calm and felt fine again. Apparently, I had successfully overcome my panic attack. Instead, I was now embarrassed for reacting so oddly to her. Fortunately, no one had noticed.

"Wine?" asked Rob's sister. "Or something stronger? I make an excellent gin and tonic."

"Then I'll take that," I said. "I've earned it after this week." Cecilia winked at me and disappeared into the kitchen, where she clinked glasses.

"In half an hour, she'll be gone, and we'll have the apartment to ourselves," Rob whispered to me.

"What do you have in mind?" I asked, letting him pull me close. His hands stroked my back and my waist, pausing on my bandage.

"How's the wound?" he asked softly.

"Very good. I went for a bandage change yesterday. My doctor is satisfied. The tattoo is unfortunately damaged. The surgeon stitched well, but there will naturally be a scar." I sighed. "I have to wait and see how it looks when the swelling goes down, but I'll probably need a cover-up. On top of everything. I'm afraid of needles."

"How did you manage to get that large tattoo done then?" he asked, frowning. "That must have taken days."

"If I knew," I replied. "That falls into the time I can't remember."

"Rob told me about that. How crazy is that?" said Cecilia, returning with the glasses. She handed me one. "I'd ask to see the tattoo, but I'd get in trouble with my big brother."

"Indeed," said Rob sternly. "You said you'd behave, Cilly."

"I'm trying, it just never works," Cecilia said theatrically, clinking her glass against mine. "Welcome to the family. I hope you like boring people."

"As soon as I meet one, I'll let you know," I said, taking a sip of the gin and tonic. It was excellent.

Cecilia caught a warning look from Rob and shrugged apologetically. "I'm terrible at small talk, you know that. What should I do?"

"Either shut up or write acceptable topics on cards," he growled. "If our parents were here, there'd be a huge argument because of you."

"But they're not here." Cecilia looked at me. "Has Rob told you about our family crest? It's unfortunately more embarrassing than cool. Our parents are very traditional. They love everything old-fashioned. Their view of family togetherness is that everyone should stick together and listen to what the patriarch says. It's not easy to live your own life."

"Cecilia!" Rob snapped.

Cecilia widened her eyes. "I thought it was okay to talk about the family..."

"But not like that!" Rob looked at me. "She's exaggerating." Behind his back, she shook her head. She wasn't, and I believed her.

"Hey, it's okay," I waved it off. "There are worse things than that. As long as they don't have a problem with my background, I can smile through a lot."

"Your mother was from India, right?" Cecilia pulled me onto the sofa. "I've never been there, but I really want to go. What's it like? Which region did she come from?"

"From Mumbai," I replied. "I went there once when I was fourteen. I'm glad I still remember that. My maternal family lives in a wealthy neighborhood, where it's nice. I have fond memories of my grandmother and aunts. In other parts of the city, it's not like that. Poverty is a big issue in India."

"I believe that," Cecilia nodded. "Still, I'd love to see it myself one day."

"Maybe you'll get to travel there," Rob suggested.

"Yes, maybe. If you didn't always snag the good assignments, I'd see interesting places too," she said, pursing her lips.

"What? You don't work together, do you?" I asked, confused.

Cecilia waved it off. "Rob sometimes works for our parents when the opportunity arises. They prefer to send him instead of me. I do too much desk work."

"You're good at it," he countered. "The best."

Cecilia shot him a scathing look. "I can do more than keep the accounts in order."

"I know. Be patient."

I felt like I shouldn't be part of this conversation. It was something the siblings needed to sort out, but I thought again how lucky they were to have each other.

I disappeared into the bathroom to give them time to talk it out. Meanwhile, I texted Skadi, who had an appointment with the baker today about the cake and looked at the pictures she sent. I was looking forward to the wedding in August.

When I returned, Rob was alone. "Where's Cecilia?"

"She had to go," he said, stretching.

"Did you make up?"

He raised his eyebrows. "We didn't fight. That bickering is normal, don't worry."

"Good." I sat on his lap and wrapped my arms around his neck. "We're alone?"

He slid his hand under my sweater. "All alone."

I kissed him and shivered under his touch. His fingers moved over my ribs to my bra and unclasped it. Goosebumps spread as he stroked my breasts. His tongue dipped into my mouth, and I dug my fingers into the fabric of his shirt.

This was how I had envisioned the evening. Now we just had to get rid of our clothes. Ideas of what I could do with him raced through my mind. My tiredness and exhaustion faded into the background, and I could finally focus on what I enjoyed: a lovely evening with my boyfriend. I would make sure he got really hot.

Sighing, I rubbed myself against him, enjoying how I reacted to him. How he felt. My hands moved under his shirt, stroking his soft skin. I inhaled deeply because he smelled so good. Every touch sent small shivers through my body, and I got hot. I had been looking forward to this for days.

We didn't see each other often enough.

I wanted to feel this every day.

Rob lifted me up, and I laughingly told him to carry me to the bedroom. I was glad everything was okay between us. And as for Cecilia, I was sure it was just my fatigue from the exhausting week.

I preferred to focus on what lay ahead.

Or, in Rob's case, what was beneath me. And he did his best to make me forget everything else.

I'm alone on the street. It's quiet.

Still night.

There's no trace of my attacker, but I distrust the silence. I don't know how I got here. Did I flee? Or did he? Does it just seem that way? He has ambushed me before. Once? Or many times, and it only came to a fight once?

I pause and think. When was the fight? Did it already happen?

Yes, I realize, it did. I feel the marks of the fight. My muscles are tense, and the places where he wounded me ache. There are several. It was apparently worse than I feared.

My thoughts falter. Worse? The worst outcome would be my death. It was a fight to the death. I close my eyes and try to figure out how it ended. I'm still alive, so I won. Right?

I look around again, filled with unease. I have no proof of his death. I don't want to be responsible for it. And yet, I went into the fight with that goal.

I must be careful. Even if he isn't dead, others could be here. After me. It might not be over yet. I must be prepared for anything.

My gaze sweeps over the empty street. Up to the sky. I focus on the rooftops. I could be attacked from up there. Whoever is after me.

Out of the corner of my eye, I notice something that captures my attention. I feel both hot and cold.

Full moon.

The phenomenon has always fascinated me, but I don't follow the lunar phases.

Today is different. Today, the bright round disc holds my gaze. I can't look away. Slowly, I move, taking a few steps.

I forget everything around me. Full moon. Nothing else is in my head. My steps quicken. I start to run. I don't know where, but I have to. I have no choice.

I woke up with a start. Another one of those dreams. I had a few days' break, but now it was back. This last one was the most intense. It still pulsed through my body, and I felt it in every fiber.

I was drenched in sweat. The previous dreams were intense too, but never this bad. My heart pounded in my throat, and I was full of adrenaline. I felt like I had run for miles and had to keep running. My muscles were warm, and my blood rushed through my veins.

I closed my eyes and tried to fall back asleep, but no chance.

What time was it? Could I get up already?

With a trembling hand, I reached for my phone and looked at the time. It was only two in the morning. I had gone to bed four and a half hours ago, tired from the long workdays behind me.

Helmut was on vacation this week, and I was handling everything. It had never been this hard, and I dreaded the rest of the week with all the tasks awaiting me. I could get up and go straight to the bookstore.

That was pointless; I needed to try to get some more rest. I rolled onto my back and closed my eyes.

"Just forget the dream," I told myself. "Ignore it until it stops."

I had talked to Mira about the other dreams on Sunday, but even with her dream interpretation book, she was at a loss for what they could mean. We tossed around theories, but none made sense. In the end, we gave up in frustration.

"Maybe you should talk to your psychologist about it," she suggested. "It could be an unresolved trauma."

The problem was, Dr. Singh was on vacation for three weeks. There was no substitute, but someone who didn't know me or my history couldn't help me anyway. I had to wait.

I deepened my breathing and tried to slip back into sleep—hopefully without the dream.

It didn't work. I was wide awake and restless. I looked at my phone again. 2:15 a.m. That wasn't a time to do anything but sleep. Especially since I had to get up at seven and the day would be exhausting again.

I breathed deeply and tried to control my pulse. It didn't help, so I tried meditating. Unsuccessfully. I had one more idea: I tensed all my muscles and then relaxed them in a controlled way. That sometimes helped. But not today.

I couldn't calm down. It was now 2:45 a.m.

Sighing, I got up. Maybe drinking a glass of water would help. If worst came to worst, I could sit with my book and read until I got tired again.

As my feet touched the floor, a surge of adrenaline shot through my body. Startled, I froze. My muscles heated up, and my heart pounded.

Please, no! Not a fainting spell now!

But it felt completely different - the exact opposite of a spell. My feet were firmly planted on the ground. It was as if I could run for miles without getting tired. I felt like I did in my dream. An urge to move overcame me.

What was happening to me?

I wanted to freak out, but I couldn't. My head was exploding with impressions, making it impossible to even feel fear.

My senses were heightened, my eyes darted around my dimly lit bedroom. Everything looked different. I saw contours and colors I couldn't possibly perceive.

Was I going crazy? Was I hallucinating? Was I even awake, or was this just a dream?

No, I was awake. Maybe more awake than ever before.

Suddenly, I couldn't stand being inside anymore. The room was too small, and I felt like I was in a cage.

Now I was scared. Mostly of what might come next. My throat tightened.

"Quick, get out of here!"

I rushed to the living room and flung open the balcony door. The cold night air filled my lungs. It was early March; my breath rose in clouds before me.

Then I saw it. The full moon.

My eyes locked onto the bright disc. I got even hotter, almost unbearably so. I couldn't look away from the moon, and then a tearing sensation went through my body. I gasped for air and doubled over.

My gaze was still fixed on the moon. I felt like it was absorbing me, like I was losing my connection to my body.

I clung to the balcony railing, or at least I tried. My hands were numb; I couldn't even curl them.

Slowly, I sank to my knees, my head tilted back. The moonlight shone on my face.

Pain shot through my body. I cried out and recoiled in shock. My cry was a snarl. My body felt different. It stretched and lengthened. It twitched and curled, only to stretch out again.

I was changing. My size, my bones, my tendons, my muscles... everything contracted, grew hotter, and then formed a new shape.

I squeezed my eyes shut and focused on coping with the pain.

I had never had a spell like this before.

I twitched and rolled on the cold concrete of the balcony. I didn't feel the cold; my body was on fire.

A cramp went through my body and took my breath away. Then it was over. The pain vanished, and I could move.

My cramped muscles relaxed, and it was as if nothing had happened.

Not entirely. My body felt different.

Completely different.

I needed to check if everything was okay with me. With a groan, I stretched and got up.

I straightened up, which meant I got on all fours. It felt perfectly natural. I turned my head from left to right. It had never felt like this before.

Scents came to my nose; it was an entire world that flooded into my brain through this sense. The pale light was enough to let me see all colors and contours.

I drew back my lips and felt long, sharp teeth in my mouth. My long tail twitched around my hind legs. The heat tingled in my body as I tested my muscles.

Finally, I managed to tear my gaze from the moon. I looked down. At my hands. They were gone. Instead, I saw black paws. I stretched my fingers, and sharp claws emerged.

I swallowed as I realized what I was. To be sure, I turned to the glass door of the balcony. I froze when I saw my reflection.

"Right guess, Neelia."

I was a panther.

A big cat.

My heart fluttered, and it felt like I was recognizing myself as I truly was. Like something was back that I already knew but had lost long ago.

"I'm back," flashed through my mind. "Finally."

Without thinking, I moved. With a graceful leap, I jumped onto the balcony railing, took aim, and pushed off with my hind legs. I landed in the old elm tree across the way and sprang down to the ground.

My body executed every planned movement gracefully. It was as if I had never done anything else.

As if I had never been anything else.

Panther. Neelia. We are one.

I sneaked down the street. No one must see me, but I had to move. I had to feel this body. "How I've missed this," flashed through my mind.

I had been a panther before. Long ago. The feeling of this body was so familiar, now that I had overcome the initial shock.

Like in my dream. I finally understood it. I had seen my second form in my dreams.

My steps quickened, and I started to run. My back muscles stretched, and I threw my forelegs far forward. My tail stabilized my run; it was entirely natural. I darted through side streets, avoiding cars and other objects long before I reached them. My whiskers were like a new sense organ, revealing things to me that I could never notice as a human.

I rounded a corner, leaping into a tree for fun and jumping down the other side. A branch crashed to the ground behind me.

I just kept running. My fur hid me from curious eyes. This was my night. I was finally myself again. Whole. Both halves of me united.

If I could, I would have cried with joy. The feeling was beyond words, and I couldn't remember the last time I'd felt so good.

Being with Rob was great, and he made me happy, but this... this was outstanding in its completeness. Body, mind... everything was in harmony.

I reached the city park. I paused briefly to make sure no one was around. Then I started running. Sand kicked up under my paws. I ran as fast as I could, enjoying the stretching and contraction of my muscles with each movement.

At the edge of my awareness, I wondered what this meant for me. What the transformation did to me. Could I only change in the light of the full moon, or was it possible on other nights too? Or even during the day?

I pushed the questions to one side and concentrated on the present. How the cold air felt on my nose and the sandy ground under my paws.

I wanted to push this body to its limits.

I wanted to hunt.

The thought startled me, but the urge was strong. I was a predator. Silent. Dangerous. Deadly. I didn't want to waste that; I wanted to use it.

I noticed movement at the edge of the park.

Gracefully, I turned towards the figure and stalked closer. I lay in wait, my steps making no sound. My whiskers twitched as I caught the scent.

"My prey. What are you?"

I recognized a rabbit as I got closer. My keen nose told me everything I needed to know. I crept closer until I was within striking distance. My heart pounded with anticipation. This was the highlight of the night.

Seek. Hunt. Kill.

I prepared to pounce when I heard footsteps. The rabbit heard them too and took off. People were approaching. I ducked into the shadow of a bush. They mustn't see me. If news spread that a panther had been spotted in the city park, it would cause a commotion that would prevent any further outings. I couldn't risk that.

I waited until the people passed. The rabbit was gone. I was disappointed, but it was okay. Next time. The opportunity would come again. I knew that for sure.

I exhausted myself on the lawns and trees of the park, marking one for fun. My claw marks were clearly visible. Let them puzzle over where they came from!

Finally, it started to dawn. I left the branch where I had made myself comfortable and jumped down. I retraced my steps and froze when a new scent reached my nose. It was very close. Danger.

'No more tonight.'

With a leap, I jumped into the nearest tree and used the shadows to slip away.

Chapter 8

Pale sunlight hit my eyelids. I blinked and took a moment to orient myself.

I recognized the wooden floor beneath me: I lay sprawled on the floor of my living room. My body was cold and stiff, and I had muscle soreness.

Groaning, I pushed myself up. Why was I lying here on the floor, and what had happened last night...?

My eyes widened as it came back to me. The impressions and feelings returned. The freedom. The movement. That sensation as my body changed.

A broad grin spread across my face as I sat back, leaning against the couch, and closed my eyes. I reflected, replaying the night.

Happiness flooded me. I felt complete for the first time in a long time.

I sensed that I had transformed into a panther before; this form was as much a part of me as my human self – one that had been missing for a long time.

Why had it vanished? How could that happen? And why had I transformed now?

Suddenly, my dreams made sense too. I wasn't Neelia in those dreams; I was the panther and someone chased me.

Goosebumps covered my arms as I wondered if the dream was both a memory and a premonition.

"Hopefully neither," I whispered, opening my eyes.

I got to my feet and went to the bathroom to warm up in the shower. I paused in front of the mirror and looked at myself.

I looked the same as yesterday. Yet I felt completely different.

I wanted to talk to someone about it, but I didn't know who. Mira? No, not even she would believe me. That ruled out Skadi from the start. And I didn't want Rob to think I was crazy.

My father? If this had happened before, he'd know - and he would have told me.

I swallowed as the thought occurred to me that my mother might have known. Only her. Maybe the knowledge of my transformation had died with her.

I sat on the toilet and stared at my dirty hands. It wasn't a good idea to talk to anyone. Not now, when I didn't know anything myself.

Maybe this was a one-time thing, and I couldn't prove it happened. I had to wait and see if I transformed again. At the next full moon. Like a werewolf.

"Like a were-panther," I corrected myself.

It was crazy. From one day to the next, my whole life changed. Again. It was better to keep this news to myself. For now. I had to find out what was behind it first.

I got in the shower and warmed up. I replayed the previous night. Happiness flooded my veins again; it felt so good. So natural and familiar.

After a long shower, I made scrambled eggs on rye bread. Starving, I also ate three slices of toast and a bowl of yogurt with oats - finally satisfied.

I was eager to get to the bookstore and arrived half an hour early. I unlocked the door, locked it behind me, and dashed to the esoteric section. Unplanned, I needed this genre I had previously always mildly smiled at. Now I wasn't looking for gifts for Mira but for volumes on shapeshifters and werewolves.

I thought I had unpacked one recently. One of Helmut's bundle purchases, which included many books I thought we didn't need. Maybe they would be useful now.

Finally, I found the book I had in mind in the box next to the shelf. A worn cover with a gaudy image of a man with a bare torso and a wolf's head. Just looking at it gave me a headache. It wasn't for me, but I had to get through it.

I set it aside and double-checked the other books. Nothing. This worn, creepy werewolf book was the only one, so I picked it up with a sigh.

"Neelia? What are you doing here already?" Helmut stood behind me, nearly causing me to drop the book in surprise.

"And you? You're supposed to be on vacation!" I exclaimed.

Helmut scratched his head. "Yeah, I know. I just wanted to stop by quickly."

"I've seen that before. You'll end up staying all day," I said, clutching the book.

"Let me work half a day, at least. It's boring at home," he complained. I shrugged; he was old enough to decide for himself, and I didn't mind the help.

Now he stretched to look at the book in my hand. "So, you're sneaking in early to read the esoteric books?"

"Caught," I muttered, embarrassed, setting it aside. "I'm looking for something on shapeshifters and werewolves. I saw a documentary on it recently."

"Where? On the Syfy channel?" Helmut scratched his head. "Ask Klara when she's here. She sorted the books the other day and can tell you if anything was there." He took my find in hand and sighed. "I really should look through the boxes more carefully."

"I'll take it," I said. "Will you ring me up?"

"For God's sake, never."

It took three minutes to convince him to charge me five euros for the thing. Then I stashed it at the bottom of my backpack. I didn't expect it to help me much, but it felt good to take some action.

All day, I watched myself, looking for changes like quicker reflexes or sharper senses. But nothing seemed different since I missed Klara passing by and bumped into her. Startled, I looked at her. I was so lost in thought that I hadn't noticed it was already afternoon. "Oh, sorry. Nice to see you."

Klara rubbed her elbow, which she had bumped against a shelf. "Hey. Helmut says I'm supposed to look for books on witches with you?"

"Shapeshifters," I corrected. "He said you just sorted through and might know if there's anything."

"I think so," she said, but we were interrupted by a customer who needed her help. I got her a cupcake from Layla to apologize for the bump. Bag in hand, I stood outside the bookstore, looking down the street.

It was early March, smelling like spring. The trees along the street were showing the first green. I wondered if the full moon and the season had something to do with my transformation. There had to be a reason why it happened yesterday.

I didn't want to ruin the memory of last night because I enjoyed it so much. But I also wanted to understand why things happened. Why now and what my dreams had to do with it.

I wondered if they would stop now. If they were just preparing me for the transformation or if they were a subconscious memory that came back because of it. And I remembered the bad feeling I had recently at Rob's place.

Now, after everything had happened, I didn't think it had anything to do with him or Cecilia. It was more likely something had been brewing inside me. That also explained why I had been so sensitive since the attack.

My eyes widened. The attack! Maybe that experience triggered the transformation! Maybe I transformed to defend myself.

I imagined turning into a panther when the guy attacked us. He would have been scared to death and fled.

I grinned grimly; this thought made me feel better. I wasn't a victim. I could defend myself, and I needed to figure out how to control the transformation so I would never end up in such a situation again. To do that, I needed more information.

I had to start with my own questions. Until then, I couldn't talk to anyone about it.

In the evening, I got a message from Rob saying he had to fly to Seville: "Last-minute job, really sorry. Hope I'm back by the weekend."

I was sad that our meeting was canceled, but it gave me a chance to delve into my new book. However, my enthusiasm waned as soon as I saw the cover with the bare-chested man. Who comes up with this stuff?

On the way home, my father called. "Are you okay?"

"Yes, why do you ask?" I replied.

"You haven't been in touch, and I'm still worried about you because of the knife attack. You have to cut your father some slack," he said.

"Oh, Dad, that's sweet, but I'm fine," I promised, then hesitated and struggled with myself. Should I talk to him about the panther? What if he knew from before? But why hadn't he ever said anything? Dad and I were always honest with each other, even when the truth hurt.

We had sworn that nothing would ever come between us. We only had each other. If he knew something, he would tell me. And that meant I had to tell him.

I couldn't.

Not before I had at least read the stupid book in my backpack.

My father sighed deeply. "How are you sleeping?" he asked. "Do you still have appointments with Dr. Singh?"

"Mostly well," I said. "I have strange dreams, but that's okay. Dr. Singh is back from vacation next week, so I can work through the attack with her. It's getting better, especially when Rob is with me."

"Good, that reassures me. Are you coming over tomorrow? I'll cook your favorite curry if you like," he offered.

"Tomorrow I'm meeting with Mira and Skadi. I'll come on Saturday, okay?" I said.

"Okay. Take care, honey."

"You too, Dad."

We said goodbye, and I resisted the urge to go to him now. Dad sounded stressed. I wanted to show him I was fine, and he didn't need to worry.

I stopped and turned around. I could just drop by for a short visit.

But there was no such thing as "just a short visit" with us. I knew exactly that I would spend at least two or three hours with him. If I then went home, I would have to take a taxi (which he would insist on), and it would be too late to read the book unless I wanted to stay up all night.

I sighed and continued my way home, deciding to send him a photo of my couch, my book, and the tea I would make to put his mind at ease.

At home, I ordered food and sat on the sofa with the book. Ten minutes later, I got up and opened a bottle of wine. The book was exactly what I had feared: pseudoscience with a lot of imagination.

I kept going until I had eaten my ordered food and drunk half the bottle of wine, then I admitted to myself that I couldn't extract anything useful from the book. Maybe Mira would enjoy it; she had fun with such things.

I set the book aside and poured more wine. I had hoped to avoid an internet search, but it seemed I had no other choice.

I typed the word "shapeshifter" into my tablet's search engine. My spirits sank immediately. 229,000 hits, the first twenty were book recommendations for novels.

My phone vibrated. A message from Rob in Seville. *"What are you doing?"*

"Surfing aimlessly on the internet," I replied. *"Important business, you know?"*

"Sure. Can I distract you anyway?"

I smiled. *"Very much so."*

"I wish you were here with me," Rob wrote. *"Seville is beautiful, you'd love it. I have a nice hotel room. Big bed, big shower. You'd probably like that too."*

My heart beat a little faster as I realized where this chat was heading. But I had no desire to type all the time.

"I'd love to hear more about it. Call me."

It took less than five seconds for the call to come through. *"Hola, chica,"* he greeted me in a deep voice. "Your Spanish lover is here."

"Wonderful. I didn't know I had one."

"Then look forward to this new experience, *mi querida*. I'll tell you more about me and my hotel room. Better draw your curtains; this will get wild."

I grinned as I followed his suggestion. On the way back to the sofa, I took off my cardigan and sweatpants and slipped under my blanket. "Done. Can't wait to hear what you have to say."

"Are you comfortable? This will blow your mind. Heavy clothing is not recommended for this; it always gets so wet and dirty."

I laughed out loud. "Oh man, where did you get that script? I hope your client doesn't check your pay-tv bills."

"Hey, I've got you on the phone; I don't need pay-tv," he teased.

"Then better stop with the jokes, or this will turn into a comedy show."

"It's my talent, you know that." He laughed. "Seriously, I wish you were here."

"Maybe I can join you on a business trip sometime," I suggested.

"Or we could take a trip together, so I have all day for you and you're not alone. You know what silly ideas you get when I leave you alone."

"Oh yeah?"

"Of course. As soon as I leave the country, you have phone sex with a Spanish lover you don't know."

"At the moment, I'm having a funny call with someone in Spain. Not sexy," I informed him.

"Then lie back and listen to my voice. I promise you'll sleep very well and be satisfied afterward. Ready?"

"Ready." I smiled as I heard his first instruction, and his voice became husky and caressing. My fingers glided over my skin, and I got goosebumps as he described what he wanted to do to me. What I should do to him when we see each other again. He gave me precise instructions on how to touch myself, when to continue, and when to stop.

It was the first time I gladly participated. It wasn't embarrassing, quite the opposite. I could have gone on forever. Even when his breathing, like mine, became faster and more intense, and I struggled to hold onto my phone.

He didn't overpromise; it was really good. So good that we arranged to do it again the next evening as we caught our breath.

The next day, I left work a bit earlier and walked to Mira's apartment. I arrived before Skadi and used the time to give Mira the embarrassing book.

"What's this?" she asked, puzzled.

"I thought you might like it, but if not, that's okay. Just throw it away," I waved it off.

Mira looked at the cover, raising her eyebrows. "Okay..." she said slowly. "Werewolves haven't been my preferred topic, but maybe they will be now." She flipped through the pages. I watched and struggled with myself again.

Maybe I could explain it to her. Mira was the most open-minded person I knew. If anyone would understand, it would be her. Even if it was something as crazy as my panther form.

"There's a reason I was looking for a book like that," I began.

She looked at me. "You're into role-playing with Rob?"

"No. Yes. I don't know; we haven't tried that yet. He's in Seville right now," I rambled.

"Then maybe you could have phone sex," she suggested eagerly. The conversation was going in the wrong direction.

"We did, but that's not what I wanted to say." I shook my head to gather myself.

"You can talk to me about anything," Mira said soothingly. "Even about phone sex. I have experience with that."

"Yes, I believe you, but..." The doorbell interrupted me. Skadi was here, and my chance to talk to Mira about my transformation was gone. Skadi would have me admitted to a psychiatric ward, if she found out. Instantly and without batting an eye.

She confirmed this right away when she saw the book on the table and rolled her eyes. "Oh God, Mira, your taste in books keeps getting worse."

Mira grinned. "I knew the title would delight you." She took the book and put it on her coffee table, then disappeared into the kitchen. I watched her go and cursed my missed opportunity. It was impossible to bring up the topic in front of Skadi.

"How are you?" she asked.

"Good," I answered truthfully. "I think I got over the shock. I've always been cautious; Rob and I had just bad luck. Next time we'll take a taxi or walk on busier streets. I'm okay, even with the wound. It's healing well, and I can get the stitches out on Monday."

"I'm glad you're coping so well," Skadi said cautiously. "But don't push yourself too hard, okay? It's okay if it takes a bit. There's nothing wrong with that."

I squeezed her hand. "I know, thank you. I'm not willing to let such crap ruin my life. Things are going too well for me right now."

"Sounds like Rob is a bomb at phone sex," Mira chimed in, carrying bottles and glasses. "Chenin blanc, ladies?"

"Oh God, yes. I hope you have more. I had a terrible week," Skadi sighed, then turned to me. "Phone sex?"

"He travels a lot," I said nonchalantly. "We have to make do somehow if we can't do it every day."

Skadi's mouth twitched. "I wish I could have that fresh-in-love feeling again," she murmured. "Instead, I'm bugging Emil about napkin colors."

"You could buy lingerie in the corresponding colors and let him decide," Mira suggested, pouring wine.

Skadi gave her a long look but then grinned. "At least it would make a good anecdote."

"I need material for Neelia's and my speech at the wedding," Mira added.

"Then no."

"Too late. I'll tell the story whether it's true or not. Good legends always need a bit of imagination." Mira smirked. "It'll be fun; I'm really looking forward to the wedding."

"Ha ha," Skadi muttered.

I remained silent, thinking that Skadi's wedding mustn't coincide with the full moon. I had to check right away.

"Neelia, are you okay?" Skadi asked as I frantically pulled out my phone.

"A sexy pic of Rob? Can I see?" Mira asked, scooting closer. She frowned when she saw my display, I was not fast enough to hide it. "Moon phases? I'd have preferred a dick pic. I mean, for you."

"Mira, you're impossible!" Skadi snapped. "I've known Rob for ten years!"

"But not naked, right?" Mira's eyes widened. "Do you? What do you do at your country club? Gangbangs? Orgies? Can I come along?"

"Emil's family isn't in a country club, and no, of course not!" Skadi's face turned bright red. Mira burst out laughing.

I had already checked the wedding date. No full moon. Luckily. I shifted focus to my friends, hoping Mira wouldn't push Skadi too far into an argument.

"The phone sex was good, but I prefer it when he's with me," I said and it worked, they both turned their attention to me. Fortunately. And maybe there would soon be an opportunity for me to talk to Mira.

Rob finally came back from Seville on Saturday. Even so, we didn't see each other until late in the evening because I went to my father's place after work, as I had promised. I would have liked to see him earlier, but my father had seemed so nervous to me that I had to go to him. On the way, I struggled with myself as to whether I should tell him about my panther form.

If it had happened before, he had to know about it. And there had to be a good reason why he hadn't told me about it. Either way, I wanted to stick to our promise that we would always be honest with each other. Things were easier to bear when you didn't have to do them alone.

I took a deep breath and decided to do it, then smiled with relief. Talking to him about it was exactly the right thing to do.

My steps became lighter and quicker; I felt like flying. My heart felt like a weight had been lifted. Dad and I were a team. If I could talk to anyone, it would be him.

I rang the doorbell and rehearsed the right words in my mind. It wouldn't be easy, but we could handle it.

I unlocked the front door and suddenly stopped as Annaya came into the hallway, smiling warmly at me. "Neelia! So good to see you. Did you have a good day?" She hugged me, took my jacket, and guided me into the living room where my father was waiting.

I gave him a kiss on the cheek, feeling my mood plummet. There was no way I could bring up the topic in front of Annaya. As much as I liked her, it just wasn't possible. Damn, why couldn't I talk to anyone alone when I needed to?

Dad and Annaya also had news that meant I had to be patient: she had surprised him with a two-week holiday in southern Germany, starting this weekend. As happy as I was for him, because he travelled far too infrequently, it annoyed me at the same time because it meant I had to wait until we could talk.

Rob picked me up at half past eight as agreed and my father persuaded him to come in briefly so that they could get to know each other. They hit it off straight away.

It wasn't how I had imagined their first meeting, but I had expected them to get along.

"Won't you stay longer?" Annaya asked when we got up.

"Next time. You're tired from the trip, right?" I jumped in before Rob could answer. I had seen him stifling a yawn, but he would never have admitted it. Now he nodded, and we said our goodbyes.

"We could have stayed longer," he said as we sat in his car. Now he yawned openly.

"No way," I said, poking him in the side. "Don't fall asleep while driving, please."

"I'll try," he promised. We were lucky to find a parking spot near my apartment. There, we kissed properly for the first time. I wrapped my arms around him, enjoying having him with me.

"Glad you're back. I missed you."

"Same here. Even the hottest phone call can't replace a kiss." He kissed me again and sighed. "Unfortunately, I have to leave again on Monday."

"What?" I couldn't believe my ears.

"Yeah, I know. This time to Tbilisi."

"Georgia? Why on earth do you have to go there?"

"Because the client wants oriental furniture with Western influences." Rob rolled his eyes. "Fortunately, there's already a shortlist. If all goes well, I just have to check the quality of the pieces and make a recommendation. I plan to be back by Wednesday, Thursday at the latest."

I nodded, even though I didn't like it. He had just come back, and now we had less than thirty-six hours together.

I remembered Skadi's warning about this very scenario. But I hadn't expected it to be nonstop.

I should have listened better. But what could I do? We'd only been together for a month. I didn't want to make a big deal out of him having a job that required travel. I had to hope he'd be back soon. In the meantime, I'd adjust. Rob had said it would be like this, and I'd insisted it wouldn't bother me. I'd have to stick to that.

He always came back to me.

And now that I had discovered the panther, it might not be bad to have more time to deal with it.

Rob placed his hand on my leg. "So, let's make tonight and tomorrow especially nice, okay? I have a few things planned that I'd like to do with you."

I grinned. "Do these plans include sushi?"

"Not until now, but it can easily be added." He stroked my knee and gave me a look that made me tingle all over.

"Then I'm ready for anything," I promised with a smile, pushing his hand higher.

We spent Sunday in bed, and he kept his promise. I was still grinning on Monday morning when I thought about it. He had even managed to distract my thoughts so thoroughly that I hadn't thought about the panther. That only returned on Monday when I opened the bookstore and walked past the esoteric section. Rob was already on his flight to Tbilisi.

I stared at the shelves with the nonsense books in frustration. Mira had read the werewolf book and had a great laugh, but it didn't help me. Nothing helped me. I only knew I had transformed during the full moon. That wasn't enough. I needed more information and had to know where this transformation came from and what to be aware of.

But there was too much to do, and I didn't get a chance on Monday to go through the boxes again to see if I had missed anything.

When I arrived at work on Tuesday, Klara was waiting for me. After my morning session with Dr. Singh, I went in a bit later. After our talks, I usually felt better, even if they sometimes stirred me up. Dealing with it helped, and Dr. Singh was the right person to show me that I could do something about it. Of course, I hadn't mentioned the transformation to my therapist.

"Hi Neelia. I have something for you!" Klara said excitedly. She was the most book-crazy person I knew, rivaling me in that regard. Her studying literature suited her perfectly. "I went through everything again because I couldn't let go of your book. And I found this." She showed me a leather-bound book without a title.

"Where did this come from?" I asked, taking it in my hands. I carefully examined it, noticing the broken lock on the side and the small golden monogram on the spine. SH. "What happened?"

"It was part of a delivery Mr. Hilmers brought when you were sick. Unfortunately, we had to break the lock. It was a shame, but there was no key in the box." Klara shrugged. "Anyway, we looked inside, and Mr. Hilmers set it aside as soon as he saw it was about shapeshifters. I had completely forgotten about it until you bought the werewolf book last week. What do you think?"

I flipped through the pages. The print looked new, modern typeface, neat layout, but there was no imprint or indication of the printer.

"Strange," I thought. "This must be a private print. How elaborate to bind it in leather and add this lock. Someone had an expensive hobby."

My heartbeat quickened when I found the table of contents. It listed topics like recognizing shapeshifters, an overview of native shapeshifters, and strategic recommendations. I turned to the overview. Someone had really gone all out, depicting various animal species. The page I opened showed a lynx, with details on the left such as size, weight, distribution, frequency (there was even an index for this. Lynxes were apparently *rare* but not *very rare*), and—I widened my eyes—recommended weapons.

"Neelia, glad you're here!" Helmut's voice interrupted my thoughts. He came around the corner, his excited face signaling that we had a lot of work to do. Then he saw the book in my hand and paused. "Another one of those crazy books?"

"Yes. I'm taking it. Apparently, this is my new hobby. Twenty?" I suggested.

"Just take it. I can't charge for this."

"Helmut, please not again. The leather binding alone..." I began.

"Klara and I had to break the lock," he interrupted. "Ten. No discussion."

"Agreed."

Klara rang me up. A blue rose tattoo peeked from under her sleeve, one I had never seen on her before. It was pretty and suited her.

"Thank you," I said. "I never would have found it."

"No problem," she replied. "Just tell me later if you like it. And let me know how you got into this topic."

I promised her, then I had to help Helmut with a problem in the storage room.

Despite our years of collaboration, our organizational systems didn't always align. Usually, we went with mine, and everything was fine, but sometimes we clashed. Like today, creating perfect chaos. So, I didn't get a chance to look at the book until I was home that evening.

It was heavy reading. If the topic wasn't so absurd, I would have thought it belonged to a hunting club and served as a manual for the novices.

I read the chapter on shapeshifters in general.

Then I needed a glass of wine.

The author described shapeshifters as monsters disguised as humans, not the other way around. He wrote about the damage they caused and the danger they posed. Why it was honorable and natural to hunt and kill them when they assumed their true form.

I set the book down, hands trembling. I wasn't sure what I had expected, but it certainly wasn't this.

Chapter 9

I needed time to get over what I had read, and I didn't pick up the book again. The unsettling idea that I might be dangerous lingered as I made my way back to the bookstore.

I remembered the hunting fever that had gripped me during my transformation. The desire to chase and kill. It scared me. I didn't want to hurt anyone, but if the author of the book had any clue about his subject, this had already happened many times. Maybe he was a shapeshifter himself who had turned against the others.

Shapeshifter sounded better than were-panther. The term covered the entire group, all people who transformed. Whether they were panthers, wolves, or something else. It was clear to me that there were other forms, even without the book.

I pushed all this aside and focused on work. Klara had her day off, so I messaged her that the book was a hit (even though a creepy one). She was a bit proud of herself for remembering and finding it.

Rob returned on Thursday, and we met at my place in the evening. He also distracted me from my strange thoughts about the book and my transformation. I was happy to let him, because my conscience was tormenting me. It didn't feel right to keep a secret from him, but I was also afraid to talk to him about what was going on with me. I was afraid that he would think I was crazy. In the worst-case-scenario, he wouldn't want to see me anymore. So I concentrated on our reunion sex and blocked out my guilty conscience.

On Friday evening, I had plans with the girls. Mira and Skadi were coming to my place. I was looking forward to it. The week had been stressful. I had convinced Helmut to continue his interrupted vacation, which meant I had to manage with Amira. Since she could only work in the mornings because of her kids, I was alone in the afternoons. Luckily, everyone would be back tomorrow, and I had the day off.

Now I was looking forward to a lovely evening with my best friends. Skadi arrived first and stood in front of me. "Oh my, you look exhausted."

"Like someone who's worked sixty hours this week," I said tiredly. It had been late several times. On Tuesday, I was in the warehouse until ten, looking for a customer reservation. I also cataloged three boxes that had been lying around for a long time and discovered a few real treasures.

"Take care of yourself," Skadi warned, hanging up her jacket. "If you burn out, you won't help anyone."

"It was just long hours, not too stressful," I replied, leading her to the living room. The doorbell rang again, and I left the door open for Mira. Skadi fetched glasses from the cupboard and told me twice more not to overdo it. Then she interrupted herself mid-sentence: "What's this? Looks intense."

I went over to see what she meant. She was standing by the shapeshifter book. Skadi set the glasses down and thoughtfully ran her fingers over the leather cover, pausing at the broken lock. "Neelia?" She looked at me in a way I hadn't seen before, as if she didn't know whether she could ask me something or not.

I didn't know how to continue the conversation either. The cover revealed nothing about the book's contents, and I was afraid of saying something wrong. Skadi was the least likely person to discuss my panther form with. She was probably wondering why there was a broken diary with a strange monogram lying around. For the first time since we met, I found it hard to be honest with her.

"Looks cool, right?" I said, hoping to draw her out. "It definitely looks good on any shelf." She muttered something incomprehensible and opened it.

Mira came in, greeting cheerfully, but Skadi ignored her. She flipped through the book and turned pale. Apparently, she had found the pages about weapons and killing methods, because she shook her head.

"Where did you get this? From Rob?" she asked.

"Rob? Why would you think that?" I laughed. "He's into books, but we've never discussed such topics. I got it from work. Klara found it and gave it to me because she remembered I bought that silly werewolf book. We had to break the lock because the key was missing. Why?"

"I just can't believe someone delves into such topics. Emil and Rob once had a phase where they played those kinds of games. Pen & paper and role-playing games," Skadi said, not looking at me. "So I thought he might have shown it to you." She closed the book and nervously turned it in her hands.

It looked like she was clinging to it.

"Do you want to take it with you?" I asked cautiously.

"No way!" she replied sharply. I raised my eyebrows, even more confused.

"Let me see that good piece that gets you so excited. SH," Mira read over Skadi's shoulder. The monogram was embossed on the book's spine. "Whose is this? Sherlock Holmes?"

"Very funny, Mira!" Skadi snapped, putting the book down in disgust. "I don't think this was meant to be sold. It doesn't seem like something that was ever meant to leave its owner's hands."

"Probably. It's a private print," I agreed. "It looks relatively new, but there's no publisher. That would have made selling it difficult, even though we sometimes have unique items that find a buyer. I'm glad Klara gave it to me. It's interesting how someone with imagination wrote down their ideas. They obviously had the necessary change to make their hobby look nice and give it a professional touch."

"If you find instructions for murder nice," Mira said, flipping through the book. "This is sick. What did the guy fantasize about? Being a demon hunter?" She paused on the page about lynxes. "My God. How bloodthirsty can you be?"

"The question is, how crazy can someone be to get so into this topic," Skadi said brusquely, slowly returning to herself. I found her behavior odd. It was almost as if the book had personally offended her. But why?

"I thought Emil was into this stuff too," Mira interjected.

"That doesn't mean I approve," Skadi replied icily.

I gave her an uncertain look. Why did the book trigger her so much? This was the first time I had heard about Emil's supposed interest in shapeshifters, and somehow, I didn't quite believe her. Rob had imagination, but not this kind. His ideas were more about our 'interpersonal interactions,' as he elegantly put it. So far, he hadn't asked me to dress up or anything like that.

What was up with my friend? My thoughts stumbled as a crazy idea occurred to me. Was she… No, that was impossible. I had known Skadi for thirteen years and had spent several full moon nights with her. She had never transformed.

That couldn't be. Unfortunately.

I couldn't imagine anything better than having someone to talk to about this. But seeing her expression, it was high time to change the subject. Mira gave me a long look, signaling she understood.

Skadi went to my kitchen to get wine. Mira watched her with raised eyebrows and put the book away. "What's up with her again?"

"I have no idea," I admitted, sliding the book into my shelf. "We should leave her be until she brings it up herself. What's new with you?"

"Not much," she said with a shrug, pushing her henna-colored hair back. Mira was the only person I knew who looked good with that. "There's another fair next weekend, and I've entered the competition. Let's see how it goes."

"Why do you always do that if you hate competitions?" I asked as Skadi returned.

"Because it's good publicity for the 'Magic Orchid.' Aylin and Antonina deserve the business," Mira loved her two bosses.

"They owe that to you too," Skadi said. She was finally herself again.

Mira smiled. "True, but we're a team. So, I'll step out of my comfort zone. Madeira isn't far off either. I need to prepare a bit more so I can see everything I want."

"When are you leaving?" I asked.

"The festival starts on April 27 and runs until the end of May. I'll be there for the first two and a half weeks." Mira beamed at us. "Hey, don't you both want to come along?"

"I can't," Skadi said regretfully. "I need that time to prepare for the wedding."

"Too bad," Mira said, looking at me. "What about you?"

"I'll think about it. Maybe not the whole time, but a short trip could be nice," I said. I liked the idea. It would be great to get away and have a bit of vacation.

"Don't think too long, or all the flights will be booked. You could stay at my hotel," she suggested. "The trip was planned for two people anyway."

"Don't you want to take someone?" Skadi asked.

"Nope. That would reduce my chances of picking up one or more hot Portuguese guys," Mira grinned. With that, the topic change was successful, and Skadi's mood improved.

Fortunately. Nevertheless, I was still unsure about her reaction. I couldn't explain it and decided to ask Rob about these ominous games.

He laughed heartily when I asked him about it the next evening. "The way Skadi said it, it sounds like Emil and I were LARPers who spent every weekend in the woods," he said amused. "Actually, a cool idea, we should have done that. Can you show me the book?"

"Sure," I said, handing it to him. "What did you really do?"

"World of Warcraft," he explained, looking slightly embarrassed. "We lived in a shared apartment in our early twenties and played it excessively every evening."

"I see," I said, disappointed by the simple explanation. After Skadi's performance yesterday, I had expected something more exciting.

I never got into video or online games. I lacked the ability to immerse myself in them and got bored quickly. Unlike books. Mira had played them for a while but stopped when she discovered her 'inner Wicca.'

"Because of Skadi's reaction, I thought there was more to it," I shrugged. Now her behavior made even less sense.

"Well, she was always pretty annoyed by it," Rob said. "We had corresponding decorations in our apartment, which probably reminded her of it. We sold everything when the two moved in together. I don't think I kept anything." He examined the book. "But this is very professionally made. If it belonged to a LARPer, they had a lot of fun with it."

"Do you really think a role-player would put so much effort into his hobby?" I asked doubtfully.

Rob shrugged. "There are people with real armor and all that stuff. They spend unbelievable amounts of money on their equipment. Writing and designing a book like this is probably just necessary for a lot of these people. It looks very professional. So what do you think of the book? Should I read it?" He turned it in his hands.

"Only if you like horror stories." I grimaced. "I found it horrible and was honestly shocked that someone would write a book on how to best slaughter people who can turn into animals. If it were real, it would simply be murder. It's disgusting and sick."

Rob stared at the open page. "Yeah, it is. Never go into my father's hunting room."

"I wasn't going to do that. I find stuffed animals just as horrible and sick." I covered my mouth. "Sorry, that just slipped out. I didn't mean it."

Rob looked at me and waved it off with a smile. "It's fine; I won't hold it against you. Besides, I don't think my dad needs to know."

Still, I felt like my words had hurt him. I climbed onto his lap and wrapped my arms around his neck. "I'm sorry. It's my vegetarian soul."

"I knew that would cause trouble," he said, smiling, and kissed me. I was glad he didn't hold it against me and set out to make him forget my remark.

That didn't change my opinion, but I didn't want us to argue. I had better plans for him.

Rob and I spent the rest of the weekend together, and it was hard to let him go on Monday morning.

We didn't bring up the book again, but when I came back from getting bread rolls on Sunday morning, it was in a different place on the shelf than before. Apparently, the stupid thing haunted him too. I understood; it had a dreadful fascination.

When I got home on Monday evening, it caught my eye again. It was the only thing I had, so I sat down with it again and looked for an entry about Panther. As a precaution, I had a glass of wine first.

There was something about my second form, but I was disappointed: *"Extremely rare, as not native to Germany,"* the note read. *"Sightings in northern Germany in the 2000s were not confirmed."*

I stared at the picture of the panther on the left page. The elegant form, the large yellow eyes, the long fangs. I looked at the paws, depicted with extended claws. I wrinkled my nose. I couldn't walk like that; I had figured it out within seconds. I only needed them to hold on to when I jumped. The picture was meant to show a monster, not a panther.

Whoever wrote this section had spent little time on it and apparently included the panther only for completeness. The pages on lynxes and even on bears, elk, and buffalo were more detailed. The wolf section spanned six pages.

The panther was found under "exotic animals" in the back of the book, along with lions, tigers, and crocodiles. I looked at the crocodile page and imagined transforming into a huge reptile in my bedroom. Here, the author's imagination had run wild.

I flipped back to the panther. *"Origin likely India or neighboring countries."*

India... Once again, I wished my mother were still alive. I kept encountering questions she would have known the answers to.

She was a special person, not just as a mother but also as a woman. Coming here alone to fulfill her dreams was just one aspect. Mom always had a different perspective on things because of her character and background compared to my German father.

She always showed me another point of view when I was stuck with questions or problems. Most importantly, she taught me to accept things and make peace with them.

The fact that I didn't remember the last few years with her was the worst thing about my amnesia and the thing that took me the longest to work through with my psychologist. That was still a big part of our conversations today.

Now I wondered if my mother had known about the panther. If she was one herself or, if not, if she knew of cases in her family. I would have told her about it. Immediately and without hesitation.

My thoughts wandered to my father, and I wondered if I could talk to him about it. But he had left for vacation with Annaya today, and if I couldn't catch him alone, I wouldn't bring it up. I didn't want him to cut his trip short, because that's exactly what he would do.

I had to wait.

I had a date with Rob at my place on Wednesday evening. Shortly before he arrived, Mira posted in our chat group and asked if we wanted to meet at her place on Friday. I agreed straight away and hoped that it would be easier this time with Skadi. Our last meeting was still on my mind.

Mira rang me at midday on Thursday. I was saying goodbye to a customer in the bookstore when my mobile phone vibrated. "Hey, I wanted to ask if you have any ideas for tomorrow evening about what I could make for dinner. I can only go shopping today. I was thinking of something light, maybe a salad?" she chatted. "Then Skadi can't accuse me of sabotaging her fitting into her wedding dress. She doesn't have to eat the chocolate mousse for dessert if she doesn't want to."

Before I could answer, I got dizzy. Cold sweat broke out, and everything went black before my eyes. "Oh no, not now!"

It was worse than ever before and came so suddenly that I couldn't manage to sit down safely on the floor. Blindly, I gripped the counter, but my phone slipped from my hand, hitting the floor hard. I heard Mira's worried voice through the rushing of blood in my ears, but I felt so sick that I gagged.

I was alone in the store. Helmut was at the bank and then grabbing something to eat, Amira and Klara had the day off.

My circulation completely collapsed, and I lost my grip on the counter. My legs gave way, and I fell. The air was forced out of my lungs, and pain shot through my upper body as I landed on my hip and shoulder. Even my reflexes weren't working anymore.

"Neelia? Oh God, what's happening over there?" I heard Mira. I had landed next to my phone, but my tongue was paralyzed.

"Aylin! Call an ambulance to Helmut Hilmers' bookstore! Something's happened to my friend, I must go!" she shouted to her boss. "Neelia, sweetie, I'm coming over. Please stay with me. Tell me if you can hear me!"

I whimpered, that was all I could manage. My body was an empty shell. It had never been this bad; even breathing was hard. I couldn't see anything, everything was blurry. My limbs were numb and tingling at the same time. I couldn't move a single muscle. My breath rattled; I wanted to cough, but I couldn't. The wheezing in my lungs scared me.

The flower shop where Mira worked was a fifteen-minute walk from the bookstore, but it couldn't have been fifteen minutes when she burst into the store and carefully placed my head on her lap. Her warm hands stroked my cheeks. I heard her muttering to herself. Her fingertips glided over my eyelids and temples. I felt warmth, and the dizziness subsided a bit.

"I'm here, sweetie, don't worry," she whispered, then continued her murmuring. I didn't understand the words, but it felt like I was sinking into cotton or warm water. Slowly and soothingly.

I opened my eyes again when two paramedics arrived. Mira waved to them. "We're here!"

"What happened?" asked a paramedic.

"I was on the phone with my friend, and suddenly she didn't respond. I heard her fall, so I came here. She was lying on the floor, so I stabilized her. She was short of breath, but that has improved," Mira reported precisely and calmly. I had never known this side of her, but I was grateful for it.

Hysteria would have finished me off.

A man knelt in front of me. "Can you hear me?"

"Yes," I said. My voice sounded like it came from a grave, but it worked.

"Has this happened before?" the paramedic asked Mira.

"Yes. She sometimes has weakness attacks, the cause of which hasn't been found yet," my friend explained.

I took a deep breath and tried to sit up. My head throbbed, and my shoulder and hip hurt, but it was possible again.

"How are you feeling?" asked the paramedic.

"Okay," I croaked.

"We're taking you in to see a doctor," his colleague decided.

"Not necessary, I'm fine," I resisted.

"Neelia, that's not a good idea," Mira shook her head. "This attack was really severe."

"True, but I know what the examination will show: nothing. Thank you for coming, but I'm fine now," I told the paramedics. They looked at me doubtfully but shrugged.

"We can't force you to accept help," the woman said. She was right. Mira looked unhappily after them as they left the bookstore. I still felt nauseous and had to lean on the counter.

"Do you really think that was a good idea? I know they've never found the cause, but I was really scared when I saw you lying there," Mira said.

"I'll wait for Helmut and then go home," I promised. "I'd rather lie there than in a hospital bed, waiting forever to see a doctor. Thank you for coming by so fast."

"Of course. You would have done the same for me," she replied immediately.

"True." I touched my head. "What did you do when you arrived? I felt better right away."

"I cast a spell on you," Mira said without batting an eye. "A healing spell that seems to have worked well."

"Indeed." I tried to smile, but she didn't seem to be joking. I broke eye contact because I got dizzy again.

The door opened again, and Helmut entered. He saw Mira and waved. "Neelia's friend, hello. I forgot your name, but…"

"Mr. Hilmers, I have to take Neelia home," Mira interrupted him firmly but kindly. "She had another weakness attack. I'll bring her home and make sure she gets to bed."

Helmut's eyes widened, and he looked at me. "Are you okay?" he asked immediately.

"Somewhat," I replied, rubbing my face.

"Then go home and rest. I'll handle things here." Helmut pushed me towards Mira. I didn't want to go, but it made no sense to stay. My legs were wobbly, and my stomach was queasy.

Mira fetched my things and took me home by taxi. "Should I call your father? Or Rob?"

"Rob's coming over tonight anyway," I said. "And I don't want to worry my father on his vacation. He would just be concerned and unable to do anything. I want to spare him that."

"Okay. I'll stay here and take care of you." Mira placed me on the sofa, covered me up, and disappeared into the kitchen. She returned with two cups of tea.

"Strange," she said, handing me my cup. "I've long believed that the moon has a lot of influence on us, but with you, it's weird. Until recently, your attacks coincided with the full moon, but tonight is a new moon." I stared at her. My mouth was dry.

"I never thought about that," I whispered.

Mira shrugged. "No surprise to me." She sat beside me and slipped under my blanket. "Probably has nothing to do with it."

I smiled weakly and tried not to think about it anymore. It wasn't working and my brain felt like it was going to burst.

Over the evening, I felt better, and when Rob arrived, I was almost back to normal. Mira told him what had happened without dramatizing. "Now that you're here, I can leave with a good feeling. Take good care of her, okay?" she said as she left.

Rob walked her to the door. "I promise."

"Thanks. Have a nice evening," she said, leaving the apartment. He closed the door behind her and came to sit with me on the sofa.

"Is everything really alright?" he asked. "Mira has asked me to look after you."

I shrugged. "I heard it." I stared at the ceiling. "I'm fine again." I closed my eyes and tried to swallow my frustration. "I hoped this would stop. Apparently, it never will. I must live with it."

"I'm always here for you," he promised. "Just call me, and I'll come to you right away."

"If you're in town," I retorted.

"Do my trips bother you?" he asked calmly, but I sensed his tension.

I sighed. "I wish you were here more often, but I knew from the start that these trips were part of your job. I have no right to complain, so I won't."

He kissed me on the mouth. "I just must hang in there a bit longer, then hopefully I'll have a status that doesn't require me to take every halfway attractive job. Then I can send others around the globe. And I'll stay with you."

I snuggled up to him. "Sounds good. I can wait for that." He wrapped his arms around me. I enjoyed the moment we had alone and was glad he was here today.

Of course, Mira would have stayed otherwise, but Rob comforted me in other ways. My hand wandered over his chest, down to the hem of his shirt. I smiled as I traced his smooth skin with rough scars. They belonged to each of us, and it was comforting that he had them too.

"One more thing before you pounce on me," he said with a smile, catching my hand. "My parents would like to meet you. So if you could hide your aversion to hunting trophies for an afternoon, I'd love to introduce you to them."

I looked at him with wide eyes. "That's fast," I said. "I didn't expect that yet."

"I've already met your father," he countered.

"True." I smiled, but a resistance stirred in me that I didn't understand. Of course, Rob wanted to introduce me to his parents.

We had been together for almost six weeks; this was the next logical step. Dad and Rob got along almost too well, and on the other hand, I liked Cecilia, despite my odd reaction recently. His parents were probably nice. The strange family stories had to be ignored. Every family had its quirks.

"Is there already a date?" I asked.

"Next Saturday for dinner. My mother is already racking her brains on how to impress you with her cooking. That you don't eat meat is a challenge for her. Usually, there's wild boar stew."

"I'm curious for the alternative," I smiled.

"And I'm glad you're coming." He kissed me and didn't stop me this time when my hand slid under his shirt. I successfully pushed aside the strange feeling in my gut.

On Friday evening, I met Skadi and Mira as planned. They had talked on the phone, and Skadi knew about my weakness attack. And she also knew about my invitation to the von Lindensteins. Rob had discussed it with Emil.

"If this keeps up, I'll have nothing left to tell," I grumbled.

"I'm not worried about that," Skadi said relaxed. "There will always be something."

"You're right." I shrugged and smiled at her.

"Are you nervous about meeting Rob's parents?" Skadi asked.

"Should I be? Do you know them?" I asked.

Skadi shook her head. "No and yes. The von Lindensteins are nice. A bit eccentric, but you'll get along well. Rob's mother is very nice, very friendly. And so chic. I've rarely met such a well-dressed woman. She has real style. His father is more reserved, seems strict, but I know he's also very warm. You know Cecilia already."

"That says something, Skadi doesn't even talk about her own family that positively," Mira teased, earning a rib poke from Skadi. She laughed. "It's true!"

"I know, but you don't have to say it out loud," Skadi muttered. She was glad not to see her parents and two brothers. The fact that they were all coming to the wedding stressed her out already. She had a better relationship with Emil's parents.

I was glad the mood was good again. The tension from that stupid book was gone. For two days, Mira's remark about the moon phases had been on my mind, so I tried to trace back the timing of each attack.

The realization was unsettling: Mira was right. Each attack aligned with the full moon. Until the last one, when I had transformed. And now it seemed to be shifting to new moon days.

I racked my brain over whether it was connected. Before, I had never thought about why. It didn't happen every full moon – or so I believed. If it was, it was tied to my transformation, I'd bet on it.

I looked over at Mira and wondered if I could confide in her. She had taken such good care of me, and she had noticed the connection. But with Skadi in the room, I couldn't. My rational friend would have no understanding. I had to wait until I could speak to Mira alone. Then I would try to tell her everything.

Chapter 10

I didn't get a chance to talk to Mira before I accompanied Rob to meet his parents. Even though I tried, we couldn't find an evening without Skadi. I had to remain patient, though it wasn't easy.

That Saturday I was to meet Rob's parents, was only a few days before the full moon. I felt good, as if my strength had come back stronger after the last low point. It was a welcome change because I was tired of feeling weak and helpless.

In the antiquarian bookstore, Helmut was circling around me as if he feared I would collapse at any moment. When I noticed that Klara and Amira were doing the same, I had to ask them to stop—firmly. I couldn't stand being treated like a child, especially when I was feeling so good. After that, they stopped.

Meanwhile, I tried to find out more about the influence of the moon on shapeshifters. This stupid book at least provided some information on that; it had a whole chapter dedicated to it.

Apparently, some shapeshifters were bound to the moon phases, while others were not. Since the chapter on panthers was so scant, they weren't listed on the table on this topic. However, I did learn that wolves were bound to the moon phases, while cats were only partially influenced.

"I always knew I was more of a dog person," I muttered and put the book away, frustrated. Like every time, I had a queasy feeling in my stomach after reading it. Even the chapter on the moon was mainly about tracking down and effectively killing shapeshifters. And by "effectively", they meant without damaging the body too much.

Whoever the author had been, he and his friends apparently considered themselves hunters who would then sell the pelts of their prey. I found it so disgusting that I almost cried. The book was wearing me down, but it was the only source I had.

Again, I wished I could talk to Mira, but she was at a fair in Berlin. I didn't want to bring up the topic over the phone when she was exhausted from the day at the fair.

Today was Saturday, and I was standing with Skadi in front of my wardrobe, looking for an outfit for my dinner with the von Lindensteins.

"I could have lent you something," she said, shaking her head as she hung two hangers back.

"Then you would have had to bring needle and thread to make one piece out of two," I replied. Skadi was so petite that I always felt huge next to her, even though I knew it was an illusion. I was satisfied with my body but standing next to an elf always made one feel broader and heavier. Mira and I shared that opinion.

"Not at all. But we'll find something for you," the elf snorted and disappeared into my wardrobe.

Finally, she pulled out a black dress that I had never worn because I never had the occasion. It had a rectangular neckline and was knee-length.

"This is it," she decided.

"Isn't it too fancy?" I asked doubtfully.

"I don't think so. And you can certainly impress them; they could be your future in-laws," she replied. I saw that she liked the idea. Then we would be even more closely connected. I hoped she understood how little that had to do with the men we were with. I loved Skadi no matter what she did. The same applied to Mira.

I put on the black dress and was ready on time. Rob picked me up in his car. His parents lived a bit outside of Hamburg, so it was easier to drive there. "This way, I can't get drunk if things go wrong, but I don't think that will happen," he said cheerfully.

"Keep it up, and I'll get scared," I said, winking, even though I was nervous.

"You don't need to. My parents are nice and have never scared anyone away," he replied.

"And why doesn't Cecilia introduce her boyfriend to them then?" I asked.

He looked at me sharply. "Cecilia doesn't have a boyfriend."

I wanted to argue, because I had inferred it from my conversations with her, but apparently her brother wasn't supposed to know. And I shouldn't meddle in other people's affairs. If Cecilia didn't want to talk about it, she probably had a reason that was none of my business. We didn't know each other well enough for me to just ask her.

"Then I was mistaken. Is she joining us tonight?" I asked.

"Yes. I asked her to because I think she'll make the situation easier for you," Rob said relaxed.

"Thanks for your thoughtfulness." I smiled, but wondered if he thought I was so shy that I needed support from his sister. The panther hadn't surfaced in front of him yet. I felt different, but I tried not to offend anyone with my behavior. I knew it would confuse others if I acted as I felt. It took effort because I felt energized and eager. I wanted to do things I had never dared before. I wanted more attention, and ideally, everyone should notice that I was strong and independent. Holding that back was difficult, but I had to proceed step by step to avoid questions.

In two days, my father would finally return from his trip, and then I definitely wanted to talk to him. He had to tell me if I had been different before my accident.

"Is everything okay?" Rob asked.

I flinched. "Yes, why?"

"You've been so quiet. Aren't you looking forward to tonight?" he asked, and for the first time, I sensed his nervousness. It somewhat relieved me.

"Of course I am. I'm very curious, but also a bit nervous," I admitted. That wasn't the whole truth, but I couldn't tell him about the panther.

That's why I felt bad. I didn't want to keep secrets from him, but I didn't know how to talk about it. I would do it eventually - it couldn't be avoided - but first, I needed certainty and more information.

"I understand, but you don't need to be," he replied. "They're excited to meet you. They know I only bring someone if it's serious."

"But I'm not getting a proposal tonight, am I?"

He looked shocked and awkward. "Well..."

My heart jumped. "Rob?"

He laughed. "You should see your face! No, of course not. It's still a bit early for that, don't you think? Give me another month to change my whole life for you."

"What nonsense," I said, feeling my cheeks flush. "I would never expect that. Everyone should be as they are. Including your life."

"And that's exactly why my parents will love you," he replied. "Because you're simply great."

I smiled at him, and a warm feeling spread in my chest. I thought he was great too, and I wanted this to work out. That included telling him about the panther. As soon as I could.

We pulled up in front of a white villa by the forest. I looked out the window, stunned. "Wow, a castle. You forgot to mention that you're filthy rich."

"Wealthy, at most," he said. "And only my parents." I gave him a long look. "Hey, I work for my money. Hard, as you know." He shrugged. "Do you want to get married now?"

"Hardly, and I know you work hard. But you probably got a bit of a head start," I said, thinking of his condo. "Which is normal in that situation I think."

"Maybe just a little." He kissed me and opened his car door. "Ready?"

I opened my door and battled my nerves. "Come on," I told myself quietly. "It's not that bad. You've never had problems with these meetings. You'll rock this."

But as soon as I stood outside, I recoiled. My senses screamed danger, adrenaline pumped through my veins, and my heart raced. My instincts urged me to leave immediately - even if it meant running through the forest. I had to get out of here.

I gripped the car roof and stared at the villa. Damn, what was this again?

"Neelia? Are you okay?" Rob's face appeared before mine, his forehead creased with concern. He placed his hands on my shoulders and held me. "Are you having an attack?"

"No, I'm fine," I tried to say. His hands calmed me, pulling me out of my panic tunnel. My heart rate slowed, and I managed to think more clearly.

"There's nothing wrong," I told myself. "Calm down. Your instincts are overreacting. There's nothing wrong." I focused on Rob.

The front door opened, and Cecilia came out. "Are you coming? Don't make things so exciting." She stopped and looked at me, scrutinizing. "Nervous? You're terribly pale."

"I had a bit of a dizzy spell," I said quickly.

"Then come in. A glass of wine and Mom's top-secret menu will perk you up. She's almost as nervous as you are." Cecilia was having a great time. "She said she feels naked without her venison roast."

"Cilly, you're impossible," Rob said, annoyed.

"I'm just lightening the mood," she said, shrugging, and linked arms with me. I followed her to the house and pulled myself together. I didn't understand what was wrong with me. I had survived such meetings before. It had never been a problem.

I wondered if it was the atmosphere. This house by the forest looked like something out of a movie; the dusk made it seem like a scene from a psycho-thriller or horror film.

I forced a smile. This was ridiculous. I should look forward to a nice evening with Rob's family. I would see them often in the future.

Robs parents stood at the door as Cecilia guided me up the steps. I looked from one to the other, surprised: Rob was the spitting image of his mother—the kind eyes and slightly unusual chin were inherited from her. Cecilia, on the other hand, took after their father, with the same prominent nose and alert eyes. And yet, the siblings looked similar. Biology was fascinating.

"Hello Neelia, nice to meet you. I'm Charlotte." Rob's mother took my hand and beamed at me. I hurried to smile back.

"Friedrich," her husband introduced himself and shook my hand.

"Hello," I managed. Goosebumps ran down my back, and I didn't understand why. The von Lindensteins were nice and welcomed me warmly; why was my body acting up?

Rob placed his hand on my back and smiled proudly as we walked into the dining room. I looked around. The room was large and inviting. The house must have been at least a hundred and fifty years old. The walls were dark paneled, and on one wall was a large fireplace like in an old film. Only men with swords at their sides were missing to complete the picture.

In stark contrast stood the modern furniture, breaking up this feudal impression so skillfully that it seemed like there was no other way to furnish this house. "Wow," I said softly.

Charlotte grinned. "I got tired of living in an Edgar Wallace castle and spruced it up a bit."

"And how. It looks great," I said, trying to finally feel comfortable. I found Rob's parents nice, and now the conversation was picking up. Both had a fondness for classic novels and had traveled extensively, so they could talk about many countries and cultures. The vegetarian goulash Charlotte served was delicious; we all agreed on that.

After dinner, we sat in the impressive living room, and I drank the best wine of my life. Friedrich was very interested in my Indian roots, and it would have been the perfect introduction if I hadn't felt like something was lurking behind me, ready to attack at any moment.

"Are you feeling better?" Rob whispered to me as his father fetched another bottle of wine.

"Everything's fine. I'm just a bit dizzy," I lied. "No problem, just don't chase me around the house."

"I hadn't planned on that tonight. Maybe sometime when my parents are out of town," he smiled. I smiled back, even though I would rather never come back here after tonight.

I was sorry for how relieved I was when we said our goodbyes at half past twelve and drove with Cecilia to Rob's apartment. His parents couldn't help it, but I just couldn't shake the uncomfortable feeling. Not even the wine could change that.

"You can drop me off at the subway," said Cecilia from the back seat, looking at her smartphone. "I'm not tired yet and meeting some friends."

Rob's eyebrow rose. He hadn't forgotten our conversation on the way there. "What friends?"

"Drug dealers and thugs," she snapped. "You know me."

"Please excuse my interest in your life," Rob said, offended. I looked out the window and hoped they wouldn't argue.

But Cecilia sighed. "Okay, okay. I'm meeting the gang. Isa, Beaver, and Henry."

I perked up because she pronounced the last name differently than the others. And it sounded familiar. "Henry, Emil's brother?" I asked. Skadi's future brother-in-law.

"Yes," said Cecilia, trying to sound casual and avoiding eye contact. So that's who she was involved with. I decided to keep it to myself. I had a feeling Rob took his job as an older brother too seriously in this regard, and Cecilia didn't like that. She was old enough to make her own decisions.

Rob dropped her off at the subway station, and we drove on alone to his place. Now I could finally relax.

"My parents like you," Rob said as he parked.

"I'm glad," I replied honestly.

"They'd like to invite you over again, but no pressure. We don't have to do this every weekend." He placed his hand on my arm and leaned over to kiss me.

I was grateful I didn't have to respond because of the kiss, and pushed aside the unease about the next meeting, which seemed unavoidable.

Late Sunday evening, Dad and Annaya returned from their vacation. Too late for me to go over and talk to him.

Monday was incredibly busy at the antiquarian bookstore, and while I visited him, I was too tired for the conversation I desperately needed to have with him. Moreover, Annaya was there, filling me with tea and dinner. Her Lebanese dishes were so good that they almost made me forget the stress.

My father watched me nervously as I ate. "And how have you been the past two weeks?" he asked. He made me nervous. It seemed like he was expecting something terrible.

"I had a severe episode," I reported honestly. "I was alone in the bookstore and luckily had Mira on the phone. She came over and called an ambulance. It was nothing, and I quickly recovered, but the bruises are still visible."

Dad made a strange face, one that took a few seconds for me to understand: relief. But why? Why was my father relieved about the episode? Or was I imagining it?

Annaya vividly recounted their vacation, and I didn't want to bring it up in front of her. I only feared that it wouldn't be possible to have our conversation before the full moon, which was on Thursday.

Thursday. My heart fluttered at the thought. I was eagerly anticipating that night and wanted to know if the transformation would happen again.

I hoped so. I wanted it desperately.

The conversation with my father had to wait because I had plans for every other evening. And if I didn't transform, the conversation would be unnecessary.

I smiled at my father and tried to convey that I was fine, and he didn't need to worry about me.

I could manage. As long as I turned into the panther.

Thursday night, I couldn't sleep. I didn't know if it was necessary to trigger the transformation. I only knew I had to avoid the moonlight until the streets were empty.

By eleven o'clock, I could risk it.

Time slipped away like sand through my fingers. I watched a movie but couldn't concentrate. I put my phone in silent mode and left it in my bedroom; I didn't want to be disturbed.

Instead, I took out the dreadful book.

"The monsters who disguise themselves as humans during the day have brought much suffering to the cities they inhabit," it read. *"It is beyond question that the transformation has a demonic origin that must be prevented from spreading. The* Skinhunters *are the only guild that can successfully resist."*

Skinhunters. What a disgusting name for a group of hunters targeting my kind. Would have, if it were only the hobby of an eccentric who had assembled equipment for his role-playing games. Somehow, I didn't believe that explanation. It would be too simple and reassuring.

But if the content of the book wasn't nonsense, I had to be careful.

I remembered my dreams. The man with the weapon. Was he one of them? If so, I knew what I had to do: attack before he did.

Finally, the clock struck eleven.

I stepped to my living room window and looked down at the street. Everything was quiet, with only the distant sounds of cars on the main road.

I could risk it. My black fur provided enough cover. Taking a deep breath, I stepped out onto the balcony. I turned my face to the moon.

Immediately, I felt the pull of the celestial body. My eyes widened, and I couldn't look away from the round orb.

It drew me in. It was a part of me.

It brought out what I truly was. Finally.

Happiness flooded me because I could experience my true form. I could feel that way again. I could be truly myself. I had been looking forward to this so much.

Now it was time.

This transformation was faster and, to my relief, painless. I only felt a tug in my muscles, like stretching during exercise. I sank to all fours and felt my fur sprout. My skull shape changed, and my muscles adapted to the new form. I became stronger and more agile. More enduring and flexible. My long tail whipped against my hind legs, and my whiskers quivered as I caught the scent.

The coast was clear. The night could begin.

Once again, I leaped gracefully into the tree across the street and from there down to the ground. I looked around and listened, ensuring I was alone. In the distance, I could hear the cars on the main road, but my street was silent. Perfect.

I stretched luxuriously from my nose to the tip of my tail. My muscles stretched deliciously, and my bones cooperated willingly with every movement. I felt fantastic. Free. Free from all constraints and obligations.

The feeling was wonderful. It was like a high that swept me away. I loved feeling this way and wished it could happen more often. But for now, I enjoyed this night.

Where to now?

The narrow streets were only interesting if I could climb trees and test my strength. The dull asphalt didn't please my paws.

I longed for something natural.

I considered running to the park near Rob's apartment, but it was tiny. Even though my playful side was tempted by the possibility that he might see me, tonight wasn't the right time to reveal myself to him. Besides, I needed to move. After the confinement of the past month in my human body, I had to awaken and then expend this energy to avoid going crazy until the next full moon.

I stretched once more, then ran off.

It was like my first transformation: the high was indescribable. Endorphins and adrenaline flooded my body and brain. If I could, I would have shouted with joy because I felt so good.

I jumped over fences and walls, used trees as intermediate stops, climbing their trunks only to jump down the other side. I ran as fast as I could, reveling in the smoothness of my body. I enjoyed how natural every movement was.

I reached the city park and frolicked across the meadow. The grass tickled under my paws, and I startled something small in the bushes that scurried away quickly.

I leaped over the bushes and landed elegantly back on my paws. I circled the planetarium and roamed through the adjacent forest. A thousand scents filled my nose, and I lifted my head to catch them all on the breeze.

A nighttime jogger with a headlamp approached, so I jumped into the bushes before he could see me and darted between the trees.

I passed the sports facility and the mini-golf course, which lay deserted in the darkness, and reached the lake. Without hesitation, I jumped into the water, enjoying the coolness, then ran on, circling the lake until I reached the landscaped gardens.

The first flowers were already budding, and I paused to revel in the scent. Slowly, I walked along the sandy paths, absorbing the nighttime silence and feeling my body.

It was perfect, and for a moment, I regretted that there was no one here to share this night with. I wished I had a companion who could feel the same joy that flowed through me. I thought of Mira. Of my father. My thoughts lingered on Rob, and I wished for a moment that he was like me. At least, I wished I could tell him the truth so he could know and share my happiness.

I had to talk to someone about this. I couldn't keep it to myself any longer.

A crack made me pause. My ears twitched, and my whiskers quivered as I tried to determine where it came from.

An animal in the underbrush? Another jogger? Or just the wind breaking a branch?

My nose caught no scent, though I turned in all directions.

"Upwind," my instincts said. Now they were on high alert. Something wasn't right.

The fur on my neck bristled, and a familiar feeling welled up in me. From my dreams.

My lips curled back as I growled. This couldn't be happening! I had only been a panther for the second time. How could he find me? Who was he?

Skinhunter.

That word was the invention of a madman who enjoyed killing people in his imagination because they changed shape. These people couldn't exist!

Another crack, and my instinct screamed. I ducked and melded with the shadow of the hedges. I wasn't an easy target in the darkness if I avoided the direct moonlight. He would have to come out of hiding to find me. And then I would get him.

If it was even a hunter. It could be a mouse or a rabbit. I could hunt it. My lips curled at the thought of the chase…

That would be the perfect end to this night. Dawn would break soon. I could catch and kill it just because I had the skills to do so. Simply because I was faster and smarter than these creatures.

I waited a moment longer, then left the shadow. I overreacted. There was no one here.

At least no one who could harm me.

I turned my head and searched for my prey. I hoped it wasn't just a mouse.

Again, the rustling. The fur on the back of my neck stood on end. My instincts were screaming so loudly that I couldn't ignore them.

I threw myself to the side just as the shot rang out. The bullet hit the sandy ground.

I growled loudly and zigzagged, approaching my attacker from the side. I was incredibly fast, and the anger made me even swifter. It multiplied my strength.

So this was it: the moment from my dream.

This encounter my subconscious had been preparing me for months.

Skinhunter.

"Just wait!" I thought, crouching for a leap. "You've caused mischief for long enough."

Now I saw my pursuer, emerging from the cover of a hedge. He wore a black coat and held a rifle. A hunting rifle.

This coward! He had planned it well.

Unfortunately, not well enough.

Finally, his scent reached my nose as I closed in on him.

The realization made me stop dead in my tracks. My heart skipped a beat in horror.

I would recognize that scent among thousands.

Leather. A certain earthy note.

I stopped three meters in front of him and stared into his face, now illuminated by the full moon.

He saw me and aimed.

My heart stopped as I recognized the face behind the rifle, just as Rob's finger found the trigger.

Part 3

Under your Skin

Chapter 11

It was like a nightmare, except I was awake.
The shock ran so deep, I forgot to breathe.
I couldn't believe my eyes.
My heart made a painful leap.
It couldn't be him.
And yet, I was looking into the eyes of the man I had fallen in love with.
He was here to kill me.
He couldn't know that I was the panther.
Or could he?
My whiskers quivered.
Rob.
Was it all just a ploy to get my fur? To display it in his father's hunting room?
Skinhunter.
"Is that what you are, Rob? A murderer?"
I looked into his eyes, but the warmth and everything I loved about him were gone. Instead, there was only icy efficiency and a distance that took my breath away.
To him, I wasn't a person, probably not even an animal.
To him, I was a monster he wanted to hunt and kill.
This was different from my dream: This had nothing to do with a fair fight. I could never hurt him. I wouldn't even try.
But he would, I saw it in his eyes.

Was everything between us fake? Even our relationship? No, that couldn't be. We had gotten together before I knew about my other form. At least I had that certainty.

But that didn't change the danger. Somehow, I had to make him understand that it was me. There was no alternative. Running away and hoping he would give up the hunt was a bad idea.

I had to reveal myself to him so that he would know he couldn't harm me. If he loved me enough for that. I had to believe it because I couldn't think of any other solution.

The click of the gun brought me to my senses. I couldn't get any further with a stare-down. He didn't recognize me in this form. I had to change back, or he would shoot at me again.

It was almost impossible to miss at this distance.

I ducked to the side and ran, at the same moment Rob fired the next shot.

The bullet whizzed past me. The sound alone made my heart race, but now I was scared. He was deadly serious. If I didn't find a way to turn back immediately, he was going to kill me.

I leapt over a hedge, darting into the nearest bushes. Every step counted to put distance between us.

I don't know how long it took to change back, but I had to do it now because he was chasing me. And he was frighteningly fast, I realized when I looked back. There was no way I could make up even a minute's lead.

Damn, I had no choice. I stopped and saw him closing in. *Now or never.*

I commanded my brain and my body to change back. Now. And quickly. Then I prayed it would work.

I winced violently and convulsed when it started. Turning back felt like plunging into ice-cold water. My nerves ached like pins and needles and my muscles felt like they were being awfully strained. I suppressed a cry of pain. I hadn't expected it to be this bad.

My body protested against this brutal haste. It felt like I was being torn apart. I bit my lip and curled up, watching as my paws turned back into fingers that dug into my arms.

My black fur disappeared, and my skin and clothes came out again. I was wearing underwear because I hadn't known what happened to clothes when I transformed. They were still there and intact, but I was almost naked.

I got goosebumps and shivered in the cold April morning. My reversal was complete, and I got to my feet. I straightened up and turned to him.

Rob stood rooted to the spot and stared at me. It took him at least as long to understand that it was me as it had taken me before. His mouth was open, and the hand with the rifle sank. He shook his head in disbelief. At least he wasn't aiming at me anymore.

"Neelia?" His voice hit me to the core, even though I had recognized him long ago.

Still, the sound made everything real.

My lower lip trembled as I finally fully understood what was happening here.

He was my lover. And my mortal enemy.

Tears welled up in my eyes, and I wrapped my arms around my torso.

Damn, how did I get into this situation?

Rob slowly walked towards me. I flinched as he shrugged off his coat and draped it over my shoulders. Now he stood right in front of me. Again, I smelled that familiar scent that had always excited and comforted me. That had always made me feel pure pleasure.

That was still there, but somewhere far behind, under all my other feelings. Fear and despair were much stronger. I felt empty and abandoned. Desperate and completely lost.

Defiantly, I swallowed the tears. I wouldn't cry; I was an adult, damn it! I would get this situation under control. In a minute.

His expression was impassive, as if none of this concerned him, but I didn't believe it. Still, I didn't want to show him how vulnerable and disturbed I was.

My gaze fell on the rifle he still held in his hand. His eyes followed my gaze, and his mouth tightened. Now, at least, his face showed an emotion again.

"We should get out of here before we get arrested," he murmured and offered his free hand to me.

I stared at it, feeling paralyzed. Should I take it? Did he mean it, or did he have a deadly ulterior motive? Would he force me to transform so he could carry out his plan?

"I want to talk to you," he said, and suddenly his indifferent mask shattered. I saw how much this was affecting him, how stunned and shocked he was. He had no idea what to do either.

Slowly, as if unsure whether it could burn me, I took his hand and let him lead me to the street. There stood his car. Rob put the rifle in the trunk. I noticed the large bag that was still there. The plastic sheeting. I didn't want to think about the fact that my corpse would be there if he hadn't recognized me in time.

I squinted and fought the urge to run. Rob closed the trunk and stood in front of me.

"You should never have seen this," he said quietly. I would have preferred that too, but now it was too late.

I backed away from him and raised my empty hands helplessly. I didn't know what to do.

I was freezing, and it was more than a kilometer to my home. Without Rob's coat, I was practically naked, I had no shoes, and not a cent of money with me. No phone either to call someone for help.

"Please get in," he said quietly. "I swear you won't regret it. Please come with me. We need to talk about this. I owe you an explanation. And you owe me one too," he added.

A helpless laugh bubbled in my throat. I had to explain myself? Who had shot at whom? I hadn't tried to kill him.

Rob read my face correctly and had the decency to blush. "I'm so sorry," he whispered. "If I had known it was you, I'd never..."

Without a word, I pulled open the passenger door and sat down in the car. I couldn't stand the cold any longer and I didn't want to hear another word.

Still, I knew we had to talk. We had to sort this out, or I would never be happy again. I couldn't just leave. I had to hear it from his lips.

"I came here to kill you. To kill what you are and keep or sell your skin as a trophy."

And then? I didn't know.

Rob got in and started the engine. I didn't dare look at him and stared out the window. We drove to his place in silence. My lips felt sealed, and my head was both so full and so empty that I couldn't think clearly.

Rob parked by the curb in front of his building. With numb limbs, I got out and hesitated as he unlocked the front door. I looked up at the facade. Was my death lurking here?

"Please don't look at me like I'm going to kill you," he said quietly. "I would never hurt you. You should know that."

"It felt different when you shot at me," I said hoarsely. Only now did I realize that I hadn't said a word. My voice was raspy, as if I had been screaming all night.

My body felt strange, hot, and too tight for me. My muscles were very unhappy with the flash transformation, and I was as tired as if I hadn't slept for days. I was an easy target if he was lying.

Rob took my hand and led me into the hallway.

It was warmer here, but the tiles under my feet radiated cold into my body. He saw me shivering, so he called the elevator and wrapped his arms around me while we waited. I closed my eyes and let the touch happen.

I wanted to believe him. The problem was that in the last half hour, my whole life had changed. Again. And this time, not for the better.

Rob pushed me into the elevator when the doors opened, and we rode up to his apartment.

"Cecilia isn't here," he said and unlocked the door. He went into the bedroom and came back with socks, a sweatshirt, and sweatpants. Gratefully, I put everything on and sat on his couch. I pulled my legs up so I could rest my chin on my knees.

I felt miserable and insecure. Rob sat down in front of me. I could see he felt the same way.

"Is Cecilia one too?" I asked.

"What do you mean?" he asked back.

"A *Skinhunter.*"

"How do you know...," he began, then raised his eyebrows. "The book. Of course. You put one and one together."

So it was real after all. Not just the fantasy of some role-player who had immersed himself too deeply in his hobby. This book was a manual for a real guild. Its contents were bitterly serious. And one of the guys who realized the madness in it was sitting opposite me and was my boyfriend.

I nodded, then something else terrible came to mind as I remembered how one of my best friends had reacted to this book. "Skadi! Is she also...?"

Rob shook his head. "Skadi, no. Emil."

I laughed helplessly, then shrugged. "I don't understand anything. We're starting at the wrong end of the story."

"You're right." Rob looked at me cautiously. "Since when have you been... like this?"

"For a month. Last full moon, I transformed for the first time. I don't know why it happened now; I haven't found out much yet. Right now, I'm just trying to cope with what I am," I replied. I couldn't read his expression. He was puzzled, as if what he saw didn't fit with what he knew. Or thought he knew.

"You think I'm a monster," I stated calmly.

He shook his head. "I know you're not. That's the crazy thing."

"This book is probably not a one-off, is it? Now that I know, Skadi's reaction makes sense. She recognized it because she had seen it before and knew something about it," I said.

"Yes. Emil has one too, just like me. It's a manual in the guild that everyone gets who takes on this task." Rob pressed his lips together.

Task. What a neutral term for bloody and senseless murder.

"That's why she asked me if I got it from you," I said. "Does Skadi know what you do?"

"She was initiated by Emil but has nothing to do with it," he replied.

"And she has nothing against him being a murderer?" I asked, unable to hold back any longer.

Rob flinched. "I wouldn't call it that," he said tightly.

"Of course not. In your self-perception, you are freeing humanity from monsters. I've read that trash book and know how you justify it to yourselves. In your eyes, I belong to those monsters that can be killed to nail their pelts to the wall."

"I told you; I know you're not one," he replied.

"Rob, how many shapeshifters have you already killed?" My heart pounded loudly with this question. I didn't want to know the answer, but I had to get through it. I needed clarity.

Rob pressed his lips together. "Does it matter if it's one, ten, or a hundred? By your understanding, each case would be murder."

"It is. You kill animals that are human except for twelve nights a year." I jumped up and paced the room because I couldn't sit on the couch anymore.

"That's not true, Neelia. I'm tasked with hunting dangerous animals that cause harm. They don't just roam around on full moon nights. They can transform at other times too. Some follow their instincts recklessly. They hunt humans. Children. Women. Men. It doesn't matter. I'm called to eliminate this danger," Rob argued loudly.

I stopped and glared at him. "I don't hunt humans; I would never do that," I replied. "But you still ambushed me and shot at me. How did you know where to look for me?"

"You've been seen. It was even in the newspaper. In the 'curiosities' column, because nobody believed the jogger who saw you. I wanted to make up my own mind. And there you were. I watched you and saw you run through the park."

"Without harming anyone, as you undoubtedly noticed," I retorted. "Yet you shot."

Rob shrugged. "You're a panther in the city. You couldn't have escaped from the zoo; I checked that, they only have leopards. You could only be a shapeshifter. And from my experience, the instinct eventually takes over and wants to hunt. And kill. Did you never think of that?"

I would never admit that I had been looking for something to hunt. I would never begrudge him this triumph. But I also knew from myself that I had been looking for a prey *animal* and not a human.

We looked at each other, neither of us knowing what to say. I was angry because I felt cheated and helpless, but we weren't getting anywhere like this.

"What happens now?" I finally asked.

Rob looked at me unhappily. "I don't know."

"Will you hurt me?" My voice was silent, and I was afraid of his answer.

He shook his head again. "Never. I love you."

I widened my eyes. "You said that for the first time," I whispered.

Rob rubbed his neck. Rob rubbed the back of his neck. "I thought long and hard about how to tell you, but believe me, this scenario wasn't one of them. Neelia, of course I'm not going to hurt you. There's no question about that. But we have other problems."

"Your job in general?" I countered, fighting the warm feeling because of his confession. My heart leaped, and I was happy because of it, but all the crazy circumstances ruined the moment. It was hard to feel heavy after all this horror and confession.

He snorted. "I already told you I'm not doing this because I enjoy hunting. We *Skinhunters* have been active for centuries, protecting people. The police are not the place to go for the supernatural. You must believe me that I do this for a reason. Like a hunter in his territory. And beyond."

"What does that mean?" I asked, startled.

"I take on international assignments," he said with suppressed pride. "Those are my business trips."

I stared at him. I felt sick. My stomach churned. "I need a break," I said flatly and stood up to go to the balcony. I closed the door behind me and held onto the railing. My throat felt tight, and now tears rolled down my cheeks.

What should I do? Here I was, loving a man who was my mortal enemy. Who hunted my kind. Internationally. On *business trips*.

There was only one thing I could do: I had to end our relationship immediately. And then... I didn't know what to do. Should I travel during the full moon? Lock myself up so I wouldn't transform, and his kind couldn't hunt me? Report Rob for murders I couldn't prove? And include Skadi's fiancé, Emil, because they were *Skinhunters*, which no one would believe me about.

Did I have to leave Hamburg now and disappear to be left alone? What would happen to my father? My job? My *life*?

I sobbed quietly.

What a shitty situation!

Behind me, the door opened, and Rob's warm hand gently turned me around. He wrapped his arms around me and held me tight.

"I'm so sorry," he whispered in my ear. "This is a shock for both of us. I swear I would never harm you. And no one else, either."

I looked into his face. "Where did the change of heart come from?"

"I can't say on one side that my girlfriend isn't a monster and on the other side hunt all those who are like her." He was serious, and all the humor had disappeared from his face. "I've been taught since childhood that shapeshifters must be fought and that it's my family's mission to do so. My father is well known in the guild, and the expectations for me were always high. I fulfilled them out of a sense of duty and because of my upbringing. I'm good at it, but now I know that the human part doesn't disappear with the transformation. How can I continue? It's impossible to reconcile the hunt with my conscience. I told you I wanted to travel less. That includes fewer hunts. If you're not a reason to stop, who is?"

"What will your parents say?" I asked. My heart was racing; I saw a silver lining of hope on the horizon. I believed Rob. If he was on my side, my identity would remain hidden, and I would be safe. I prayed I wasn't making a mistake.

"I'll need a good excuse to leave active duty," he said. "Usually, we do this job until we can't anymore. Either we get old, injured, or die."

"You don't meet any of those criteria," I said.

He nodded. "No, but I'll think of something. And I'll keep you out of it. No one will know about your panther form. But you also must be extremely careful. Cecilia must never find out. And it's better if Skadi doesn't either." At Skadi's name, my insides clenched painfully.

"Is Cecilia one too?" I asked softly, repeating one of my very first questions. Rob didn't answer it yet. Now he nodded seriously.

"Yes. And she's very ambitious because she's understandably annoyed with always being compared to me. She's been waiting for an opportunity to show our parents and the guild how good she is. We work for money, too. Those with the best reputation get the best assignments."

I looked over his shoulder into his luxurious apartment and wondered if I could ever feel comfortable here again. But for sure I would never set foot in his parents' house again.

"I understand your feelings," Rob said quietly, holding me tighter. "How is it that you've only been transforming since last month? As far as I know, it usually starts during adolescence."

I shivered, and he pulled me back into the living room. My stomach felt queasy as I sat on the couch. "I don't know," I began. "It just happened. For the first time, as far as I know."

Rob frowned. "But you can't remember two years of your life."

"If that's the case, it doesn't help us," I said unhappily. "And it doesn't explain why there was a ten-year gap."

He rubbed his stubbled chin. "Could it be because of me?" he murmured. "Maybe your subconscious recognized me as a threat and..."

"No, not you," I interrupted him. "But Cecilia and your parents. I had panic attacks when we first met. That's why I felt so bad at dinner."

Rob looked at me with wide eyes. "That's not very flattering for my relatives," he said with a weak smile. "Still, something must have suppressed the transformation. Usually, it's done through a magical spell. It must be anchored, for example, through a talisman you always carry with you." He paused. "Or a..."

I widened my eyes. "Or a tattoo?" I finished his sentence. Rob nodded. Automatically, I touched my side, where the robber's knife had injured my skin. He had damaged the tattoo. If it was indeed a spell, he had destroyed it.

"It fits the timeline perfectly." My lips felt numb, and this feeling spread as a realization dawned on me. I jumped up. "There's only one person who can tell us more about the tattoo. Rob, we need to go to my father immediately!"

My father wasn't home when I rang the bell. It was early in the morning, but we were still too late; he had already left for work. I couldn't even call him because I didn't have my phone with me.

That brought me to my next problem: I didn't have a key with me either because I had left the apartment through the balcony.

"We need to go to Mira's and get my spare key," I said calmly. It was after eight, so she had already left for work too.

I navigated Rob to the florist shop and knocked on the door until Mira came from the back and opened it, looking confused. "What do you look like? What happened?" she asked alarmed.

"Long story. I'll tell you tomorrow when we see each other. Do you have my apartment key with you?"

Mira nodded; she had it on her keychain and fetched it. I saw her relief that Rob was with me. In her eyes, it apparently minimized the risk that I had gone crazy.

We then drove to my place, and I was relieved to be in my own apartment. Rob came with me; he had no assignments today.

"Do you really work with antiques, or is that all fake?" I asked while I changed clothes.

"Yes, the company exists, and I know about antique furniture. But the business belongs to the *Skinhunters*, and my department serves as a cover. My parents, on the other hand, have a real antique shop alongside the calling." He shrugged. "It's like a parallel universe. We grow up with it and mainly have contact with others in the guild. I attended a regular school but spent every afternoon in *Skinhunter* training."

"How did your parents react to me? Wouldn't it be easier if you dated one of *the guild*?" I asked chewing on the expression.

"I tried, but there aren't that many of us. That's why it's common for 'outsiders' to join. That's how it was with Skadi back then. A partnership doesn't automatically mean you get initiated. Emil waited three years before telling her."

I knew I had no right to be angry about it, but it hurt me that one of my best friends was on the team that wanted me dead. Skadi had no idea how the situation was, but she had never made a hint. I now understood even less why she had so little understanding for Mira and her inclination toward magic. That belonged to the same world.

Oh God, I couldn't possibly attend her wedding! Emil's entire family was probably *Skinhunters*! What if they found out? Would they kill me right next to the buffet?

"You're overthinking," Rob said quietly. "Skadi isn't your problem. There are other more important issues. But please do me a favor: Don't talk to her about it. Don't try to convince her to turn away or persuade Emil to quit. That will go wrong."

"You don't know that. She's my best friend," I replied defiantly.

"Friendships have broken over less," he insisted. "The more people know about the panther, the greater the danger. Even if Skadi were on your side, she only needs to say one wrong word, and you have Emil's entire family on your back. And more people. I can't protect you then."

"I can take care of myself," I countered.

"That's true up to a point. But you don't know how the *Skinhunters* operate and what you can expect." He took my hand. "I just don't want anything to happen to you. And my people are incredibly dangerous."

"You shoot without thinking."

"Cut the nonsense; I'm serious." He let go of my hand and looked hurt. "I know you're angry. Is this standing between us? I mean, is this going to be a problem for you that we can't solve?"

I looked at him and listened to my inner self. It was difficult because my feelings were all over the place. Just like my thoughts.

"I hope not," I whispered. "But for that, I need to feel safe and know one hundred percent that you keep your promise."

"I will, and I'll make sure no one hunts you." He frowned. "We need to talk to your father and clarify this. Can you call him and ask him to come over?"

"I'll try." I got my phone and called my father. He didn't answer. I looked at my watch. "I must go to work soon. As soon as he calls back, I'll let you know. We'll talk to him together, I promise. Then we'll hopefully know more."

I could see that Rob didn't like waiting, but he nodded. I got ready for work, and he drove me there. It was hard for me to say goodbye to him, but at the same time, I desperately needed time for myself. And distance. Then, hopefully, I could bring some order to the chaos in my head.

My head felt like it was about to burst, and it was as if I had entered a strange state of suspension. I had lost my footing and had no idea how to regain it.

My panther form was something I hadn't fully processed yet and meant a lot of uncertainty for me, and now *this*. When I closed my eyes, Rob stood before me, and I looked into the barrel of his rifle.

I shook my head, forcing myself to focus on work. Helmut wouldn't be in until noon; Amira and Klara had the day off. At least I didn't have to make conversation; I didn't have the head for that right now. I hoped many customers would come to distract me for a bit and then leave me alone again.

Then it was a matter of waiting until my father called back.

It was afternoon when my phone finally rang. I apologized to Helmut and went to the back room.

"Hey, please excuse me. I've been with a client all morning, and it was hairy. I couldn't call. What is it?" my father asked.

"I need to talk to you urgently," I replied. "It's about panthers." There was silence on the other end of the line for a long time. "Dad?" I asked when I couldn't bear the silence any longer.

"You transformed?" he asked thinly.

Something shattered inside me. "You knew," I whispered. "But... how could you..."

"We really need to talk," he sighed. "I can't leave right now, but in two hours, it should be possible. Can you be here at six?"

"I wish it could be sooner," I murmured. I felt numb. He knew and had kept it a secret. The betrayal hurt, and I dug my nails into my palms to release the pressure.

"Me too. Sorry, honey. I'll be there as soon as I can," he said.

"Alright. Rob and I will come then."

"Rob? Why? Does he..."

"Yes," I interrupted. "We have a problem, so please hurry." He promised, and we hung up. My stomach clenched with ice, and my eyes burned.

Why did everyone keep secrets from me? Rob, Skadi, even my father, whom I thought we were absolutely honest with each other!

I sank into a chair and hugged myself, feeling so alone and abandoned. I still had my phone in hand and considered calling Mira, the only person who didn't lie to me.

I didn't, because I suddenly feared she might have a dark secret too. In the end, I called Rob, updating him on what would happen next.

Chapter 12

W e arrived exactly at six.

Rob held my hand and gave me an encouraging smile. "After this conversation, you'll finally know more," he said.

I tried to smile back, but I couldn't. My insides twisted, and I felt sick. I hadn't been able to eat a bite all day, so I was also dizzy.

The situation was unbearable, and I dreaded the conversation. For the first time, I had a bad feeling about talking to my father. That hurt.

Rob rang the doorbell, and this time, I waited for Dad to open the door. It felt strange, but today I couldn't use my key. This apartment, which had been a second home to me, now felt like enemy territory. I could have cried.

My father's face was tense as he let us in, his gaze shifting between me and Rob. He was wondering why my boyfriend was here, but I didn't want to give him that information over the phone.

"Come in," Dad said, leading us into the living room and waiting for us to sit down. He had water ready, which was good because my mouth was dry. We looked at each other, not knowing where to start.

Rob broke the silence. "Abel, we're here because of Neelia's transformation. We have questions that we hope you can answer."

"Were you with her when it happened?" Dad asked.

"Not exactly," Rob said, looking at me.

Now it was my turn. "We'll get to that later. Dad, how do you know about the panther and why am I only finding out about this now?"

Dad took a deep breath and raised his hands, then sank into his wheelchair like a heap of misery. "Because I hoped we would never have this conversation," he murmured. "I'm sorry I kept it from you, but after the accident, I thought it was the best thing I could do."

"Please start from the beginning so I can understand," I said, trying to approach the situation neutrally. The accident had something to do with it—and Dad must have had a good reason for the ban.

Dad took a deep breath, as if he needed to muster courage. I understood that. I could see that he was afraid of this conversation. We both had to go through it now. Rob reached for my hand. Despite everything, I was glad he was by my side.

"Your mother was also a shapeshifter," Dad confirmed my suspicion. "It runs in the family. As far as I know, it affects all female relatives. She only told me after we were married and you were born. It was a shock for me, I would never have suspected such a thing. Your mother was always careful and managed to keep it a secret that she was here. When you turned sixteen, you transformed for the first time. We expected that. Shanti guided you and taught you everything you needed to know. Despite that, you were noticed. Then the hunt for you began."

"*Skinhunters*," I said tonelessly. Rob squeezed my hand.

Dad nodded. "So you know about them. Good, then you know what to watch out for. How did you find out?"

"By chance." I took a breath. "Rob is a *Skinhunter*."

My father flinched, and if he could have, he would have jumped up. His eyes widened, and he clenched his hands into fists.

"Abel, please!" Rob said, raising his hands. "I'm here because I want to protect Neelia. I would never harm her. Never. But to protect her from my family, I need to know everything."

Dad gave me a wild look. "*Skinhunters* caused the accident back then! They hunted your mother and you so ruthlessly that I accompanied you. You were too fast for them, so they took the car. You ran to me and transformed back. I had just started the engine of our car when they crashed into us." He sank back, defeated. "You know the rest: your mother died, and I broke my spine. You were injured too." He clenched his hands into fists. "After that, I contacted Shanti's family, and they sent a shaman. She placed the ban under your skin. It was strong, almost unbreakable, that's why the tattoo is so large. I never expected a knife attack. It must have hit the heart of the ban exactly. What incredible bad luck." He looked down.

I sat there in silence, trying to understand the story. So much information. Too much to digest all at once.

I looked at Rob, feeling helpless. He shrugged. "It wasn't us. When that happened, we were abroad, I checked that already." His mouth twisted. "At least that's something. I couldn't forgive myself if I had anything to do with it."

"Whether it was you or someone else, who cares?" Dad retorted bitterly. "Fine for your conscience, but I'm still in this wheelchair, and my wife is dead. That's on your people, Rob!"

"I know!" Rob snapped. "I wish I could make it right, but all I can do is be there for Neelia now. This shaman, where is she? Can she help us again?"

"Wait, what do you mean?" I asked, startled.

"Your father had the ban placed for a good reason," Rob said. "Maybe we can renew it. Or the shaman might have an idea how to protect you even better."

"Stop for a sec!" I raised my hand and stood up. "Can I maybe have a moment to think about what I've just heard? I need to process this. This... Dad, this changes everything. You lied to me all this time."

"I omitted what I thought should be forgotten, but yes." Dad hung his head. "You're right. I'm sorry."

I looked at my father. He had been punished more than enough. I understood why he had done it, but it didn't change the fact that he had kept a part of me from myself. For ten years. That hurt and it made me angry.

"I was almost eighteen," I said. "We could have decided together."

"No, honey, we couldn't. You would never have agreed, and I couldn't protect you otherwise. You have every right to be angry with me, but I stand by my decision. They kept looking for you for a long time, so the ban was the only way to protect you. The urge to transform is too strong, and you were too young to control it. Eventually, they gave up the search because your mother's family erased all traces." He looked at Rob. "Until now."

"I can only repeat myself," Rob said emphatically. "I will make sure nothing happens to Neelia."

"But surely you're not the only one who knows about the panther, right?" Dad shot back. "How will you keep the others from hunting her?"

Rob pressed his lips together. "No, I'm not the only one, and as long as there's no proof that the panther has been killed, they won't stop. But I can make sure they search in the wrong places." He looked at me. "And we could leave the city on full moon nights."

"That's not enough," my father said. "I know how it was back then. How they searched for Neelia and Shanti. After every transformation, my wife reported hunters, sometimes seeing them even between the moons. She knew their faces."

"Do you know who they were?" I asked.

My father shook his head. "I was only there on the night of the accident. Otherwise, they could have found out who you were through me."

I glanced at Rob, seeking something to hold on to. He nodded. "We don't give up easily once we have a target," he said, then he turned to Dad. "What happened after the accident?"

Dad's mouth turned even more. "Both Shanti and Neelia were in their human forms when the accident happened. Of course, your people noticed that, maybe even investigated in the right direction, but it wasn't obvious that they had gotten into my car and we had anything to do with their hunt. We had a very thin lead. Maybe having three of us confused them. Perhaps that's how I at least saved Neelia." He looked at me, and all his pain was in his eyes. "When no panther appeared again, they eventually gave up. And moving out of town was a good idea."

"Is that why we moved to Berlin after the accident?" I asked. I had spent my last school year in the capital because Dad had taken an assignment there that lasted almost three-quarters of a year after his rehab was completed. During his rehab, he had sent me to a neighboring town for a retreat. He said at the time that we needed distance from Hamburg to move on. I always thought we had returned because of Dad's family.

My father nodded at my question. "Yes, I wanted the greatest possible protection. Moving was the best decision. After a year and the certainty that the ban held, I felt safe enough to return."

"That was smart," Rob confirmed. "And if the panther disappears from the scene again, no *Skinhunter* will spend much time looking for a vanished animal. For that, the workload..." He broke off and bit his lip.

"Too high?" I offered, trying not to freak out over it. Rob nodded again. "Can you find out who hunted my mother and me back then?" I quickly changed the subject before I lost my composure.

"Yes, I can, but what good will it do? Do you want to find them? And then what?" he asked.

"I don't know," I admitted. "I just want to know."

"I'll find out," Rob promised, but I could see he had doubts about whether it was good for me to know. And what if it really had been his family?

"It's more important to focus on the present," my father interjected. "I think it's a good idea for you to leave the city on full moon nights. You have to disappear, Neelia. I can't let anything happen to you too." He gave Rob a sharp look. "And I hope that applies to you as well."

"It does," Rob said immediately.

But the unspoken truth remained that he couldn't keep an eye on all the *Skinhunters* at once.

That night, I slept restlessly, despite being physically and mentally exhausted. Rob lay next to me, and I could sense that he was awake too, but I couldn't bring myself to speak to him.

We had talked all evening, and my words were spent. All the plans had been made; all the concerns shared. I didn't want to burden him with my feelings any longer. I needed to sort through it alone and decide my next step.

Having him with me was comforting, but at the same time, it reminded me that someone was after me. The shock of the previous night was still too deep. I didn't know if I could overcome it.

Rob left after breakfast to fulfill his promise to find out who had hunted us back then. He also wanted to find out the status regarding the hunt for me. He had been the first to report, but after an unsuccessful attempt, others could get involved.

"I assume they will," he said. "Panthers are rare and receive high bids." He looked at me with alarm, as if he had said too much. He had.

I winced but maintained my composure. I should get used to being spoken of like a commodity; that way, it wouldn't hurt as much when Rob slipped up. This was no longer his opinion, but it was so ingrained in him that it was hard for him to let go.

After he left, I snuggled into the cushions of my couch and tried to calm down. So much had happened in the past thirty-six hours that I couldn't keep up.

Rob's profession weighed heavily on me. I hadn't told him yet, but I loved him too. After this revelation, though, I was glad I hadn't said it. I didn't want it to stand between us, and I believed him when he said he wouldn't hurt me. But I knew he stood alone in that. I barely knew Cecilia and his parents, and as much as I wished they would accept my second form like he did, I was sure they wouldn't. In the worst-case scenario, I wouldn't survive the revelation.

My insides twisted.

It would be best to draw a line and leave—just like my father had done back then.

Dad wanted the ban renewed. I thought about it. It would make everything easier and bring me to safety. The problem was that just the thought of it made me feel resistance.

I had just found the panther again. It was all I had left of my mother. A connection that had outlasted her death. I wished I could remember the time before the accident, but the amnesia had nothing to do with the ban. I had to accept that.

I stayed on the couch, pulling myself together until it was time to head to Skadi's.

I was almost at Mira's door to pick her up when I remembered that Skadi was involved too. Sure, she didn't shoot at my kind, but she was about to marry into this guild. And she did so knowingly, as Emil had initiated her.

"Hey, is everything okay?" Mira asked as she greeted me. "You look like you've seen a ghost."

I took a deep breath and started walking. "There's a lot going on right now."

"Sure, but I know your stress face," she said, tapping my nose. "This isn't it. This is your 'something-bad-happened' face. Please talk to me. Did something happen between you and Rob?" Sometimes her intuition was almost creepy.

"Yes, but it's not worth mentioning," I deflected.

"Of course it does," she muttered. "But I can't force you. Skadi will."

Internally, I flinched at her name. The next problem. I had no idea how to face her.

Normally, I would address any problem. But not this one. Not with Mira there. Not without telling her that her fiancé was probably hunting for me. Not without accusing her of joining a horrible organization.

I could only stay silent and hope to get through it until I figured out how to deal with the situation.

We reached Skadi's apartment building. For the first time, I prayed that Emil wasn't there. I couldn't bear to see him.

Luckily, there were still almost four months until the wedding. Either I would find a solution by then, or I would have to stay away from the celebration. Just the thought of ten or more *Skinhunters* being present, each of them eager to kill me, was too much.

I had a lump in my throat as Mira rang the doorbell and we climbed the stairs. I wanted to run away, but I didn't know where to go.

Skadi greeted us with a radiant smile. I had never felt so awful seeing her. I felt Mira's gaze on me, and Skadi's smile shrank considerably when she saw my face. I had never been good at hiding my emotions.

"Something's up with Rob," Mira announced dramatically. I avoided eye contact but couldn't maintain it. In Skadi's face was a question I didn't want to see: 'Did he tell you?'

I pretended not to see it.

"Did you two have a fight?" Skadi asked gently as we sat at the dining table. I didn't know where to start. I had to say something; they wouldn't let it go.

"Not exactly," I mumbled. "It's about his family." I saw Skadi perk up. That slipped out. Now I couldn't get out of it.

"What about his family?" Mira asked. "You said his parents were nice."

"Yes, they are, but they're not my type," I said, slowly gaining momentum. "They live in a completely different world, and I feel out of place when I'm there. I don't think I can warm up to them."

"That's hard to avoid if you want to be with him," Skadi said slowly. "Rob and his parents are close."

"I know, and I don't want him to distance himself from them because of me. I just don't want to..."

"Have anything to do with them?" Mira suggested, frowning. "This isn't like you. What's so bad about them?"

"Is it because of the hunting trophies?" Skadi asked. I flinched. There it was: the question I could answer in different ways. I wanted to talk to her about it, but I was scared.

Fear won out.

"Partly. You know about the hunting room? I wasn't there, but he told me about it. Just the thought of it gives me chills. Even if I weren't a vegetarian, I would find it horrible." I saw Skadi's confusion. She was trying to figure out if I had answered her implied question or the literal one.

"Maybe you could get used to it?" she asked cautiously.

"Get used to dead animals? Am I missing something?" Mira interjected. I needed to react convincingly, or the discussion would never end. Mira always fluctuated between being a flexitarian and a vegan. She said it had to do with the moon phases and her period.

"No," I said firmly. "I find the whole thing so outdated. It has no place in today's world. The stuffed animals are creepy, and I find it undignified to do that with corpses. It was kind of Charlotte to cook a vegetarian dish, but the whole house felt like a mortuary to me." I shuddered, and it had nothing to do with the *Skinhunters*. "I can't handle that."

Skadi looked at me for a long time, trying to understand me. I met her gaze as best I could and tried to look innocent. Mira raised her eyebrow. "Is everything okay?"

I smiled at her. "Sure, why?"

But Mira looked at Skadi. "Is there something going on that I shouldn't know about?"

Skadi tore her gaze away from me. "No. Everything's fine." She forced a grin. "I thought your problem was more serious, but I understand this too. Emil's parents also have a thing for hunting, that's how the families know each other. It's not my thing either."

"What we do for love," Mira grumbled. I shrugged.

"Hey, I understand that you can't relate to it and that it bothers you," Skadi said, returning to her usual self. She had concluded that I wasn't aware. I had had enough discussion for today. "But talk to Rob again and explain it to him," she continued. "You two have been so happy since you got together, you're good for each other. I'm sure you'll find a solution because, as far as I can tell, he's crazy about you."

"He told me he loves me," I whispered.

Skadi covered her mouth in delight. "Oh, how wonderful! So, what will you do?"

"I'll talk to him again," I seemingly agreed and ignored the tense look on Mira's face. "Did you know that Cecilia and Henry are seeing each other?" I asked Skadi, because I couldn't think of anything else to change the subject and improve the mood.

Skadi's eyes widened, exactly as I expected. 'What?'"

I hurried to bring Mira into the loop and tell her about my discovery. I felt bad about it. Both for the things between me and my best friend, and for making Cecilia a target. Then again, that applied to me in her case too. I wondered if Cecilia would shoot me if she knew who I was.

My gaze shifted to Skadi. Would she betray me to Emil and have me executed if she knew? And worst, it was impossible to find an answer to this horrible question.

Rob came to see me at noon on Sunday. "I haven't found anything yet," he said dismissively when I bombarded him with questions at the door. "My parents are out of town and Cecilia is on an assignment in Hungary. I haven't found anything in the guild, there's no register I can check."

I took his coat and felt discouraged. I had hoped for answers.

"Well, at any rate, no one from your family is hunting me down. Or not this weekend, at least."

It was supposed to sound casual, as if none of it bothered me, but instead, I sounded forced and bitter. I bit my lip. I didn't want to be like this.

You're safe right now; no one hunts while the moon is waning," Rob said gently.

"What, do *Skinhunters* only work once a month?" I asked defiantly.

"No, there are also new moon hunts."

"Do I want to know more about that?"

Rob shook his head. "No, better not. Just trust me - you're safe. By the next full moon, we'll have a plan to protect you."

"Good to know," I said. "But it doesn't save anyone else's life."

He took me in his arms. "I had a feeling you would say that sooner or later. Can we save your life first before we take care of anything else?"

"Is there a chance your friends and family will stop killing?" I asked.

He took a breath, and I could see how hard everything was for him. For him, it was much more complicated than for me. Rob had to go against everything his family stood for and what he had learned from childhood. I couldn't forget that, even though my frustration was great.

"I retract the question," I muttered. "Do you get in trouble for not catching me?"

"No. Unsuccessful hunts are part of it. Especially with an exotic like a panther, no one expects it to work the first time. The fact that I even found you in a metropolis like Hamburg is a sensation."

I looked at him in shock. "Did you tell the others you saw me?"

"That would be pretty stupid of me, wouldn't it? Of course not." Now he was irritated. "The less they know, the safer you are. But they don't give up easily, so we need a plan for next time."

I looked down. "I don't even know if I want a next time."

That was a lie. Everything in me longed to transform again. But my fear was real, and it stayed with me.

On Wednesday morning, my father texted me and asked me to come to him after work. '*If Rob has time, he can accompany you. If you think that's a good idea,*' the note said.

So it was going on. I called Rob, who immediately agreed, and then wrote to my father that we would be there at half past five. I couldn't leave the antiquarian bookstore any earlier.

I stood among the books and felt miserable. I didn't know why, but I felt like my time was running out. It felt as if the books whispered that I'd never live to see their age.

Although I knew I wasn't in danger at the moment, it felt like a dark cloud was hanging over me. Like someone could come in at any moment, put me in chains, and calmly wait until the next full moon. Just three weeks to go.

I wondered what Dad was planning to tell us.

Rob picked me up from work, and we walked over to my father's. He smiled encouragingly. "Surely it's good news."

"Do you have any idea what it could be?" I asked.

He shook his head. "I try not to think too much about things I can't influence. Keeps the mind clear for everything else."

"Nice if it's that easy," I grumbled and unlocked the door after ringing the bell.

Dad waited for us in the living room. I felt a weight lift off my shoulders when I saw his face. He was excited, but positively so. Apparently, Rob was right.

"I have good news," Dad began. Rob looked triumphantly at me, but I wanted to hear what it was first. Nothing that came to mind was good news and solved my problems. Whatever Dad was about to announce, it had to be good.

"I contacted our family in India," Dad continued. "It took a while to reach your grandmother. I told her about our problem. She knows about the *Skinhunters* because they've been fighting them for ages. She said that if you came to them, the family could protect you. I told her that's not really an option. She then said the old solution was the best and contacted the shaman who originally placed the ban," he said eagerly. "She can renew it and prevent you from transforming again. That way, you're safe, and all problems are solved."

He beamed at me. The room fell silent as he waited for my reaction. Both he and Rob stared at me, but I was at a loss for words.

"Honey?" Dad said. "Isn't that good news?"

I looked at Rob, who was nodding enthusiastically. "That would solve all the problems. That's perfect, Abel," he said so eagerly that it felt like a knife twisting in me.

Chapter 13

No, it's not," I said with numb lips. "Absolutely not." I shook my head, feeling the heat rising within me. "Not at all!" My voice was louder than I'd intended.

Dad and Rob looked at me in shock. My reaction surprised them. Of course, they had no idea about my feelings and only saw their own perspective.

"But..." Rob began. "This would take you out of the line of fire. We wouldn't have to worry anymore."

Typical. Men always look for the easiest solution - get it done, check it off, move on. But it wasn't that easy.

"How nice, and you could continue with your job," I snapped. "This is of course a setback for the *Skinhunters* ... No new trophy, but at least one less monster. Then the panther disappears, and everyone goes on as before. Almost everyone. What about me? For eleven years, I felt like something was wrong with me. I was constantly afraid of fainting. Those episodes would come back if the ban was renewed, wouldn't they?" Dad nodded thoughtfully. I shook my head. "But I don't want that! I'm tired of feeling weak! I finally found myself. I'm fine now. The only problem is the *Skinhunters!* Why should I make this sacrifice because of them?"

"To be safe," Rob said slowly. He just didn't understand. How could he?

"Exactly, that's the problem: It's not just about safety, Rob. You're asking me to give up who I am, so a bunch of murderous bastards won't hunt me anymore. Sorry, Rob, I just had to say that." I jumped up because I couldn't take it anymore. It was all too much for me. "Please excuse me, I need a break."

I grabbed my jacket and left the apartment. I had to leave before I lost control completely. It wouldn't help if I yelled at Rob, but the situation was so unfair.

Yes, a panther was a predator, but that didn't mean I went hunting humans during a full moon. I hadn't even hunted an animal!

My departure was far from mature; I knew that. Rob and Dad just wanted to help, but they were making it harder right now. They weren't in my situation and didn't understand how great my sacrifice would be if I had the ban renewed. I couldn't make such a decision on the spur of the moment.

Rob messaged me: *I know it's a lot to ask. I'm sorry. Think about it calmly. I'm always here for you. Just reach out -whenever. Your favorite bastard.'*

I had to grin, even though I was so angry. Despite his casual message, I at least had the feeling that he knew what I was talking about. That was a small solace.

Still, I needed time for myself. I couldn't go back, or it would all start again.

'Thanks. Tell my father I'm sorry, okay?'

Then I walked through the evening, wondering what else would happen before this mess was over.

It took me until Friday to calm down. Then I texted Rob to see if we could see each other. He agreed immediately and suggested we meet at his place.

I didn't like going to his apartment, but I wanted to make this concession after my outburst. I arrived a little after seven and rang his doorbell.

Cecilia opened the door. My insides clenched at the sight of her. Another *Skinhunter*, someone who had no problem shooting someone.

Rob's sister smiled casually and let me in. "He's still out but should be back any minute," she said. "Wine while you wait?"

"Sure," I said, seeing no alternative. But Rob had kept his promise. She didn't know anything; her face was as friendly as ever.

Cecilia went to the kitchen and poured some white wine.

"Do you have plans for tonight?" I asked.

"Yes, don't worry, I won't be in your way," she said, raising her glass to me.

"That's not what I meant," I replied. But it was exactly what I meant. I couldn't wait to see her leave.

"I'm meeting some friends, probably going to be a late night."

"With Henry?" I asked without thinking.

She looked at me, surprised, and blushed. "Why would you think Henry?" she asked, bewildered and terribly fake. At least now I knew how she reacted when caught. In the end, she was just a young woman like any other. No, not quite.

"Well, you know, I...," I stammered.

"Fuck," she sighed. "Alright. I guess I'm not as discreet as I thought. Does Rob know?" I shook my head. Cecilia looked relieved. "Good. Do me a favor and keep it that way?"

"Is your relationship a secret?" I asked. I knew Henry. He was nice and good-looking, though a bit taciturn. But I couldn't imagine the von Lindensteins having anything against this relationship. On the contrary, a son-in-law from the same asshole guild must be the jackpot for Friedrich and Charlotte.

Cecilia just snorted. "We're not together. Neither of us has the time or inclination. We are just having sex. It's uncomplicated and convenient for both of us."

"Okay, I understand why you want to keep it quiet," I conceded.

"Our parents are friends. The discussions would be endless," she sighed. Her phone rang. "Sorry, I need to take this. I hope it's my realtor. It's about time I found my own place." She took the call as she left the room and went into her bedroom. She closed the door, but it didn't latch properly, and I could hear her.

"Hey. Yeah, I'm coming over later. Anything new? ... No idea, Rob says he hasn't seen it. ... Yeah, I know, but even my glorious brother doesn't complete every task on the first try. I'll take over. ... I swear, this time it's mine. Do you have all the info? ... Thanks. My parents will see I'm good too. I'll be on the council, not Rob. ... I know, big brothers suck. ... You're the best. I'll thank you later. ... Oh, already? Then I'll head out. Bye."

I realized I had been holding my breath and exhaled. I had a feeling I knew what her conversation was about: me. And from her words, I deduced that she had spoken to Henry and got him on board. She was determined to get ahead of Rob. The thought of the council and her steely tone made my skin prickle.

I stared out the kitchen window, trying to ground myself and calm the pounding in my chest.

"Hey, Neelia. Sorry, did I scare you?" she asked as I jumped at the sound of her voice. She stood in the kitchen doorway; I hadn't heard her return. "I need to go, but Rob will be here any minute." She downed her wine. "Have a nice evening. And you know..."

"My lips are sealed. Thanks, you too," I stammered, barely managing to force a smile. Cecilia disappeared into the hallway. Shortly after, I heard the front door close.

With trembling fingers, I reached for my wine glass and downed its contents. My lips quivered, and the fear returned with full force. "Shit," I whispered. "What am I going to do now?"

The front door opened. "Neelia?" It was Rob's voice.

"Here!" I said weakly.

He came into the kitchen, but his smile faded when he saw me. "Is everything okay? You look like you've seen a ghost."

It took me two tries to tell him about Cecilia's phone call. "Apparently, she sees me as a steppingstone to that council, whatever it is," I said, shrugging helplessly. "Rob, I..."

He took me in his arms. "She won't get you," he whispered in my ear. "Not as long as I'm alive."

"She's determined. Because older brothers suck," I murmured.

"Do you know who she was talking to?" he asked.

"Henry. He seems to be supporting her."

Rob nodded grimly. "That makes sense. Henry is a follower. I can imagine how easy it was for Cecilia to convince him." He had no idea what strings his sister had pulled to make Henry her accomplice.

"I know you don't want to hear this, but maybe the ban is the solution. At least temporarily," he said gently. "If we wait six months for the excitement to die down, we can think of something else in the meantime. We'll find a solution that takes you out of the line of fire."

"And then? Even after six months, they could come after me again. I don't see an alternative. No matter how you look at it, I always have to hide," I replied.

"You have to anyway," he said. "No matter where you are, you can never walk down the street as a panther. If it's not the *Skinhunters*, then it's the authorities who will send hunters. A wild animal of that size is out of the question. You know that yourself. Or do you want to reveal yourself as a shapeshifter? You'd get media attention for sure. And a gilded cage, in the best cage."

"It'd be just as bad as ending up with your people," I rubbed the back of my head. "There are good reasons why it's kept secret."

"Exactly," Rob confirmed. "And that applies to both sides."

"It's so unfair. I haven't done anything to anyone."

"But you could. It's like having a gun license," he replied. "You can't just walk around with a gun in your hand."

"Says the man with the rifle in the trunk. I thought I was in an episode of 'Dexter' when I saw your equipment," I said bitterly.

Rob sighed. "You could at least talk to the shaman and hear what she has to say. Your father said even your grandmother thinks it's the best solution, and she's a shapeshifter herself." He poured me more wine and got himself a glass. "I know how shitty the situation is for you, but your safety is my top priority. Sometimes we have to make sacrifices, you know that. I'll pull back as much as I can and not take any more assignments. That's all I can do at the moment. I need to stay in to know what's happening. And to keep an eye on Cecilia and Henry."

"It's so unfair," I repeated, tears running down my cheeks.

He brushed his thumb over my lower lip and kissed me. "Yes, it is, and I wish I had a perfect solution, but I can't think of anything. I could never forgive myself if something happened to you. Please talk to the shaman. At least explore what options you have."

I pressed myself against him, fighting with myself. I didn't want any of this. I wanted it to stop, to not have to confront this mess anymore.

The dumb thing was, I knew that wasn't going to happen.

The days passed without me making a decision. I just couldn't. The very thought paralyzed me and made me so angry that I couldn't move forward. I didn't want to feel this way. I just wanted to be myself, but that seemed impossible without putting myself in danger.

"I still have time," I told myself. "Enough time to think everything through. It wasn't even New Moon yet. I need to let everything sink in so I can make an informed decision. Not now. Not today."

But the weekend, Monday, Tuesday, and Wednesday went by, and I made no progress. I was nervous and irritable. It was hard for me to control my temper. I acted like an actress. And I was bad at pretending.

I hadn't seen Cecilia again; she stayed at Henry's on the nights I was with Rob, presumably. That was fine with me; I couldn't look her in the face after hearing what she planned.

Rob's parents invited us again, but he came up with something so the meeting didn't happen. Luckily, I didn't want to see them either. Never again.

On Wednesday, I glanced at the calendar.

Tomorrow was New Moon.

I dreaded it; the memory of the last one was still fresh. I absolutely didn't want to be at home, alone with my thoughts and fear. There was only one person I felt completely safe with.

I pulled out my phone and called my father.

"Hello?"

"Can I stay with you tonight and tomorrow?" I asked. "You're working from home, right?"

"Yes, of course. Come over, we'll figure it all out. It's because of the New Moon, isn't it?" he asked.

"Yes. Last time was enough for me," I replied. "I'll just grab a few things after work and then come over."

"No need, I have everything here. Just come by."

"Thanks. See you later."

I picked up some toiletries from the drugstore across the street and headed to my dad's place after work. I rang the bell, climbed the stairs, and was glad to see my father's face. Since our last meeting, we had only spoken on the phone. Now he smiled cautiously at me. "I'm glad you're here."

"You'll always be my safe harbor," I said, kissing his cheek.

"Where's Rob?" he asked, making room for me to hang up my jacket.

"I think he's at home. I thought about going to him, but his sister is probably there, and I feel safer with you." I had told him about Cecilia's phone call.

My father nodded seriously as we reached the living room. "You are safe here. If she's set on finding the panther, she'll do some research. She might notice the connection between the moon phase and your physical condition."

"She'd have to have me on her radar first, but it's not impossible. I don't want to take the risk." Exhausted, I sat down on the sofa and held my head. "It's all too much," I murmured, closing my eyes. "So much has happened in the last two weeks, more than I can digest." Dad eased himself next to me. With a sigh, I leaned against his shoulder.

"Glad to have you," I murmured.

"What are you doing about work tomorrow?" he asked.

"I have the day off and will work on Saturday. It fits without causing a fuss."

"Good. Let's order some food and have a nice evening."

When I woke up the next morning, I felt terrible. This time the fainting spell announced itself. How kind of it. I stayed in bed, not trusting my circulation. Luckily, I was at Dad's.

There was a knock on the door, and my father came in with a tray on his knees. "Tea? Toast?" he offered.

"You're the best." You're the best." I took the tray, hands trembling as I lifted the cup. My hand trembled, and my head throbbed.

"It's starting already, isn't it?" Dad asked.

"Yes. Is it always like this? Every New Moon?" I finally managed to bring the cup to my mouth and took a sip. The warmth of the tea felt like a gentle anchor in all that chaos.

"Only at the beginning when the body is adjusting to the change. When you were sixteen, it took a few months for your body to adjust. Your mother always said the New Moon was like a second period for the body, but that's all. Your body would have adjusted soon if..."

"If I don't decide to renew the ban," I finished his sentence.

Dad nodded seriously. "Now's not the right time to discuss this," he said. "I have a web conference in five minutes. I have the shaman's phone number. Calling her will take three minutes." He kissed my cheek. "Rest and text me if you need anything. I'll come as soon as I can."

"Thanks," I murmured, watching him leave the room. Only two weeks until the next full moon. Time was running out.

My phone buzzed with a message from Mira. *'How are you today?'*

'Not well. I'm at my father's.'

'I thought so. Tonight is New Moon,' she answered.

I stared at the display, struggling with myself. I wanted to be honest with her, but I was afraid of her reaction. And even more so that she might have a secret that could endanger me.

I closed my eyes and took a deep breath. When had it happened that I assumed everyone had a problem with me because of the panther?

Because it's true, I realized. So far, no one had been completely surprised and uninvolved. I can't trust anyone except dad and Rob. Not even Skadi. Not even Mira.

Shit.

'Can I come by this afternoon to make sure you're okay?' she wrote at that moment. I swallowed. What should I do?

I typed quickly, deciding before I could change my mind. *'Sure. I'd love to see you.'*

'I'll be there at 4:30,' she replied promptly.

That settled it.

Mira was her usual fifteen minutes late, but it didn't matter. Dad was still at a video conference but managed to open the door for her before returning to his computer. Shortly after, my friend was sitting by my bed, looking at me thoughtfully.

"New Moon again," she said.

"I know," I replied.

"Alright, then it's time for you to confess you're a were-wolf," she said.

My eyes widened. "Excuse me, what?"

"Well, it's obvious: The book you gave me, your fainting spells during the New Moon... Let me guess: Rob is one too, and he infected you, right?" She said this deadpan.

"Mira, you're crazy," I sighed, but then bit my lip. She watched me closely.

"Crazy good at putting things together," she said with a light smile. I sighed and stared at my hands. There it was: the moment to tell her. To confide in someone who (hopefully) had nothing to do with the whole scene.

"Panther."

Mira blinked. "Sorry?"

"Not werewolf. Were-panther."

She looked at me speechlessly. Her lips moved, but no sound came out. I started to panic and was about to wave it off when she suddenly nodded. "A panther suits you much better than a wolf."

"Is that your whole conclusion?" I asked weakly.

She sighed. "I've been racking my brain about your spells for ages. Eventually, I came up with the moon phase theory, but there were inconsistencies. And you never said anything."

"Because I didn't know myself," I replied. "I've only known what's going on with me for about a month and a half."

"Does it have something to do with Rob or the attack?"

"You're really good," I admitted. "Both."

"Oh, I didn't expect that." Mira brushed her henna-red hair back. I noticed a new tattoo on her wrist: a crescent moon. She saw me looking. "I like the moon," she said. "And my new circle is a crescent moon circle."

"How serious are you about that?" I asked.

"Do you think I'd spend so much time on it if I weren't serious?" she replied.

"No," I conceded.

"See. So Rob and the attack triggered your transformation - how?"

"The injury damaged my tattoo. It was a ban that suppressed it," I explained. "And Rob is..."

I took a deep breath and tried again. "Rob is a *Skinhunter.*"

Mira furrowed her brow. "Like Emil?"

My insides were freezing. "How do you know that?" I whispered.

"I heard him talking about it once. I was at Skadi's, and he was on the phone in the next room. He didn't know I was there; Skadi was in the bathroom. His door wasn't properly closed. I heard the word and found it so strange that I googled it."

"What did you find out?" I whispered. That idea hadn't occurred to me. I had my source. My pulse calmed. Mira wasn't involved. She was just in the right place at the right time. Or the wrong one, depending on how you looked at it.

Mira's face grew serious. "That shapeshifters should stay away from them. I didn't find much, but the name says it all, doesn't it? Big game hunters for magical creatures. Someone at a gathering recently knew the word. He was a sorcerer and said *Skinhunters* can procure all kinds of animal parts for bans and potions if you pay them enough. I thought it was crazy, like poachers getting ivory. Now I can put it in context. Honestly, I hoped Emil was talking about a browser game." She paused. "But if Emil is a real *Skinhunter* in this real world - and Rob too - I wonder what role our dear friend plays in all this."

"Rob says she knows but isn't involved. He still told me not to talk to her," I replied.

Mira grabbed my hand. "Rob says? He knows?"

I told her about the full moon night and everything that had happened since. Mira listened, her face pale. "Neelia," she whispered. "You have to break up with him. I'm sorry to say this, but... You must."

"I didn't expect this from you, Mira. Of all people?" I couldn't believe my ears.

My friend looked at me, unhappy. "I know, and I'm sorry. But how can you be with Rob, knowing this about him and his family? How can you face Skadi, knowing she's involved? I know she doesn't do anything herself, but she knows, and there's a reason Rob warned you not to talk to her. You have to assume she'll tell Emil, and he'll target you." She nervously kneaded her fingers. "What a shitty situation. I didn't expect this."

"What *did* you expect?" I asked.

"Well, I figured you might be a shapeshifter, but I didn't know what kind. I didn't anticipate this nasty side effect. Honestly, I never imagined it would be this bad."

"How could you?" I sighed.

"I can't tell you what to decide, Neelia, but if I can say something as your best friend: I would put as much distance as possible between myself and anyone hunting me. Skadi's connection to these criminals drives me crazy, and Rob being one of them... From my perspective, a complete break is the only option. The quicker and more radical, the better. You can never be safe if you keep contact with them."

Her words took a long time to settle in. I felt worse as sunset and moonrise approached, making thinking difficult.

"You're right," I murmured, touching my hot forehead. "But that's easier said than done. I don't want to, Mira. And honestly, I don't know how."

"Neither do I," Mira admitted. "But if you let me, I'll help you. I want to give you the support that's missing from the others. Together with your father, we'll figure something out."

I nodded and sank into my pillow. It got worse, and thinking became impossible.

Mira held my hand. "I'm here. Try to relax," she said and put her other hand on my forehead. Once again, I was overcome by a feeling of sleepy calmness. Breathing became easier and the pain subsided. I slowly dozed off and was grateful that Mira was there.

Chapter 14

The fainting spell was severe and lasted all night. I lay in bed in a kind of daze. Still, it was nice to have someone there.

Mira stayed with me, taking turns with my father. I could hear the two of them talking, with Mira explaining her perspective. The more time I had to think about it, the better I understood what she meant.

It was easier to endure the spell when it didn't come out of nowhere. Lying in a soft bed instead of on the floor and having someone to care for me made everything more bearable.

I still felt weak; my eyes were strained, and my whole body tingled. But I wasn't as scared as usual and somehow I got through more easily.

The next morning, I was fit enough to go to work. The attack was over, leaving no aftereffects this time – and thankfully, no injuries. It felt as if the pain was lifting like fog and making room for a new, completely unexpected idea: What if I left Hamburg? If I went somewhere where no one knew me, I could have peace. If I was careful during the full moon and stayed in the woods, I should be safe.

My grandmother had offered me protection from our family. Moving to India or flying there for every full moon wasn't an option, but maybe there were other shapeshifting families in Germany and packs I could join, even if I was the only panther.

I needed to talk to my father about this the next time we met. And then discuss it with Rob, explaining that I was considering this option. Explaining it to him would be much harder.

On Saturday, Rob picked me up from work. He had been on a business trip for the last few days - a real one, he assured me, genuinely involving furniture. I tried to believe him.

Now he was back.

Still, I had a strange feeling in my stomach when Rob walked through the shop door. The more I thought about leaving, the more sensible it seemed, even if it meant leaving everything I loved behind. I needed to make a clean break. It felt like there was no alternative.

Rob was not part of this plan. That was a painful realization, but I had come to see that Mira was right about this too.

I could never be 100% sure that nothing would leak, and his family would leave me alone. There was always the risk that they would find out and start hunting me. Besides, I didn't want anything to do with them anymore.

Rob came to me and kissed me. Despite all the shit that had happened and everything between us, that little feeling of happiness surfaced when he touched me. I was in love with him. That made everything harder.

"Is everything okay?" he asked on the way to the car.

"No, not really," I replied hesitantly. How should I phrase what was going through my mind without him taking it the wrong way?

"Just say it; we'll figure it out." He opened the car and held the passenger door for me. I got in, searching for the right words.

"Is Cecilia home today?" I asked as he settled into the driver's seat.

"No, she's traveling. And she finally found an apartment. She can move in on May fifteenth." He started the engine. "Finally, I'm tired of the shared apartment." He placed his hand on my leg. "But you are always welcome, you know that."

"I'm thinking about leaving," I blurted out.

Rob hit the brakes and stared at me. "What?"

"That's not how I wanted to say it," I mumbled. "Sorry, I lacked context. Mira was with me the day before yesterday; I told her everything."

"And what does your witch friend say about it? And why did you tell her? Is that a good idea? She's friends with Skadi, isn't she?" he asked, frowning.

"Don't call her that. She's just into magic and everything related to it. And yes, it was a good idea. She was able to help me," I defended her.

"Neelia, I don't know." Rob shook his head vigorously. He pulled out of the parking space and merged into traffic. "If she talks to Skadi about it…"

"She won't," I interrupted him. "And that's not the point. She asked me why I should renew the ban against my will. I'm not the one posing a danger. Only your people are."

"You transform into a predator that can easily seriously injure or kill a person," he retorted.

"I would never do that. You walk around armed, the same applies to you. One wrong decision is enough. I'm no more dangerous than you or any driver distracted for a moment."

"That's not the same, and you know it. *Skinhunters* primarily ensure safety. There's a simple reason for that: not every shapeshifter is harmless. Some kill, Neelia. For fun. And since the others don't know you're the panther, they keep that possibility in mind with everything they do."

"And what they do involves hunting me until I'm dead. Or gone," I said, frustrated. "Your own sister has it in for me. And probably three others."

Rob's mouth became a thin line that set off alarm bells. He knew something I wouldn't like. "Rob?"

"More than three," he said through gritted teeth. "The hunt for the panther is now a top priority, and they're coming from all over Germany. Two Danes arrived yesterday, and Dutch hunters are coming tomorrow."

I stared at him, speechless. "You can't be serious," I whispered. "This is like a hunting tournament. Will there be snacks served? Does your mother make her famous goulash from slain shapeshifters?" I grabbed the door handle, but we were driving, and I couldn't jump out.

"Of course not!" Rob hissed. I didn't believe him.

"You know better," I said icily. "You can tell me how they'll hunt and kill me."

"I'm doing everything I can to prevent that!!" He gripped the steering wheel and clenched his teeth. "All I think about is how to protect you. I can't think of another solution besides renewing the ban." He looked at me. "I'm begging you, Neelia. Not for my sake, but to save yourself. Please be reasonable and renew the ban until things calm down here. Please!"

I looked out the window, fighting my anger and frustration. "I don't want to leave Hamburg," I said quietly. "Really, I don't. My father is here, my job, my friends… and you. But if I stay, I'll either be killed sooner or later, or I'll have to give up part of myself. I can't do that; you must understand."

"I understand that this is all hard for you, but I don't understand why you're willing to risk your life for it." Rob paused and pulled into a parking space on his street. "Or give up your life completely." He looked at me. "Let me guess: I'm not part of this consideration, am I?"

My heart ached as I shook my head. "No, you're not." Saying it hurt more than I expected, but it was the truth – a cruel truth I couldn't ignore.

The evening was tense, and I debated going home. Rob's question and my answer hung between us. We were on the brink of breaking up. That hurt more than I expected, considering we'd only been together for two months.

I leaned against him. "I wish this hadn't happened," I murmured. "I wish these problems didn't exist. Then I could just enjoy how nice it is with you."

He pulled me close, and I took the opportunity to distract us both. I suspected Rob had the same idea and was putting in extra effort, so tonight we had the best sex of our relationship. It was breathtaking, and we didn't get tired, starting over and over again.

It almost felt like this was our last night together, but it wasn't. We spent the next two nights at my place to avoid Cecilia, but on Tuesday, Rob left for a trip. He swore it wasn't a *Skinhunter* assignment. I tried to believe him.

On Tuesday afternoon, my father called. "I have important news," he began. "When can you finish work?"

"I'm meeting Mira later, but I'm sure we can meet an hour later. I'll come to you at half-past five," I replied. "What is it?"

"I've found a pack in southern Germany and made contact. I'll tell you everything in detail. Come as soon as you can. I'm at home."

I could hardly stand it and jumped at the chance when Helmut said it was quiet today. Klara was there, and everything I had originally planned could easily be done tomorrow. So I told him I urgently needed to see my father and left at four.

The way seemed endless. Since our conversation, I'd been wondering where Papa knew the pack from, what they had told him, what he had asked, and what kind of pack it was. They couldn't be panthers; at least I didn't think so.

My mouth went dry.

Southern Germany. That was far away. It meant breaking camp here if they considered taking me in.

What did that mean for me and for my dad?

I stopped and looked around. Cold fear spread in my belly. This was my home. I was born and raised here. The places that reminded me of my mother were here. And death lurked here. It was hot on my heels.

I swallowed and kept walking. First, I should listen to what news dad had, then I could ponder further.

Finally, I reached his building and stood before him in his living room. Dad was on the phone and gestured for me to sit on the sofa. It took a moment before he could end the call. Every minute felt like an hour.

Finally, he hung up and turned to me. "You couldn't stand it anymore, could you? I understand. I'm sorry I had to be so secretive, but I wanted to be cautious."

"It's okay. You said you talked to a pack. I'm here for the context," I said, grabbing a couch cushion to squeeze.

Dad's mouth twitched. "Context is always good. I know the pack from the past, through your mother. When she came to Germany, she contacted other shapeshifters. Réka is one of them. She's a lynx and lives on the edge of the Black Forest. The Southern Pack is special because it's not a family but a coalition. The shapeshifters are interconnected and warn each other of dangers. We lost contact after your mother's death and your banishment, but Réka remembered me. Thankfully."

I tried to curb my imagination about what Réka might have said to my father. I suspected what it was.

"I told Réka about our situation and the idea of leaving Hamburg to protect you from the *Skinhunters*," he continued. "She's willing to take you into the pack's protection, but only under one condition."

"Rob must not know where I am," I said. There was no other way.

Dad nodded. "Exactly. I know you've decided to trust him, and I believe he won't harm you, but the risk is too great. Someone might find out and follow him. Réka wants to protect the pack, of course. And since this condition applies to Rob, it also applies to Skadi and everyone else we know." My Dad looked troubled.

I needed a moment to understand it all.

"You would come with me?" I finally asked cautiously. I didn't want him to feel forced, but he had always spoken of 'us.' I needed assurance that I wasn't mistaken.

He nodded, surprised. "Of course. What did you think?"

"That it's bad enough if one of us has to give up their life," I said. "What about Annaya? You're thinking about moving in together. That will be difficult if she can't know where you are. Or does the offer apply to her too?"

The sorrow on his face deepened, but he forced a terribly strained smile that pierced me to the core. "No, just for the two of us."

"But Dad, I can't ask that of you."

"There's no alternative, honey. You don't want to renew the ban, and I understand. But I can't let Rob's clan harm you either. Hoping it will blow over already failed horribly once. That can't happen again." He placed his hand on my arm. "Losing you would be a thousand times worse than not seeing Annaya. That's the sacrifice I have to make."

But I felt terrible, wondering if I was being selfish for rejecting the ban. "When do we have to tell Réka?"

"The offer stands and isn't time-limited," he replied. "But the next full moon is in less than two weeks. If you do this, it's a final decision. Meeting them beforehand is out of the question due to your connection with Rob. If you go, you have to stay."

I took a deep breath, trying to decide.

"It doesn't have to be now," Dad said. "But I feel like time is running out for us."

Mira said the same when I told her. I couldn't keep it to myself; at least with her, I had to talk since I couldn't do it with Rob.

My friend listened until I finished and rubbed her chin. "Oh man," she murmured. "That's tough."

"I know," I replied helplessly.

"But your father is right," she continued. "Time is running out. The *Skinhunters* are getting ready."

"How do you know that?" I asked.

"I was at Skadi's on Saturday and Sunday," Mira replied, shrugging when I looked at her in shock. "I'm your wing woman, sweetie, so I went undercover as a spy. Luckily, Skadi needs help with a thousand things for her wedding, and I offered. Bam, I was in the den of the beast-killer. Emil was there too, and I grilled him."

"Mira…" I said uncomfortably. Mira was anything but inconspicuous, and her motives were always crystal clear. I prayed she hadn't accidentally betrayed me.

"I know what you're thinking," she waved off. "But no one noticed anything. That's the good thing about most people thinking I'm a nutcase."

"No one thinks you're…," I began, but she shook her head.

"It's okay. I know it, you know it, and it was an advantage here, so let's move on. Anyway, I took a thousand detours to approach his hunting hobby and feigned interest."

"Skadi will never buy that," I argued.

"No, she usually doesn't, but here's where the nutcase comes in. I told them I met a guy who's into role-playing and hunting stuff. And because I want to sleep with him, I need some insider knowledge. They bought it. Anyway, after a long and disturbing lecture on gutting game, I got to what Emil really wants to hunt. I circled around and found out they're planning an 'event' for the full moon. No, my imaginary boyfriend and I can't come; it's exclusive to the hunting club." She looked at me seriously. "Neelia … they are organizing a hunt - for you. Rob and his sister are part of it."

My mouth went dry. "Rob certainly won't participate."

"He's signed up. I suspect to get information, but there's the old problem again: he's caught between two worlds. I believe he loves you, but when push comes to shove, who will he choose? The woman he's known for a few months or his family? I'm afraid we both know the answer. And it's not in your favor."

I swallowed, feeling wretched. "I told him I'm considering leaving. Without him."

"He didn't like that, did he?" Mira asked softly.

"No. He asked me again to renew the ban. And I wonder if I should just do it. Then I could stay here. With you, with Rob, even with Skadi. Papa wouldn't have to give up Annaya. I could go on and take over the antiquarian bookstore when Helmut retires. I wouldn't have to move to the other end of Germany to stay safe. I would be safe here."

"But always near the *Skinhunters* and not as you want to be," Mira argued.

"Yes, but without the guilt of hurting many people. I can't even go to Skadi's wedding." I stared at my hands. "I would disappoint so many people."

"You know what, you should screw that." I flinched at Mira's words. She didn't usually talk like that. "Sorry, you know what I mean. This isn't about scheduling a vacation around a wedding. It's about not wanting to be murdered. Even if you get banned, you've seen it can be broken. What if it happens again and the *Skinhunters* find out? What if it comes out by a dumb coincidence? Those guys are crazy enough for anything; I wouldn't put it past them to break the ban themselves. I don't believe the ban can protect you forever."

"I need to think about it," I said quietly.

"I know," Mira replied, hugging me. "But the answer is pretty clear."

I racked my brain until Friday, then asked my father for Réka's number. I had nothing planned today, and because I was getting desperate, I decided to call her and talk.

Maybe I wouldn't like her, making the decision easier. Then I'd know I was staying. Somehow, I clung to this thought, even though I knew it didn't solve my problem. Because next week was already the full moon, and I still had no idea how to protect myself from the *Skinhunters*. Rob had offered to take me away, but it wouldn't work: the other hunters had firmly planned him for the hunt, and he had no plausible reason to stay away without making the others suspicious.

I didn't know how many there were, but I knew about Emil, Cecilia, and Henry, plus the *Skinhunters* from other cities and countries who had shown interest. The full moon night in Hamburg was set to become a deadly hunt. An event everyone looked forward to. Except me. And Rob was getting more and more nervous too.

I had to leave the city, one way or another.

The question was whether I should go alone to a place where I hoped no one would see me but where I was unfamiliar. Or if I should secure my safety once and for all. To Réka. Far away from Hamburg.

That would be the end of my relationship with Rob.

I sat on my sofa, my smartphone in hand, and fought back tears.

It wasn't good to leave the city during the full moon and go to a different place each time. There was always the risk of someone seeing me and the news of a roaming panther spreading. Eventually, they would find me because I always stayed where it appeared.

Mira had offered to accompany and protect me as best she could, but I didn't want to put her in danger too.

The only one who could effectively protect me was Rob. But that was just as dangerous as staying in Hamburg because Cecilia and the others saw him as a competitor. Wherever he went, they would follow, making protection futile.

I pulled my knees to my chin and sniffed. It didn't look like I had a choice.

It was possible to renew the ban before next week, but time was running out. If only I didn't have such an aversion to this solution. I didn't want it, but my options were limited to the ban or joining the pack.

I had to decide quickly whether I wanted to give up my whole life. No, I didn't. Just thinking about it hurt.

I called my father. "What should I do?" I whispered. My voice trembled.

"I don't know," he admitted. "But the options are dwindling. I contacted the shaman; she can't renew the ban before the full moon. She's missing an ingredient for the ink that she can only gather during the new moon. That means this option is off the table. At least for this month. We waited too long."

I closed my burning eyes. "Shit."

"Have you decided to renew the ban?" Papa asked. "Then I'll let her know. We'll get through this full moon night, sweetheart; don't worry. We'll figure something out. Even if it means finding a place for you to spend the night, we'll manage."

I sat quietly for a while, not knowing how to feel about it. I was discouraged. Afraid. I felt surrounded, as if a gun were pointed at my face. Again.

I hadn't forgotten that situation. It haunted me, and I often dreamed about it. It was better when Rob was next to me when I woke up in a cold sweat, but he wasn't with me every night.

"Sweetheart?" Papa asked, and I realized I hadn't said anything for a long time.

"I'm going to call Réka," I said. "Now. I'll decide tomorrow."

"Do that. We'll need to prepare a lot if you decide to go. Please call me after." I promised and ended the call. I took a deep breath. Then I dialed her number.

"Hello?"

"Hello, this is Neelia Jacobi. Réka?"

"Yes. Neelia… You're the panther." Réka's voice was full and silky, yet there was something lurking in it. I understood immediately; a lynx is also a cat. I felt triggered. The panther wondered if the lynx was a companion or a rival.

"Yes, that's me. I wanted to talk to you and…"

"Your father told me about your situation," she interrupted kindly. "I must admit the story touched me. You combine a lot of unusual things; I had to discuss it with the pack."

My courage sank to the bottom. I felt like I had unexpectedly stepped into a hole.

"Your connection to the *Skinhunters* caused a stir," Réka continued. "That's why we had to tell your father that our offer comes with the condition that you break all contact with your boyfriend. You understand that, don't you?"

"Yes. You want to protect the pack," I replied. "I understand, of course."

"Neelia, you're welcome. Here, we don't just survive; we find peace, a life without hiding. It's a life you won't find elsewhere I want you to have this chance, too. The price is high, but we all pay it. It opens new paths. You can find a job and live under our protection. We're a family and support each other. It's appreciated and expected that you will contribute. The most important thing is that you don't have to worry during your transformation, as long as you follow the rules: be cautious and no trips to town. That's all."

"That sounds good," I said slowly.

"I know it's a leap of faith for you. If you come, you must stay. If you leave, you can't come back. We must protect ourselves. Especially given the illustrious company you've kept."

"That wasn't intentional," I replied.

"Of course not," she snorted. "Which shapeshifter would voluntarily get involved with a *Skinhunter*? Sorry for being so strict. Normally, I'd invite you to meet us, but they've already noticed you. How do you plan to spend the full moon?"

"I don't know yet," I admitted. "Probably have to lock myself up somewhere."

"That's terrible," she replied. "You wouldn't have to do that here. We have a lot of land where we spend the moons. Here, you never have to restrict yourself."

"I have the option of renewing the ban," I said.

There was a moment of silence on the line. "And you're seriously considering it?" she finally asked.

"That way, I could continue my life and even keep my relationship," I replied.

"But because of this guy, you're in danger in the first place," she countered. "And you want to give yourself up for him? Don't you enjoy your second form?"

"Yes, I love it. And when I transformed again, it was like being reborn," I said.

"Why would you give that up? Compromises are part of relationships, sure, but this... If you don't do it, his friends will kill you. That's not a compromise. Sorry," she interrupted herself. "I know that was harsh, but the thought chills me to the bone."

"I understand," I murmured, looking up. It was dark outside, and I saw my reflection in the window.

A ban was not an option, I realized. I didn't want to lose the panther. With the amnesia, that was possible, but not now. And staying here was not an option. My heart ached with this realization.

"Réka, I'm coming to you. I'll somehow survive the full moon and prepare everything. I'll be with you in at most two months."

"I hoped you'd decide that way. I look forward to seeing you, Neelia."

I smiled at my reflection, trying to ignore the breaking of my heart. I'd lost so much already - my mother, my memories. But the panther was mine, and I'd fought too hard to lose that now. No one would ever take it from me.

Part 4

My true blood

Chapter 15

I slept badly that night; my head was buzzing too much to rest. Panic rose up inside me. What was I thinking? Could I really do this?

Leaving meant safety, a new life, and freedom. But it also meant giving up everything I'd ever known. I clung to the memories of Skadi's laughter, Mira's unwavering friendship, and the moments Rob and I had shared. The shapeshifters I'm going to meet at Réka's place knew how to protect themselves from the *Skinhunters*. On the other hand, it'd also become my job to ensure that this security remained stable. I could never forgive myself for endangering anyone.

Then came the doubts as to whether I could give up my life in Hamburg. Whether I could leave my friends, my job and my plans behind.

And Rob... My heart ached for him as much as it did for Skadi and Mira.

Yes, we had only been a couple for a short time, but it had been enough to make me happy and make me believe that we could have a future together.

Now I felt like everything had been taken from me. Only one thing mattered: survival. And the worst part: He was one of the reasons there was no other topic in my life.

Rob took away my choice. He stole our future. Because of him, I had to take this path.

At the same time, I was glad that I could at least keep the panther. And my father.

It was true, as I had told Réka: Banishment was out of the question. That was also the case before her judgement, but her words had only cemented my decision. There were few people for whom one should make such sacrifices. And since Rob had caused everything, I could not give myself up for him.

I never thought I was so strong, but now I realized that I was. I would not be a victim, and I did not want to submit to something that repulsed me. If being myself meant I had to break up with him, then that was right. Then we were not meant for each other.

It hurt now, but I had to learn to deal with it. I could manage on my own. It was that way before our relationship, and it would be that way afterward.

On Saturday, I had a day off. Rob was at a meeting with the *Skinhunters* and was trying to find out more about the accident back then. That gave me time to make arrangements. I called my father, then went to the antiquarian bookstore and talked with a heavy heart to Helmut. As expected, he was completely taken aback, and it took a while to calm the waters.

"Are you coming back?" he asked hopefully.

"I don't know," I admitted. "At the moment, probably not. If that changes, I'll be here."

Helmut was not happy with that either, but I had him calmed down so that he was no longer angry. I explained to him that the attack had brought back the trauma of the accident, and I needed distance and a change of scenery to cope with it. In principle, that was true, albeit in a different way than he thought.

Then I called Mira on facetime. We were meeting tonight at Skadi's, a meeting I was afraid of because it was now clear that I would not be attending her wedding.

"You don't have to tell her today," Mira said. "I know it kills you to lie, but that's what she's doing to us."

"She doesn't know I'm the panther Emil is hunting."

"And that's a good thing," Mira sighed. "So you're leaving. That's right, but I can't be happy about it right now. I can't continue meeting with Skadi if her husband is partly to blame for that. And without you as a buffer, we'll be at each other's throats all the time. That's it for our trio." She looked at her wrist, where she had a tattoo of a stylized 3. "I'll have to think of another meaning for it. Of all my tattoos, this is the one I least expected to change."

I wanted to comfort her, but nothing came to mind. I hoped to keep her in my life. But Mira was right: Skadi was not an option, no matter how much it hurt.

"But one more thing," Mira said. "Talk to Rob first, then Skadi. Otherwise, she'll tell Emil about it, and he'll spill the beans on Rob. He should hear it from you, not from his former roommate."

I nodded and held myself together all evening at Skadi's. I felt terrible pretending to be looking forward to the wedding. I was ashamed of the hypocrisy, but Mira was right: Skadi would tell Emil, and I didn't want to risk him beating me to it.

I was glad when the girls' night was over, though the next day loomed, when I was to meet Rob.

We met in the afternoon because he couldn't get back from the meeting any earlier. He called when he was almost in

Hamburg, and I headed to his place. Cecilia wouldn't be there; she had other plans for the weekend.

Still, I was nervous when I arrived. My stomach fluttered, and I felt sick. Today, I had to tell him I was leaving. Without him.

He hadn't taken it well when it was just a consideration. I didn't expect it to be any better now. It meant we had to break up.

That hurt me too.

He opened the door with a smile and pulled me into his arms. When our lips touched, I almost burst into tears. His thumb wandered over my cheek and lingered there. Then he looked at me in alarm.

"I hope you're crying because you missed me so much," he tried to joke. So, I was crying. Rob pulled me into the living room and set me to the couch. "You want to tell me something, right?"

"Yes." I took a deep breath. "I'm leaving. For good."

Rob looked at me speechlessly. He opened his mouth several times to say something but remained silent. He shook his head and tried again. "I didn't see that coming," he said. "I thought you'd agree to the banishment and need my support."

"I can't do that," I said. "Besides, it wouldn't work before the next full moon; the shaman is missing an ingredient she needs for the ink."

"Then we'll bridge that one night, and..." he began, but I interrupted him: "No, it's not an option."

"But, what then, Neelia? You want to leave? Where to? To whom? And without me?"

"I'm joining a mixed pack that will protect me. Protect me from your people," I clarified. "And they won't allow a

Skinhunter near them, whether you're still active or not. Don't think this is an easy decision for me. Except for Dad, I'm leaving everything important to me behind. My job, my friends, everything I've built. And you."

"But you don't have to do that!" he said excitedly. "There are options! If banishment is out of the question, we'll think of something else. We could travel during the nights of the full moon so that no one notices. Or I could organize a hideout for those days."

"We could do that once, but you know that's not a permanent solution. The panther wants to be free. If I lock myself up every full moon, it's like being bound. But I need to express my second form."

He took my hand. "And if I ask you not to go?" he asked softly.

"Then I still have to. For my own sake," I replied, squeezing his fingers. "I'm so sorry, Rob. I love being with you and don't want to leave, but the *Skinhunters* give me no choice. I heard about your hunting event next week."

"I'm only there to keep an eye on things," he said.

"I understand, but I don't see how you can get rid of them," I replied. "And even if you could come with me, your parents wouldn't accept that, would they? Eventually, they'd catch on, and then what? Would you stand against your family to protect me?"

"They would never find out!" Rob gritted.

"That's a moral conflict I don't want to put you through," I said. "And I want to avoid the constant fear of being discovered and killed. And by the people of the man I love. Neither of us should have to make that sacrifice, Rob."

He seemed to want to argue but then pressed his lips together. "What a mess," he muttered. "I've known for a long time that this would ruin my life, but I thought I'd lose an arm. That it would separate me from the woman I want to be with—I didn't see that coming. Now I hate it even more. Especially after this weekend."

"What was discussed at the meeting?" I asked quietly, unsure if I wanted to know.

"A lot of general stuff, but you were discussed too. Cecilia swore she'd be the one to get the panther. During that conversation, I found out who hunted you back then."

My heart was pounding in my throat.

"It was Emil's family. That's why they're so keen to support Cecilia now. It may only be half the glory, but..." Rob stopped when he saw my face. "Neelia?"

"I suspected it," I said through gritted teeth. "I knew it was them. It all fits and makes everything ten times worse." I clenched my fists and felt helpless with rage. "Of all people, my best friend's fiancé is responsible for my mother's death and my father's paralysis. That I missed the last two years with my mother!" I jumped up because I couldn't stay on the couch any longer. Hatred burned fiercely within me. Rob looked at me in shock, but I didn't care. I couldn't contain my anger.

"I'm leaving!" I said loudly. "And if only to never have anything to do with *Skinhunters* again. Have you ever thought about how many families you've already taken mothers and fathers, sons and daughters from? Can you even imagine the suffering you bring to people with your damn hunt? And for what? For furs and ingredients that even traditional Chinese medicine balks at. You're a bunch of murderers, and I hate you for what you've done to me and others. And you want me to bind myself? That will never happen, Robert von

Lindenstein, I swear to you! And you'll never see this panther again!"

I had become so loud that I couldn't hear anything else. Now I saw that Rob's face was even more horrified.

I had nothing more to say and turned around.

I looked directly into Cecilia's face, who looked at me as shocked as her brother.

"Fuck!" Rob jumped up.

Cecilia didn't take her wide eyes off me. Slowly, she shook her head. "Neelia..." she said quietly. I had never seen her so subdued. How much had she overheard of my shouting?

It didn't matter, I realized, because the crucial information was in my last sentence: She definitely knew I was the panther. And she couldn't believe it.

Her face was a picture of pure disbelief, her lower lip trembled, and her cheeks were flushed.

The same dilemma Rob had faced: Suddenly, the monster was a person of flesh and blood.

Someone she knew. Someone she liked.

I saw the shock on her face. The realization came slowly.

"Neelia, you should go," Rob said emphatically. He came closer, every muscle tense.

"You're the panther?" Cecilia asked in a low voice, her lips barely moving. "And you know about the *Skinhunters*?" Her gaze darted to Rob. She looked completely overwhelmed and helpless.

I didn't know what was wrong with Rob, I expected anything but danger. Still, my panther senses awakened and were cautious. But Cecilia looked more like she was fighting back tears. Sympathy rose in me; I wanted to comfort her. She looked so lost. Her whole world had collapsed.

Rob looked at me warningly and shook his head. A vein throbbed at his temple. Did he think so poorly of his own sister?

"I never would have guessed," she whispered, looking at her brother with wide eyes. "How long have you known?"

He only shrugged and slowly positioned himself between us. "Neelia, you should go," he hissed.

I didn't understand his tension. Cecilia stood there like a bundle of nerves; she was anything but a threat. He had to see that. Now she was staring at her empty hands. They were trembling.

"Oh God, what will Mom and Dad say?" she muttered, then sniffled softly. "And the others, what..."

"Nothing, because they won't find out," Rob snapped.

Cecilia looked up. Her face was flushed, and her eyes were glassy. "You can't be serious!" she shouted. "Neelia is the panther and..."

"They don't understand," Rob kept his eyes on his sister. His jaw was clenched. "The consequences are unforeseeable. This information will not leave this room! Cecilia, you must..."

Suddenly, Cecilia moved her hand so fast that I could barely follow the motion with my eyes. At the same time, all my senses went on high alert. Rob jumped between us, blocking my view.

"I knew it," he growled.

I looked over his shoulder and stared into the barrel of a gun. Cecilia was aiming straight at my face. Her cheeks were flushed, and her eyes gleamed—with joy.

"Got you," she whispered. My heart skipped at least two beats. I stared at her, unable to believe what she was doing. Now I shook my head slowly.

"Get out of the way, Rob," she said icily.

"No way. Neelia will leave this apartment now. Alone and unharmed."

"Are you crazy? She's the panther! Everyone is looking for her! We could be the ones to catch her! Imagine the uproar. No one would ever get past the von Lindensteins again." Cecilia's voice grew louder and more excited. I felt sick. She talked about me as if I were a trophy. Her determined look told me that, in her eyes, I had lost all humanity. All sympathy between us was gone. I was just her prey. Her ticket to the highest circles of the *Skinhunters*.

The panther. The object of desire.

"We have to lock her up until the full moon and..." Cecilia continued.

"Murder her?" I spat. She flinched.

"Taking shapeshifters out of circulation isn't murder," she said through gritted teeth. "You're unnatural. Beasts that injure and kill people. I've seen what your kind does to helpless people. To children. Killing you is a service to the community. You're a bigger threat than a serial killer."

"Says the woman pointing a gun at two unarmed people," I countered. Anger rose in me again. The *Skinhunters* were a community of insane big-game hunters who had lost touch with reality, like a cult. The same monotonous explanations to legitimize their actions. The same prejudgment Rob had pushed. The logic didn't add up.

"Look at me, I'm human. Your brother's girlfriend," I tried again. I had gotten through to Rob. Cecilia wasn't stupid. Maybe I could make her understand. Rob was so tense that I heard him grind his teeth.

"You're a monster," Cecilia snarled. "And you're on my hit list."

"Wrong," Rob interjected. "Cecilia, you will lower that gun, damn it! This is my apartment, and no one is threatened or shot here."

"Either you're a miserable traitor or so selfish you want the glory all to yourself!" she screamed at him.

"You disgust me!" Rob snapped. "This is the woman I love."

"Then a traitor. And I can't tell you how much you disgust me right now." Cecilia screamed as Rob grabbed her arm roughly and pointed the gun at the floor.

"Leave my apartment immediately," he growled. "Before I completely lose it."

Cecilia pulled away and raised the gun again—this time, she aimed at Rob's face.

"You're crazy!" I gasped. "That's your brother!"

She looked at me with utter disgust, her cheeks red. "Do you think I want to do this? What did you do to him, huh? What did you do to make him turn against his family to protect a monster? Rob," she said pleadingly. "Hey, it doesn't have to be this way. We're just doing our job. I'm sorry it's Neelia. I liked her, honestly, but she's one of them. Think about the code."

"Cecilia," Rob said firmly. "Leave my apartment. Neelia is no threat. No one will hunt her, and no one will harm her. I will personally ensure that."

"You can't be serious!" Cecilia's hand trembled on the trigger. "All the *Skinhunters* are after the panther. There's no hiding place in this city. And we will never stop. Do it yourself and make sure it's quick. It's that simple."

I felt sick as I heard her talk about me like that. Like a task that needed to be done. In her eyes, I was no longer human but a monster. Convincing her otherwise was hopeless. And she was determined to kill me. Not today, but on the full moon.

Horror mixed with my anger. How could she even think about it? How could she decide my death without batting an eye?

My loathing for the *Skinhunters* grew immeasurably. They were the brutes. They were the murderers. Not me and certainly not most of those they had on their conscience. A deep growl escaped my throat, surprising even me.

"Cecilia, for the last time: Get out of here. And if you tell anyone what you learned, I will make your life hell," Rob threatened.

Cecilia's eyes widened. "Now you're threatening me too?" She looked at me with hatred. "I'll find out what you did to him. Before the full moon. And you'll pay for it."

Rob slowly reached for her gun, keeping his eyes on her. He had to be sure she wouldn't shoot him. I didn't share that certainty.

"Rob, stop it, damn it!" Cecilia tried to break free. I ducked as the gun shook. If a shot went off now, it could only...

The shot made me flinch. For a moment, time stood still.

I saw the muzzle flash.

I heard Cecilia's startled cry.

I saw Rob's body jerk back.

I smelled blood.

My paws barely touched the ground as I leaped at Cecilia with extended claws. I knocked her to the floor and pinned her with my paws. It wasn't a choice – my instincts took over with just one thought: *'Protect Rob!'*

Her eyes widened, her mouth open in shock. But the shock turned into something darker - deadly hatred. Her face hardened and she gritted her teeth as she struggled against me.

Then she screamed in pain as I dug my claws into her shoulders.

Only now did I realize I had transformed. Without the full moon. To protect Rob. I had to neutralize Cecilia. She still had the...

I jumped to the side as she fired again. Pain shot through my body, and I roared.

The shot had missed, but she had grazed me. Warm blood trickled down my flank. I saw red. She would pay for this! My blood would not be spilled by a *Skinhunter* but the other way around!

Flashbacks of my dreams flashed before my eyes. The same threat as back then. The same insane desire to kill. They were all the same. It didn't matter which *Skinhunter* it was. It could have been Cecilia who hunted me back then. Or Emil. It didn't matter at all.

I wanted to finally put an end to it all. To solve this problem once and for all. I had no other choice, because Cecilia knew my identity. I was no longer safe anywhere. Unless I killed her, just as they had killed my mother back then. An eye for an eye.

She had shot her own brother. Maybe killed him. She didn't deserve to live. I would be doing the world a favor by ending it now.

Growling, I prepared to pounce.

Out of the corner of my eye, I saw movement. Rob was getting to his feet, cursing loudly and holding his shoulder.

"Damn, are you insane?" he snapped at Cecilia, who was just getting to her knees.

He was alive. I allowed myself a moment of relief. Maybe I wouldn't have to kill her after all. But she wouldn't give up,

I realized, as she looked at me with hatred. I growled again, my claws scraping the floor. Rob stood in front of me and shook his head.

"Don't even think about it," he said dangerously softly, then turned to his sister. "Are you crazy, shooting at her? In my apartment?"

The smell of his blood made me dizzy. The wound on my flank throbbed, and I felt my blood running into my fur.

"She attacked me!" Cecilia screamed, getting up. Her face was bright red, and I saw a thin trickle of blood seeping into the light fabric of her shirt. I had grabbed her harder than I thought. Served her right. She deserved much more pain than that. But her face told me she wasn't done with me yet.

The gun, where is the gun?

The cold barrel of the gun pointed at me again. I tasted the metallic taste of my own blood, felt the heat of my wounds and heard the tension in Rob's voice as he once again ordered Cecilia to stop.

A warning growl came from my throat. Next time, I wouldn't hold back. My claws would find their target: Cecilia's carotid artery.

Rob stood in front of me. "Forget it, Cecilia!"

"You miserable traitor!" she screamed. "You're protecting a monster over your own sister! I hate you!" She aimed the gun at his face. "Get out of the way, you idiot! You're going to get us all killed!"

"You fired, not me!"

"Because she attacked me! Why can't you see what a monster she is?" Cecilia's hand trembled on the trigger. "Rob, I'm going to shoot. Please make sure I don't hit you."

The next few seconds passed as if someone had turned off the lights.

I heard the shot.

I felt my paws lose contact with the ground.

The scream pierced through me, though I was full of adrenaline.

The dull thud as the body hit the floor turned the lights back on.

I opened my mouth and howled - a sound full of heartache and anger that crushed my heart and took my breath away.

Chapter 16

Cecilia lay on the floor, Rob standing over her, yet she kept the gun aimed at his face. The last shot had missed, but I finally realized just how close it had been.

The bullet had lodged in the ceiling, and plaster was crumbling down.

I stayed close to him, sniffing to make sure he was okay. At least as okay as he could be. His wound was still bleeding.

Three shots. The police would be on their way soon—if they hadn't been called already.

Jail would mean safety, at least. But they'd never let it get that far. They would prevent it. Her parents. The other *Skinhunters*.

I swallowed hard. If I got out of here alive, I would be fair game. I couldn't kill Rob's sister in front of him. I didn't want to, either.

Cecilia's face was a mask of pure rage and disappointment. She seemed unable to decide if she hated Rob or me more.

Now she swung the barrel of the gun back at me. "I have one bullet left," she growled and pulled the trigger.

Rob yelled and kicked the gun out of her hand. Just in time, the shot shattered the window. The sound of the breaking glass was deafening and pounded in my skull.

I scrambled up. My instincts were so quick that I barely noticed I had leaped across the room. Now the door was right behind me.

"Stop!" Rob kicked the gun, sending it skidding under the sofa. He whirled around to me. "Get out of here, for God's sake!"

I turned and bolted without looking back. The front door was ajar, so I threw myself against it and stormed out. I sprinted down the stairs, then hesitated at the front door. I couldn't open it as I was; I needed my hands.

Upstairs, Cecilia's shouts echoed; Rob must have been holding her back, buying me time.

I couldn't go out on the street in my panther shape. It was broad daylight, and the police were surely on their way here. I forced myself to calm down and transformed back. Once in human form again, sharp pain shot through my body. The wound on my thigh burned and bled profusely. My clothes were soaking up my blood. At least I had something on, but my bag was missing.

I looked up the stairs, fear shooting cold through my guts. I couldn't escape like this - bleeding and without my things. I had to risk it and go back. Pain coursed through me as I ran back up the stairs. My bag was in the hallway. I just needed to grab it quickly.

"I'll tell everyone what you did!" I heard Cecilia scream. "Our parents, the other hunters—everyone, do you hear me? You won't get away with this. They should all know what you did!"

I turned my head to the living room and froze. Rob had bound Cecilia's hands and legs, leaving her struggling on the floor.

Rob turned around. Our eyes met. I saw pain in his eyes. I felt the same. This was the last time we would see each other.

"I love you," I whispered. "Despite everything." He nodded, his eyes telling me more than words ever could. There was no excuse for what had just happened. He was protecting me and making sure I could get away. That was all he could do for me now.

I ran to him and kissed him on the lips. Then I turned and rushed down the stairs, my bag in hand. Outside, I saw several police cars turning into the street. I turned and ran the other way.

The pain from my wound was driving me nearly insane. I didn't know how Rob would explain the shots. I didn't care.

I made it to the park and pulled my phone out of my bag with trembling hands. "Dad, I need you. Please pick me up!"

Dad came and took me to his apartment. He tended to my wound and called Réka. Meanwhile, I informed Mira. She needed to know what had happened. And I wanted to say goodbye to her.

"I'm coming over," she said immediately. "Don't think you can just leave without saying goodbye."

No, I hadn't expected that, but I had to leave Hamburg. As soon as possible. Rob couldn't hold Cecilia forever. And once she was free, the hunt for me would begin. I dared not imagine all the *Skinhunters* currently in Hamburg searching for me. My window of time was frighteningly small.

Dad and Réka saw it the same way. "The pack is aware and expecting you," he said, handing me a note. "That's where we'll find them. Now we need to take care of everything else." He looked stressed and pale. My heart ached seeing him like that. My father had already endured so much suffering. And because of me, it continued. I knew how much he cared for Annaya. Yet he was leaving her to be with me. I owed him a debt I could never repay.

Mira came to us and brought a leather suitcase. It was old and worn. I saw patches and badges that made me inwardly groan because they looked like they were from her conventions.

"What's that?" I asked, exhausted. The painkillers were finally helping. It took a long time.

"My supplies for spells. I'm going to cast a protection spell for you," she replied. I gave her a long look. Did she really think this was a joke? Her mouth twitched. "After everything you've experienced and learned, do you still not believe I might be capable of magic?"

"At this point, I'm willing to believe anything," I replied. "But I had hoped you were who I thought you were." I sank onto the sofa, feeling miserable.

"I am. And I've never lied to you. You just didn't believe me," she replied, and for the first time, I noticed her hurt because of it.

"I'm sorry," I said quietly. She was right. We had always smiled and dismissed it as a quirk. I should have known better by now.

"You don't need to apologize. Let's keep going." Mira rummaged through the suitcase. "I'm going to give you a disguise so you can get to the pack in one piece. Now, write your father and me a power of attorney so we can take care of everything." She handed me a folder. I opened it and saw resignation letters and other documents. Among them were some in Mira's name for her apartment and her job.

"But what ...," I began.

"I'm coming with you. Everything is already arranged," she said casually. "I decided that as soon as you told me everything. I can't stay here any longer either. Nothing's keeping me here. My family is spread across Germany, it doesn't matter if I move away. After this, I can never look Skadi in the eye again. Sooner or later she'll find out that I had something to do with your disappearance. That's stress I want to avoid. Besides, it's time for a change of scenery. I've been wanting to leave for a while, but you two were the reason I stayed. That's changed now. I've already prepared a lot. You didn't even notice I didn't fly to Madeira, did you?"

I looked at her, stunned. My problems had been so overwhelming that I had completely forgotten. "I'm so sorry," I repeated. "And you ..."

"I'm coming with you," she said again. "Abel has already arranged it. Réka sees the value in having a good Wicca. I'll go with you, start fresh, and make sure you're okay. And honestly, where else would I feel more at home than among people who are just as crazy as I am? I mean, my best friend is a were-panther. It doesn't get much crazier than that, right?"

"I'll make it up to you," I murmured.

Mira piled pouches and bundles on the dining table. "Yes, you will. And I'll make sure you can," she said, pulling a leather-bound book out of the suitcase. "I've already prepared a spell, and the amulet is half-finished." She placed a small leather pouch on the table and continued searching through the suitcase. "A few small things are missing, but that's no problem. I have everything here. We'll activate the spell when you go to your apartment to get your things."

Her words made me feel cold. I hadn't thought about the fact that I could only go there one last time. I loved my apartment. It had been my home for six years. All my things were there. My clothes, my books, my memories.

I swallowed and fought back tears. It was too much. It was just too damn much of everything.

Mira stopped her preparations and hugged me. "I know," she whispered in my ear. "And I'm so sorry it came to this. The worst isn't over yet. You still have to get out of here. I'll make sure that happens." She wiped a tear from my cheek. "You have to stay strong, Neelia. It's not over yet."

"It feels like it is," I said. "I feel like I'm losing almost everything. I must give up my whole life or die. You should have seen Rob's face when we said goodbye. I wish I had ..."

Mira put her fingers on my lips and shook her head firmly. "Don't say it. Don't say something you'll regret. You're better than that, that's why you didn't do it. And because they're so bad, you must do something that shouldn't be necessary." She lowered her hand and looked at me sadly. "In this situation, there are only losers, as sad as it is."

"I wonder what they'll do to Rob," I whispered.

"Probably nothing. They won't kill him," she said. "But that's not your problem. We need to use the little time you have left. The best thing is for you to leave tonight. You have to go to your apartment first." She grabbed the leather pouch. "Ready?"

"No, but that doesn't matter."

My heart pounded as I turned into my street. The last time. Mira was with me; she had insisted. I had argued against it, but now I was grateful.

I looked around nervously. I had no idea what the *Skinhunters* looked like. Where they hid when they ambushed someone. I didn't know if Rob had already released Cecilia.

The shooting had been hours ago. I swallowed, but my mouth was still dry. She could have freed herself and informed Henry and Emil. They could already be on their way here. Maybe she had injured Rob even more. Maybe she had shot him in rage after all. Rob's apartment was full of weapons. Cecilia knew where they were.

I felt paralyzed and barely dared to take a step. Mira grabbed my hand. "Do you want to transform?" she asked quietly.

"Then I'd be an easy target. They can't just shoot a human," I said calmly.

Mira nodded seriously. Now she was dragging me along. It was already nine in the evening, and it was getting dark. It was becoming far too easy for the hunters to ambush us. And with every minute that passed, the risk grew.

I ran to my front door and unlocked it with trembling fingers. We nearly fell into the hallway. With a racing heart, I closed the door again and took a few seconds to catch my breath.

Mira pulled on my hand. "Come on, we don't have time for a heart attack!" she urged. We quickly ran up the stairs.

I unlocked and opened the door a bit, then I let my panther senses take over - sniffing, listening, lurking. Was someone waiting here, gun ready? Was someone hiding here to kill me right away?

No, they would capture me and wait for the full moon. For Mira, it would be dire, I can't imagine that they would leave her alive. They didn't want eyewitnesses for sure. It was foolish to bring her here.

"Is everything okay?" she whispered.

There was no one in the apartment that I could sense. We had no choice but to risk it. I nodded and pushed the door fully open. Inside, I looked around. The apartment was empty. Apparently, Rob could still keep Cecilia at bay. Or she was on her way here.

I hurried to my bedroom and yanked my suitcase out of the closet. Blindly, I began stuffing clothes into it. Mira went to the bathroom and gathered my toothbrush and other toiletries. I paused and stared at the suitcase. These were the wrong things.

They were just things. Nothing that mattered to me.

I went to my dresser and yanked the top drawer open. Here were the important things. The keepsakes from my mother. The photos. A piece of her sari that she had worn at her wedding with my father. The jewelry I had from her. The book she had given me for my twelfth birthday. The pictures of Skadi, Mira, and me. And a bunch of other things. I pulled the drawer out and dumped it into the suitcase.

"What are you doing?" Mira stood in the doorway, shaking her head.

"I can't leave these behind," I said, feeling on the verge of a breakdown.

Mira placed the toiletries in the suitcase and hugged me. "I know someone who handles moves. We can do it discreetly. No one will know where the things are being delivered. Nothing will be lost, I promise you. But now you need to pack things you actually need. Everything else will come later, once you get out of here safely." She let me go and helped me pack the suitcase.

Voices came from the hallway. We froze in mid-movement. My heart hammered as I edged closer to the window. I turned around and looked down at the street. There was a black minivan. No logo. A man stood in front of it, his face in shadow. It could be Emil. Or his brother Henry.

They were here.

It was a terrible mistake to come here. One wrong move could cost us our lives.

"What now?" I whispered, panicked.

Mira pulled the leather pouch from her jacket pocket and looped it around my neck. "Hope that I'm as good as I think," she said, taking a deep breath. "Ready?"

"For what?" I asked.

"We're going to walk out of here as if none of this concerns us," she said.

I shook my head. "Then we're dead, Mira!"

"If we just sit here and wait, we are too." She pushed me toward the door. "Come on!"

I dragged my suitcase behind me. This could only end badly. If the *Skinhunters* were at the door ...

Mira opened the apartment door and looked around the stairwell. The voices again. Several men, no women. None of the voices sounded familiar.

Mira grabbed the second handle of my suitcase and helped me haul it down the stairs. I panted, sweat breaking out on my forehead.

Downstairs in front of the house stood the black minivan. The guy standing in front of it was smoking. He was neither Henry nor Emil and didn't give us a second glance.

Mira quickly pushed the suitcase over the uneven path, and I hurried to follow her. Dad's car was parked in the next street. We had to make it there. We couldn't slow down now.

I took one last look back at my street and tried to say good-bye. I couldn't. Numb, I turned into the side street, realizing I was leaving behind not just clothes and furniture, but my entire life.

And it felt utterly miserable.

We reached Dad's car and loaded the suitcase in. Panting heavily, I sank onto the back seat, Mira plopped down next to me. Dad was in the driver's seat and breathed a sigh of relief. No one else could drive this car, but it had been out of the question for him to accompany us. He was driving the getaway car.

"I was terrified when the van showed up," he said, driving off. "I thought it was them."

"So did we," I said. "I thought we were done."

"But we weren't," Mira said bravely. "Now we've almost made it."

Dad drove us to Mira's place, where I waited until my train departed. I took the first one, but it wasn't until six in the morning because it was May 1st, a public holiday. I tried to sleep a little, but I could only doze off.

Finally, it was time to get ready. I called a taxi, said goodbye to Mira, and got in. On the way to the main station, I passed Skadi's house. I pressed my hands to my face and tried not to cry.

"Everything okay?" the taxi driver asked.

"I'm just tired. This is not my time of day," I forced myself to say.

"I understand. Maybe you can sleep on the train," she suggested.

"I'll try," I replied.

My heart was as heavy as a ton of bricks when I boarded the train half an hour later. The doors of the train closed with a hiss, and I looked out at Hamburg's main station.

This is it,' I thought. *These are my last minutes in Hamburg. I can never come back.*' I fought back tears, knowing my life had turned into a disaster within twelve hours.

We slowly pulled away from the platform and picked up speed. "Welcome to the Intercity Express to Basel," came an announcement. "We wish you a pleasant journey."

I wasn't going to the end station. I would get off earlier. Réka was going to pick me up and take me to the pack. To my new life. The train was the best way of travelling because I didn't need an ID. A ticket paid for in cash at the counter was enough to disappear.

I touched the amulet with Mira's protection spell. I didn't know if it worked, but I wanted to believe it did. It diverted attention from me. People noticed I was there, but it was like she had coated me with a lotus effect. That was the theory.

When the conductor passed me for the third time without checking my ticket, I knew it worked.

I pulled my jacket tighter around me and stared out the window. Just a few more hours, then I would reach my new home. Hopefully, I could leave the fear behind.

Mira and Dad would take care of everything else and then follow. They would terminate the leases, organize the move, and do the same for me. I had written a message to Helmut, trying to explain that I had to leave immediately and was deeply sorry for leaving him in the lurch. Then I destroyed my SIM card and got a prepaid card at the station. Only Dad, Mira, and Réka had the new number.

I hadn't said goodbye to Skadi and wouldn't contact her. That hurt, but I didn't dare. Mira had to hold out until she could leave. And Dad had to try to keep a low profile. I hoped with all my heart that the *Skinhunter*s would leave him alone. I hoped the plan would work.

I kept wondering how Rob was doing. Had he released Cecilia? Or was she still tied up on his living room floor? I didn't know how long he could keep it up.

I had to keep pushing away the thought that she might have hurt him. Or that she and her friends were currently wrecking my apartment. That they had captured Rob and taken him to the *Skinhunters*. That they were doing something to my father or somehow finding out where I was headed.

I pushed the thoughts aside. What would the police do? I kept checking the news app, but there was no report of gunfire in Barmbek. That didn't mean anything; the von Lindensteins had money. They could handle such things differently.

If she was free, Cecilia would surely have told her parents what had happened, but I had no idea what that meant for Rob. I didn't think his parents would denounce him, as Cecilia had threatened. People like them wouldn't let that get out; they maintained their good reputation. I could see them pressuring him, expecting him to change his mind and look for me. His parents had as little understanding of his decision as his sister did.

If they wanted to sweep it under the rug, that would be good for me. They would withdraw from the hunt so no one would draw conclusions. They would never broadcast that Rob had been involved with a shapeshifter. Cecilia wouldn't want everyone to know that Rob had brought shame to the family. But Cecilia might inform Henry and Emil about my identity despite everything. Then Skadi would also find out what had happened.

That thought strangely reassured me. At least she wouldn't have to wonder why I had just left. Maybe she would even understand. Maybe it would make her think about who she was involved with.

I hoped I would never find out, because that would mean they had found me. That could never happen.

I looked out the window at the breaking dawn and felt incredibly exhausted. For now, there was nothing more I could do. I had to see where this would take me. With that thought, I finally fell asleep.

Chapter 17

Réka looked different from what I'd imagined. Though I hadn't pictured her in any particular way, I was still surprised when she stood before me. Moreover, her appearance triggered something within me, awakening my instincts. I was glad to finally leave the train and walked toward her with long strides, memorizing her face.

She was about my height, sturdily built, with wild brown-blond curls falling onto her shoulders. Her brown eyes had a feline quality, as if the lynx was peeking through even in her human form. Her wide mouth curled into a smile, behind which I almost expected to see fangs. She didn't have them, but I wondered if one could see the panther in me if they knew about it. Maybe she could answer that question for me.

"Neelia," she said. It wasn't a question but a statement. She had recognized me too.

"Yes, hello Réka." I smiled with relief when she nodded. It really was her; my instincts were reliable.

"Glad you're here. Come on, let's go to the car." She started moving, and I hurried to follow. "Are you okay?" she asked. "Your father told me what happened. That was quite the ordeal." Her lynx eyes scrutinized me.

"That's true." I touched my hip. The wound still hurt, but it was bearable. "It will heal. Yes, the injury was bad, but the shock was worse. I can't handle firearms. I fear if I had stayed in Hamburg, I would have encountered them more often.

Thank you for letting me come so spontaneously. It must have been a surprise for you too."

"It's understandable, given what you've been through," Réka said. "Even among shapeshifters in different packs, there's a sense of solidarity. And the *Skinhunters* are our common enemies. I told the others about it. Believe me, the vote was unanimous, but that's why we're being extra cautious today. You'll stay with me for now. Zsófia, my sister, is a real estate agent and is already looking for an apartment in town for you. Things are looking good; she can pull some strings."

"That's great, thank you," I said, surprised. "I didn't expect full service."

Réka shrugged. "It's part of the deal. We can't take you in and just leave you hanging. Many of us have skills that help each other. I'm a ranger and keep an eye on our forest."

"I'm a bookseller," I said apologetically. "It's not that useful for the community."

Réka smiled at me. "Wait and see; it's often the ones who think they won't be useful who end up making the biggest difference."

We reached the parking lot, and I noticed Réka keeping an eye on people. "Are you assuming that I'm being followed?" I asked. "Mira, my wicca friend, gave me an amulet that keeps unfriendly eyes off me. And it works."

"I noticed; it took me a bit to find you. Almost until you were right in front of me," she replied. "But we must be prepared for anything. I can imagine they're all eager to get a panther. We're taking it step by step. Zsófia is also looking for an apartment for your father. Your girlfriend is moving in with you, right?"

It took me a few seconds to understand what she meant. "I think she'll appreciate the privacy of her own place. She's my best friend, not my partner," I clarified, frowning.

What did Réka think of me? She knew I had a relationship with Rob, and my father surely hadn't introduced Mira as my lover. But apparently, Réka thought it possible. Maybe I should take it as a compliment. Mira would.

"A great sacrifice she's making," Réka said, surprised. "That's why I thought there was love between you two."

"Yes, that's true, and it is love, but a friendly kind. I hope florists are in demand here. And booksellers," I said, smiling. Honestly, I didn't care what I did for a living for now, if I could make ends meet. I didn't want to overstay Réka's hospitality. It was the same for Mira. My dad could work from here. He took over a client base that revealed nothing about our whereabouts. I didn't know if the *Skinhunters* would continue to pursue us and how much access they had to registration data and such.

"We'll find something," Réka said, unlocking a pickup truck. "As I said, we're well-connected. Do you need anything before we go? We have a bit of a drive ahead."

"Is the place where the pack lives so far away from cities?" I asked, surprised.

"No, but I had you get off at a different station than necessary. I said we're being extra cautious. Your father and friend will go to a different place." She looked at me calmly as I climbed into the passenger seat next to her. "We've been keeping the *Skinhunters* at bay for some time now, thanks to various helpers in strategic positions, even outside our pack. Each of us has a handful of confidants who assist us. We'll hide you, so they can't track you. You won't need a new identity, if you were wondering about that."

"I was, and I'm glad that's not necessary." I looked out the window as we drove off. I had worried about Skadi. As a banker, she had different ways to find me if she wanted to. It was easy for her to look up my social security number, probably even my tax ID. I hoped she would remain loyal enough not to exploit that. But it reassured me that Réka was also prepared for it.

"We've never had a Wicca before," Réka said, driving off the parking lot. "I'm very curious about her."

"I believe it. I'm biased, of course, but I love her dearly."

Réka smiled again and accelerated on the country road. I looked out the window.

Again, my thoughts wandered to Rob. My heart ached. I kept thinking about our last kiss. How desperate he looked when we said goodbye. Everything happened too fast. I felt as if I had been torn from my life. He left a gaping wound in my heart.

Was he okay? Or would I be left forever worrying, never knowing?

When I closed my eyes, Cecilia's gun barrel haunted me. Her face twisted with rage. I didn't know what she hated me more for: being a shapeshifter or that her brother sided with me and wanted to turn his back on the *Skinhunters*. I had seen how hurt she was because of it.

Something was taken from her too. It wasn't my fault. I didn't want to take anything from anyone. I just wanted to live in peace. I hoped that it would be possible here.

But I feared she wouldn't let it go. Cecilia had something manic about her, this urge to prove to everyone how good she was. I was afraid she would move heaven and earth to find me. And I feared she didn't care in the least what her parents said. She surely had one supporter, as Henry was always by her side. I wondered if that also applied to Emil. If he would tell Skadi when the information reached him.

I had known Emil for years and had always got on well with him. I was sure that he didn't mind any more than Cecilia did.

"Try to relax," Réka said. "No one's following us. You got here safely."

"I can't truly relax until Mira and my dad are here," I replied.

"I understand. But for now, you can't do anything. Rest; the evening will surely be exciting. Zsófia will come to us later. I think you'll like her," Réka said. I nodded and looked out the window at the passing landscape.

The drive took two hours, and I was exhausted when we arrived in the small town that was now to be my home. It was tiny, no comparison to Hamburg, but I hadn't expected that.

"Is everyone here a shapeshifter?" I asked, looking around. The town seemed quite normal to me.

"No, there aren't that many of us," she replied, steering the pickup away from the town center. "Including you, we're twenty-six in the pack. It was unexpected, but by now, I'm very happy about it. Zsófia and I are originally from Hungary. Our parents are dead, and it was a coincidence that we met the wolves. They already lived here and had no problem with two lynxes. There are also two sisters who transform, and their children. Later, the deer brothers joined. Two bears the year before last. There's also an eagle and a wildcat. Their families live here too, but they're the only shapeshifters."

"I thought it ran in families," I said, puzzled.

"Yes, that's true. But sometimes the genes lie dormant for one or more generations. Lily, the wildcat, doesn't know her father. It's possible he passed it on to her."

"It was my mother for me," I said. "Apparently, all the women in my family are panthers. But they live in India. That would have been my emergency plan if you hadn't wanted me."

"India. That's something," Réka murmured. "Almost forgot: There's also a wild boar in the pack." I stared at her to see if she was joking. "Yes, I'm serious," she said.

"I'm always surprised at how diverse the transformations are," I replied. "I accidentally got my hands on a book from the *Skinhunters*. It's very detailed and contains a lot of information about them. It's not pleasant reading, but helpful. I brought it with me; I thought it might interest you."

Réka raised her eyebrows. "Definitely. The better we know our enemies, the better we can defend ourselves. See? You already helped us." She drove up a hill. "I live on the edge of the forest; it's a very short commute. Lynxes are also loners, and I like my peace and quiet. How is it with panthers?"

"Not so much. I like having friends around me. And my dad," I replied.

Réka nodded. "You haven't been in your true form for long. That means some aspects of your personality were overshadowed because your instincts were buried. That might change. If it does, embrace it, Neelia. Anything else will make you unhappy. I speak from experience." She stopped in front of a rustic house before I could respond. I saw red brick and half-timbering.

"Welcome to your new life," Réka said, opening her door.

"Thank you." I was glad to get out and stretch my legs.

"Zsófia can't wait to meet you. You'll meet everyone else on Friday when we gather for the full moon. Are you tired from the trip?" Réka took my suitcase and unlocked the door.

"Yes, but also quite wired. I haven't been able to relax since yesterday," I replied.

"That's understandable. I wouldn't be able to shake it off so easily either if someone shot at me. But you're safe here. Try to relax a little."

She opened the door, and I entered a cozy living room with a fireplace that adjoined an open kitchen. I liked it instantly and was grateful to Réka for letting me stay with her.

Réka's sister Zsófia came for dinner. She had the same wild curls, but the resemblance ended there. While Réka seemed somewhat aloof and reserved, Zsófia came over with an open smile and pulled me into a warm hug.

"Welcome, Neelia. Despite the circumstances, I'm glad you're here," she said warmly.

I liked her instantly. She brought photos of the apartment I could move into in June. It was nice and well-laid out, close to the outskirts of town. For a comparable apartment in Hamburg, I would pay twice as much. I preferred not to think about it, as it made my heart heavy.

"I'm also looking for places for your father and your friend," Zsófia said. "You're a bookseller, right? I have a friend who knows someone who…never mind. Anyway, there's a bookstore in the neighboring town looking for someone. If you're interested, let me know."

Her words warmed my heart. "Thank you, that's so kind. I didn't expect you to take care of me so well. I don't know how I'll ever repay you."

"By doing the same for another shapeshifter in need," Réka replied. "That's how our community and our pack's philosophy work."

"There's a code and an oath," Zsófia said. "The main idea is to be there for each other and to protect each other. We stick together and support each other wherever we can. We promised that under the full moon and bind ourselves to it."

"Is it a magical oath?" I asked, intrigued. That would be something for Mira, and she would surely feel at home if there were other Wiccas, warlocks, or magically gifted people here.

"No, but one that comes from the heart," Zsófia replied. Her words warmed my heart again. They were sincere and came straight from her soul. If all shapeshifters were like the lynx sisters, I was incredibly lucky to be taken in here.

"Maybe your Wicca friend can help us make it a magical oath," Réka interjected.

"Mira would definitely be interested in that. Once she's here, we can discuss it with her," I said.

"Absolutely. I don't know any Wiccas and don't know what to expect," Réka said.

"Until recently, I didn't know how serious she was either. I long thought it was just a hobby. I have a lot to learn about it too," I admitted. "The stories Mira tells about her expositions, fairs and gatherings are very entertaining. You'll surely enjoy them. Is there such a community around here somewhere?"

"I'm not sure, but our energies are probably interesting to magically gifted people," Réka said. "I can imagine she'll find like-minded people if she looks for them. We've never done that."

"Maybe through you, we'll discover whole new possibilities," Zsófia smiled.

I smiled back, but my insides twisted.

Hopefully, these possibilities didn't include deadly dangers for the other shapeshifters. I could never forgive myself for that. We all had to be aware that this danger was real. I was sure Réka had that in mind.

"How are you?" Zsófia asked, having observed me. She could probably read my thoughts from my face, even though she had only known me for a few hours. "This all went much faster than planned. You probably have emotional whiplash, right?"

"That's a good way to put it." I stared at the tabletop. "Right now, I don't know how I feel, to be honest. I'm simultaneously exhausted and wired. I can't quite wrap my head around it. Everything still feels completely surreal."

"Give yourself time," Réka advised. "It all has to sink in first. Then it will probably get really tough again. We're here for you, Neelia. Promise."

"Those aren't words," Zsófia said. "Accept the help. We've learned that things are always easier when you don't face them alone."

"Thank you. Again," I said, trying not to let all the emotions brewing under the surface come out.

The lynx sisters made an effort to give me a pleasant evening and a warm welcome. I liked them and managed to shed some tension. Now I knew I was safe. For now, at least.

Everything would be a bit easier once my dad and Mira were here.

Knowing I had an apartment and possibly even a job lined up made everything more bearable. Eventually, this cold lump in my stomach would surely dissolve and disappear.

But later, as I lay in bed in the guest room and stared at the ceiling, I realized for the first time what had happened. Leaving Hamburg abruptly was the right thing to do, but it left a wound on my soul. Another one. I felt like they were piling up.

The shock still gripped my limbs. Had the fight with Cecilia only been yesterday?

I pulled out my phone. My dad had texted me. We had stayed in constant contact, as had Mira.

'Everything will be alright, my dear. Mira and I are taking care of everything,' my dad had written. *'Now have a good night and rest. I'll call you tomorrow. I'm glad you're safe.'*

I wished him a good night too and put the phone away. I stared at the ceiling again. I had arrived. It wasn't what I wanted, but being here was the best thing that could have happened.

I felt welcome in the pack, and thanks to my dad and Mira, I didn't have to completely leave my old life behind. It could continue to exist.

I felt tears streaming down my cheeks and decided that it was okay. I could mourn what I had lost. I could cry for my friend Skadi, whom I couldn't even say goodbye to. We had been close friends for over ten years; she left a gaping wound in my life.

I cried for the chance to take over the beloved bookshop one day. I had invested so much time and effort into making it successful. Now, I would probably never know what happened to it.

And I cried for the roots I had to cut, all the places that reminded me of my mom that I could never visit again, and the future I had carefully planned.

And for Rob, whom I loved, even though it was foolish. He had been part of that future plan. It was far too soon, but I had already thought about moving in together. About children. About a thousand things I wanted to do with him.

That was not going to happen now.

I couldn't take over the bookshop. I could never see Skadi again. I couldn't have a future with Rob. It was so unfair, but I was too sad to be angry.

It didn't change anything. My old life in Hamburg, and everything that came with it, was over. I had a new chance. I should be smart enough to take it and build something new.

Still, I kept crying.

I sobbed, my body shaking with it.

I didn't try to stop it. It was okay. It was necessary for me to move on. I tried to make peace with the situation, and finally, at some point, the crying subsided, and warmth spread through my body.

My breathing became a little easier and I no longer felt quite so terrible. It was okay. I accepted things as they were.

It was the best thing I could do.

And if I sometimes cried again, that was okay.

I would be okay again.

Eventually.

And Réka, Zsófia, my dad, and Mira would help me.

With that comforting thought, I finally fell asleep.

The next morning, I woke up and started my new life: I visited the apartment with Zsófia and decided to take it. It might even be ready a few days earlier. I walked through the rooms and knew I could feel comfortable there.

After that, I felt better. It felt like I had more solid ground under my feet again.

"We'll make it easy for you," Zsófia promised.

"I can see that," I replied. "I already see myself looking for a place to buy thank-you baskets."

I also talked on the phone with the bookstore owner in the neighboring town. We hit it off immediately and set a meeting for next week to get to know each other. The bookstore was in the next town, a few kilometers away. I would need to find a ride or cycle if that worked, but that was okay with me. I just needed a plan to keep myself from thinking about anything foolish.

Mira and my dad were coming as soon as possible; it looked like early June. I knew it was just a blink of an eye, but the four weeks until then felt like forever.

I didn't expect everyone to leave as abruptly as I did.

Mira had to quit her job and take care of her and my move. Her acquaintance with the moving company was informed. He would handle everything discreetly. That also took a load off my mind. Mira knew he had nothing to do with the *Skinhunters*, and we were on the safe side with him. Another advantage we had through the magical community. And because the *Skinhunters* weren't popular everywhere.

I didn't hear from Rob. That was a good thing, because anything else would have thrown me off course.

I suspected Mira would hear a lot from Skadi, but she kept it under wraps. Mira was currently playing dumb, and I didn't know how much Skadi knew. We had to be incredibly careful, so Mira avoided meeting with Skadi.

Once that was over, a huge weight would lift off all our shoulders. It bothered me that I could do almost nothing from here. I visited apartments for my dad and Mira, but not much more.

We all had to be patient. No matter how hard it was.

Chapter 18

On Friday after my arrival, the time had finally come: my first full moon night was about to begin. Tonight, I would meet the entire pack of shapeshifters.

I felt so nervous as I walked with Réka and Zsófia to the gathering spot in the forest. My hands were shaking and my mouth was dry. What awaited me there? Will they accept me as one of their own?

Everyone had agreed to my arrival and expected me to officially join the pack. Still, I was about to face twenty strangers who were supposed to become my family from today onward.

So far, I hadn't crossed paths with any of them, as the pack only gathered outside full moon nights for very important matters. Since Réka had already arranged my admission before I arrived, no additional meeting was necessary. We met two hours before moonrise, which gave me time to get to know the others a bit.

"Don't worry, we don't bite," Zsófia said encouragingly. "Everyone is really excited to meet you."

I smiled. "I feel the same way. I hope I can live up to everyone's expectations."

"You will," Réka said. "You align with the pack's values and are a shapeshifter. Being a unique one makes it even easier; you don't pose any competition within the pack." Réka was the Alpha, and I had no intention of challenging her position. At least I was clear on that point.

We reached the edge of a clearing. We weren't the first ones there; four people were already waiting. Réka introduced me to twin brothers who shifted into stags. Both were tall, and I could imagine the magnificent animals they would become after the transformation. That was likely the reason why, as prey animals, they were still part of a pack of hunters.

After them, I met a mother-son duo who turned into bears. These two were more unassuming, and I was curious to see them in their second forms.

Next arrived a family of six – two sisters and their four children, all wolves under the full moon. The sisters were friendly and greeted me warmly, while the children hung back a little. The youngest boy had only been shifting for three months. I sympathized with him.

Then, the man who turned into an eagle arrived. I knew immediately that Mira would fall head over heels for him as soon as she saw him. He had that mysterious aura she found so attractive. He nodded to me seriously and managed to maintain his stern demeanor for a few seconds before we started talking. He was intelligent and sharp-witted. Mira was as good as lost.

Lastly, there was a young girl who turned into a wildcat. Her name was Lily, and she looked at me cautiously. Of course, compared to her second form, I was a giant. I decided to make friends with her.

"That's everyone," Réka said.

"No wild boar?" I whispered to Zsófia, who had been introducing each newcomer like a news anchor.

She shook her head. "Jakob is traveling."

"I hope he didn't choose a big city," I replied.

She laughed. "Who knows? You can ask him next time."

Réka introduced me to everyone. "Here she is, as promised. Neelia, I warmly welcome you to our circle once again."

"Thank you. Now I'd like to thank you for literally saving my life. I'm so grateful to be here with you," I said to the group, managing to keep my voice steady.

"That's natural," Zsófia said. "What happened to you is what we all hope never to experience. We swore to stand together against the *Skinhunters*. You're joining us and our code, which means you would do the same for each of us."

Réka had thoroughly explained the code to me, and I fully supported it, so I nodded. "I do, and I'm ready to take the oath."

Réka called everyone closer, and I looked into the faces of the people to whom I was entrusting my fate. Each was different from the others. I could tell there were many fascinating characters here, and I looked forward to getting to know them all.

Réka held out her hand. In her palm lay a predator's tooth, carved with runes. I knew it had no magical powers, but it still seemed infinitely precious.

"Neelia Jacobi, panther. Do you join our pack and swear loyalty to us? Do you place your fate in the hands of the community? Will you submit to the authority of the pack, which I also represent as its Alpha? Do you swear to protect us with all you have and to help us live in safety and peace? Do you promise to accept our rules and never turn against a member of the pack?"

"Yes, I do," I said solemnly, placing my hand in hers. I felt my sense of belonging grow. The other pack members came to greet me again, this time even more warmly.

"I can't wait to see a panther," said Lily, the wildcat, when it was her turn. I smiled and turned my face to the moon, which was rising above the treetops. I was ready.

"We'll spread out a bit, so we all have enough space," Zsófia said, motioning for me to join her. The others dispersed around the clearing.

Then it began. I closed my eyes and concentrated on the fantastic feeling in my muscles as the transformation finally began. My senses sharpened and my bones shifted, stretching and reshaping. My muscles stretched and heat spread through me. Then came the overwhelming joy of being me again. Although it had only been a few days since my last transformation, I had missed this form incredibly. I couldn't wait to celebrate this night.

I smelled the others as they shifted too. My pulse quickened. Panthers hunted alone, but I wanted to welcome this company and was eager to join the pack under the open sky.

I stretched my body feeling each muscle come alive, and yawned deeply, tasting the cool night air. I immediately recognized Réka and Zsófia, even if I hadn't known they were lynxes. It was their eyes that gave them away. Zsófia gave me a catlike grin, which I returned. Behind them, the wolf family gathered alongside the wildcat. The stags stood a bit farther back, even larger than I had expected. Even farther away were the two brown bears.

Above us, the eagle glided gracefully through the air.

We were ready.

I caught up with the lynxes and let the others sniff me. They had respect for me, but I felt the same toward them. For now, I wanted to be cautious, but perhaps later I'd indulge the young wolf's curiosity and measure my strength against his.

Now, I just wanted to run and use my muscles. I wanted to feel free. For the first time, without fear and without constantly being on guard. A tingling sensation lingered at the edge of my awareness, but it could just be the flood of impressions surrounding me.

Réka snarled, and we took off. I leaped and followed her in long, graceful bounds.

I never felt better. I was exactly where I belonged.

My decision to come here was right. It had been the right decision, even before the fight against Cecilia had taken place.

Banishment would have been madness.

This feeling of being in my second form was something I never wanted to give up. The panther was a part of me that I would never bury again. I deserved to feel whole. And to be happy.

I was happy; I could admit that to myself.

I was in the right place.

The lynxes, the stags, the wolves, they all ran with me. The eagle soared above us, and the bears trotted along behind. The wildcat darted through the undergrowth.

What a dynamic.

What a wonderful feeling.

I was curious about what this would lead to, what possibilities we would have together.

I wished Dad and Mira were already here.

I tried not to think about it, however much I wished Rob was here to see what shape shifters were really like: friendly, family-oriented and lovable. That none of us deserved to be hunted and shot at. We were a wild pack, but not a threat. I wished there was a way to make the *Skinhunters* understand that.

We used the night to celebrate our second forms. I ran, I jumped, and I climbed. I playfully tussled with the wolf pup and the lynxes. I had to be careful around the bears, but I was fast enough to dodge their swipes.

Finally, I took a break in the clearing where we had met. I sat down on my hind legs and watched the wolf cubs play. The wildcat purred and circled me, then sat down beside me. I looked down at her and felt her contentment.

Réka and Zsófia leaped beside us and lazily stretched out on the grass. The cats had had enough of wasting energy. My urge to move was satisfied; now the cat wanted to do what it did best: sleep and let the world be.

The eagle perched above us on a branch, watching over us. I was already looking forward to seeing him meet Mira in his human form. Only a few more weeks until she was here with me. Maybe she could accompany me to the next full moon and meet the pack. I knew she wouldn't be afraid. She would run with us if we let her.

The wolves howled in chorus to bid the night farewell. The moon slowly dipped behind the treetops, and I sensed it was time to return to my human form.

I hadn't tried shifting back without the full moon yet. I knew it was possible, but it required much more energy.

I looked over to Réka and waited for her command. This was still new to me, but I would get used to coordinating with her.

Above us, the eagle gave a warning cry, making me sit up. The lynxes stood again, and the wolves stopped howling.

What was happening? I exchanged a look with Zsófia. Was this normal? But she and Réka looked concerned. Their noses twitched, and their claws were extended.

Danger.

I looked around and sniffed the air. A bad feeling crept down my spine, but I couldn't smell anything.

The wind was against us.

But the eagle wasn't affected by scents. His sharp eyes were unforgiving.

The sun cast its first rays across the meadow, and the bears shifted back. Then the others followed. Beside us, the eagle landed on the ground. Zsófia appeared in her human form next to me, so I hurried to shift back as well. It felt strange to stand on two legs again, but there was no time for that now.

"What's going on, Alex?" Zsófia asked tensely.

Alex, the eagle, furrowed his brow. "There's someone at the edge of the forest. A man," he said, pointing.

"A man?" Réka turned in the direction he indicated, a growl rising in her throat. A chill ran down my spine.

The other shapeshifters gathered with us. They'd also noticed the stranger. Now we were coming together, ready to protect one another.

My heart pounded. Had they found us? Had I led the *Skinhunters* straight to the pack?

I stepped beside Réka, ready to take responsibility first. If necessary, I would buy the others as much time as possible. She looked at me with concern, but then my attention was caught by movement.

The man stepped into the clearing. I recognized him instantly. His walk, his silhouette. His scent drifted over to us now. My senses were still sharp enough to identify him.

My heart skipped in shock, and I covered my mouth with my hand. "Oh God!"

"Neelia?" Zsófia asked from behind me. "Who is that?"

"It's Rob," I whispered, my mouth dry, not knowing what to do. My heart hammered in my chest and sweat broke out. What now?

What did this mean?

Why was he here?

"Rob?" Réka asked tensely. "The *Skinhunter*?"

"Yes."

Behind us, murmuring began, and the others grew increasingly uneasy. Someone whispered that we should get out of here.

"How many of them?" Réka asked in Alex's direction.

"Just him," he replied.

"How did he find us?" Réka asked me.

"I don't know. I didn't tell him anything," I whispered, unable to take my eyes off him. He was getting closer. The danger was rising on both sides.

Réka looked at me intently, then nodded. "I believe you. Then he'll have to explain it himself."

"Yes, he will." I took a deep breath and walked toward him. Réka followed me. I heard her instructing the others to stay back.

We stopped about ten meters apart. Rob's gaze swept over my face. I could see relief in his eyes. He had found me. His search was over. I felt torn apart, unsure of what to make of his presence here.

"You look like you have something to say," Réka said as she caught up to me. "And I sincerely hope you haven't shown up here with your *Skinhunter* friends looking for trouble."

"I waited until dawn specifically to prove I don't want any trouble," Rob replied calmly. I knew him too well to fully believe that. "I'm here to make you an offer," he said, looking at me. "To you all, but especially to you." He stepped a bit closer. "It took a lot to find you. And a lot of persuasion with your father."

Réka's expression hardened. Again, that growling tension filled the air.

"I've left Hamburg and the *Skinhunters*. For good," Rob said quickly. He paused, his eyes flicking from Réka to me, gauging the mood of the pack. "And I'm unarmed, see?" He spread his arms, showing his empty pockets. He turned around once to prove he wasn't hiding any weapons.

"I came alone. I had to let my sister go. She and my parents know about Neelia. My parents are currently trying to keep that information contained—not to protect Neelia, but to preserve the family's reputation. I don't expect them to succeed forever. Not as long as my sister is losing control. Cecilia's with my parents, but she won't stay there forever. For me, it's clear I no longer belong with them. Instead, I want to help you protect yourselves from them. So I can be with you, Neelia."

I stared at him. That was too much information to process all at once.

"Why?" Réka asked, her eyes narrowing. "Nothing you've just said convinces me to give you this chance. Quite the opposite: you're putting us all in maximum danger. Why should I expose my pack to that?"

"I understand. And I can explain, Alpha. I don't want to be a killer. I want to be with the woman I love. I know I realized it late, but it's here now. I thought for a long time about your words, Neelia, and you were right. I don't know how many families I tore loved ones away from. I can't change that. I can only make sure there won't be any more. Especially not you." He looked steadily at Réka. "I'm asking to stay with you. I'll take any oath necessary to convince you. Neelia's friend is a Wicca who can seal the oath magically, if you wish. I want to help you protect yourselves better from the *Skinhunters*. I found you (albeit with help), so others could too." He looked at her, then his gaze went back to me. "Please let me help ensure this pack remains safe. I'm also offering my services to any other pack that would accept them."

A hush fell over us. I looked at Réka, and she seemed uncertain. "Neelia?" she asked.

I took a breath. The shock was deep, but now I had to ensure we found a solution. And I had to protect Rob; he had put himself in danger to find me. And to be with me. Unexpectedly, a new opportunity arose. I had to seize it, or I would never forgive myself.

I looked at Rob's face and my heart skipped a beat. Here he was. Alone. Promising he'll leave his past behind. To live with me and the people of which he always thought they were brutal beasts only worth to be slaughtered.

Could he really do this? And what about me?

I wanted it so much but a part of me feared what would happen if I was wrong.

I didn't need to look back to feel the pack's tension. I could sense it. They were afraid, on the verge of losing their nerve.

I had to ensure Réka stayed calm. One word from her, and all hell would break loose.

"He's sincere," I said clearly and loudly. Hopefully, the others could hear me too. "Rob protected me from his sister and helped me escape. He had already promised me he wouldn't hunt anymore. And I believe him… I believe you mean it, truly." I looked into his face, the face I loved so much.

I couldn't believe he was making this sacrifice for me, risking this danger. There was no guarantee that Réka and the others would believe him. Nor would they simply let him go if they rejected his offer. Rob was a huge risk to the pack. And he had willingly placed himself in Réka's hands to prove he was serious.

I wanted to run to him. I missed his touch.

I didn't dare, but I would protect him as best I could.

Réka motioned for the others to come closer. She couldn't make this decision alone. The shapeshifters approached cautiously. I felt their mistrust, and it now extended to me. I was new and unpredictable. Despite the oath, they held me responsible. And it was true. Rob was here because of me.

I had to stick to the code.

I had to follow my heart.

I wasn't sure the two could align.

"So, this is Rob," Zsófia said, standing behind me.

Réka summarized what he had said to the others. Despite the number of us, it was silent. I didn't hear anyone whisper.

"I know, I showed up uninvited," Rob began, "and I apologize for just barging in here. I couldn't announce myself because I didn't have Neelia's number, and it was difficult to find my way here without leaving a trail."

So, you're saying no one knows you're here?" Réka asked, wary.

"No one. I had a rough idea of where Neelia went, and I researched articles to pinpoint this place. Animal sightings and such. That's how *Skinhunters* track their prey. I know all the strategies and how to avoid them. If you let me stay, I'll increase your security."

Réka and Zsófia exchanged glances, and now the others began murmuring among themselves.

"We'll discuss it," Réka said. "Wait here." She waved the rest of us to her, and we moved out of earshot. The Alpha looked at me. "Neelia, you need to say something."

"What?" I asked quietly. "I'm anything but unbiased."

"You trust him?" Alex asked.

"Yes, but what does that change? We can't let him leave, can we?" I asked. "The risk is too great. He needs somewhere to go, and that would be Hamburg. That's where the *Skinhunters* are, looking for me. We have two choices: either he stays here, or he and I leave. If we leave, I swear on my life that I will do everything to keep the *Skinhunters* away from this place."

"You're right," Réka said to the group when the silence stretched. "Those are our options."

"I don't want to make such a big decision out in a meadow at dawn," said Ursula, the bear. "I suggest we go home, and your friend stays under your close watch, Neelia, until we meet again soon to make a decision."

Réka considered this, then nodded. "She's right. We'll come back together tonight and decide as a group."

Everyone agreed, and we dispersed, though I could see some reluctance. Réka, Zsófia, and I returned to Rob.

"Your offer is interesting, but the pack decides democratically," Réka said. "I see the value you could bring and believe you're sincere. I'll advocate for you."

"Me too," Zsófia said, shaking her head. "Crazy, all this happening. First a panther, now suddenly a *Skinhunter*. It's unexpected."

"Ex-*Skinhunter*," Rob corrected. "I left the Guild. For good. You need to know that."

"Understood," Réka said, turning to leave. "Talk to each other, Neelia. It's up to you to ease any doubts by tonight's gathering." The sisters disappeared among the trees, and I turned to Rob.

"Hey," he said softly.

"Hey." I smiled, and my eyes stung. "I didn't expect to see you again."

"Me neither, but you know me: Some things I just can't leave unresolved." That mischievous grin I loved spread across his face. I stood on tiptoe and kissed him.

It felt so good to touch him. Now I could admit how much I'd missed him.

"Do you want me here?" he asked. "You know, I can't go back, and that would be awkward if you said no now."

I kissed him again. "So you have an excuse to show up unannounced again? You heard them: You're stuck with me now. I hope we can both stay."

He pulled me into another kiss. "I hope so too. I never thought I'd give up my whole life for an amazing woman and move to southern Germany to live with her and a pack of wolves."

"It's too late to regret it, unless you plan to kill us all," I replied.

"Neelia, I can't go back," he said seriously. "Imagine my parents' reaction when Cecilia told them everything. They want to force me to find you and bring your pelt back. Only the shame of me being with a shapeshifter and protecting her is stopping them from going public and putting a bounty on you."

Fear cut through me like a cold knife. "Then they'll do it now that you're gone," I whispered. Rob held me tighter.

"No, they won't. They must process the shock that I'm gone. Then they'll try to sweep it under the rug for as long as possible. I'm more worried about Cecilia. She's completely losing it over this."

"I am too," I admitted.

"Please, let's stay here." He gave a crooked smile. "I don't have anywhere else to go."

"I'll do everything to convince the others tonight," I said. "But with Réka and Zsófia on our side, that's a good start. We have a chance. If they understand that you're a friend who wants to protect the pack, you'll surely be allowed to stay. I'll do whatever it takes for us to stay here together," I repeated.

The sun's rays warmed my skin as Rob pulled me back into his arms. "That's what I was hoping for," he whispered in my ear. "Otherwise, I wouldn't have searched for you, my panther girl."

I pressed myself against him, feeling his heartbeat against my cheek. "I'm glad you did."

My new life lay ahead of me, full of chances and opportunities. However, there were still decisions to be made and questions to be answered. It wasn't going to be easy, but for the first time I felt complete - like a panther, with Rob by my side.

Whatever lay ahead of me, it was worth the risk.

It was worth being brave.

Epilogue

He was gone. Just like that.

I couldn't believe it.

I stood in his apartment. It wasn't empty, but it felt that way.

I had come here to make one last attempt to get him to see reason, to try one last appeal, to convince my brother that he couldn't just throw everything away.

His family. His heritage. Me.

I bit my lip, realizing what a fool I'd been.

He had made his decision long ago. Even before last Sunday, when my life became a huge pile of crap.

My shoulders still ached from her damn claws. I hated her with all my heart.

It was because of her that all of this had happened. Because of her, I had no chance now to prove to everyone that I was better than Rob. Because of her, I now had to bear my parents' expectation to make everything right again.

There was no making things right anymore. We were miles away from that.

Only one thing was left for me to do: I could get revenge.

The hunt would go on. I had talked to Henry; he was on my side.

Together, we would find the panther and bring her down. And if, in doing so, I found my brother and showed him just what a mistake he had made, all the better.

Sometimes, realization only comes with pain.

That's just how it was. My realization—that he was a traitor—hadn't been any easier for me.

I never would have pegged him as someone who'd let himself be swayed by a woman. Apparently, sex with a shapeshifter softened the brain.

I clenched my fists and looked at the bullet holes I'd caused. The shattered window still hadn't been fixed.

I'd made mistakes, too - acted rashly, let anger cloud my judgment. But I wouldn't make the same mistake again. Next time, I'd be smarter. Cold. Precise.

It was really quite simple.

I had a problem. I knew the solution.

Neelia. A shot to the head.

It was that simple.

The fact that she could shift without a full moon only made it easier.

If I found him, I'd find her.

I forced a grin, even though I felt utterly wretched.

I would solve this problem.

And then I'd keep going until I reached my goal.

Simple.

I turned and left Rob's apartment.

My goal was clear. And, this time, so very simple.